PRAISE FOR NAIMA SIMONE

"Passion, heat, and deep emotion—Naima Simone is a gem!"
—Maisey Yates, *New York Times* bestselling author

"Simone balances crackling, electric love scenes with exquisitely rendered characters."

—*Entertainment Weekly*

ravaged

OTHER TITLES BY NAIMA SIMONE

Secrets and Sins

Gabriel

Malachim

Raphael

Chayot

Guarding Her Body

Witness to Passion

Killer Curves

Bachelor Auction

Beauty and the Bachelor

The Millionaire Makeover

The Bachelor's Promise

A Millionaire at Midnight

Lick

Only for a Night

Only for Your Touch

Only for You

WAGS

Scoring with the Wrong Twin

Scoring Off the Field

Scoring the Player's Baby

The Sweetest Taboo

Sin and Ink
Passion and Ink

Blackout Billionaires

The Billionaire's Bargain
Black Tie Billionaire
Blame It on the Billionaire
Ruthless Pride
Trust Fund Fiancé

Billionaires of Boston

Vows in Name Only
Secrets of a One Night Stand
The Perfect Fake Date
The Black Sheep Bargain
Back in the Texan's Bed
Broody Brit

Rose Bend

Slow Dance at Rose Bend
The Road to Rose Bend
A Kiss to Remember
Christmas in Rose Bend
The Love List
With Love from Rose Bend

Fairy Tales Unleashed

Bargain with the Beast
A Perfect Fit
Grading Curves
Sweet Surrender
Flirting with Sin

BURNED Inc.

Heated

Trapper Keeper Diaries

Jesse's Girl

ravaged

BURNED Inc.

NAIMA SIMONE

Published by Montlake, Seattle

www.apub.com

Amazon, the Amazon logo, and Montlake are trademarks of Amazon.com, Inc., or its affiliates.

ISBN-13: 9781542030687
ISBN-10: 1542030684

Cover design by Elizabeth Turner Stokes

Printed in the United States of America

To Gary. 143.
To Connie Marie Butts.
I will miss you forever and love you even longer.

CHAPTER ONE

MIRIAM

"World-devastating war. Cataclysmic earthquakes. Evil wizards and their minions bent on total annihilation. Mankind has survived them all. Yet love . . . fucking love will be the end of us all."

—Sarafina Rose, *Ravaged Lands*

There are times when I wish my job was as a psycho clown with a particularly virulent hatred for vigilantes dressed like bats so I could throat punch them. Guilt-free.

I mean, being one-third owner of Breaking Up, Reversing Nuptials & Evading Disasters—or BURNED Inc., a full-service breakup company—isn't always shits and giggles. There is the enormous amount of paperwork; the occasional asshole clients my sister, Zora, won't allow me to drag 'cause of their assholery; the sometimes stifling constraints of the marketing and promotional projects. The "Who's handling Miriam?" side-eye traded by my older brother and sister.

Yeah. Not always shits and giggles.

But today is not that day.

Or rather night.

I pick up a chilled bottle of champagne out of the black-and-gold ice bucket on the low smoked-glass table in front of me. The light from the overhead fixtures hits the liquid, and for a moment, I'm captivated by the pale shade. It's so fragile. So innocent, almost. And yet strong, capable of felling a person if not prudently handled. I love this color. No, no. I respect this color.

And maybe I just need to pour the champagne.

Carefully, I pour the bubbly into two waiting flutes, not stopping until the gold alcohol almost meets the rims. With a satisfied grin, I replace the bottle in the bucket and hand one of the glasses over to the gorgeous brunette perched next to me on the black leather sofa.

"Cheers." I clink my glass to hers and sip the wine, humming as the light, delicious liquid flows over my tongue. "Ooh. This is good."

I'm glad I demanded my client not skimp on the amenities. Top bottle service. The most expensive and private VIP booth with the best view of the popular Denver nightclub dance floor teeming with gyrating bodies. The soundproof glass prevents most of the sonorous bass and music spun by one of the country's top DJs from infiltrating the luxuriously appointed space. More leather furniture, opaque switchable privacy windows . . . oh yes, my client went all out.

As he should since he's dumping this poor girl like last night's Chinese-food takeout.

Which is probably how long he dated her too.

Fucking athletes.

But hey. Clients are clients.

Still, millionaires or not, when I'm breaking up with their "girl-friends," it's going to be done with dignity and respect for these women who have the misfortune to fall for the bullshit lines these players dish out like free pancake breakfasts. And while I love free shit as much as the next person, what I've learned is it will probably give you worms. Or worse.

Ronnie—doubt that's her government name—eyes me over the rim of her glass. "Thanks for this." She tips her head to the side, and her sheet of thick, shiny dark hair flows over a shoulder. That's a trick I've never been able to master. Even if I straightened my natural shoulder-length curls, I'd still never achieve that move. And not only because of the hair. It requires a coyness that I'm incapable of. "And not to sound ungrateful, because I'm very appreciative. But will Linc be arriving soon?"

Lincoln "Linc" Young. Star point guard for the Nuggets, another of Jordan Ransom's teammates. And my client.

As one of the three owners of BURNED, I'm not usually responsible for the actual breaking up with people; we have staff for this who carry out any number of packages that range from ending relationships through text to a fancy dinner to even skywriting. Okay, fine, not skywriting. Zora and Levi vetoed my idea, but we have broken up with someone by singing telegram. Singing. Telegram, folks. I kid you not. But I digress . . .

This—sitting in the superelite and private VIP section of the hottest nightclub in the city on a Friday evening—isn't my usual gig. But when your clientele encompasses celebrity athletes who, thanks to your best friend, have not only discovered your company as a way of avoiding messy "scenes" but have adopted you as their unofficial little sister, then you give the customer what they want. And my customers happen to want my personal touch. Which means I'm stuck breaking up with their girlfriends. Or hookups. Or hookups who stay too long and believe they're girlfriends.

Fucking athletes.

"Listen, Ronnie." I cross one black-leather-clad leg over the other, prop my arm on it, and lean forward. Even though the soundproofing in here is excellent and she can hear me perfectly. "You're gorgeous, got a body that could make a priest rethink the whole celibacy thing, have confidence that rocks your sexy factor from a ten to a fifteen, and just from the time we've spent together, you're not only beautiful but smart and witty too." I snort, catching the slight stiffening of her shoulders and the small shifting of her body away from mine. "Calm down, sis. I'm not hitting on you. Although, you should be so lucky. I'm a great fucking catch."

I really am.

But only for a night or two. Then I'd throw my own self back overboard.

"Oh." She lets out a breathy and relieved laugh. I'm trying hard not to be offended. "I didn't think you were. I just didn't know where you were going for a moment there."

"It shouldn't be an odd thing for us to compliment each other. Especially women. We should normalize straightening each other's crown, not suspecting an ulterior motive but instead knowing I'm not going to let anyone try to knock it off. Anyone." Ronnie starts to frown, and I softly inhale and let it out. "Lincoln's not coming, Ronnie," I say. And not softly, not gently. Not in any manner she can mistake for pity. Because the last thing this woman wants—or needs—is pity. "This is his way of letting you go and asking you to move on from him. He wanted to treat you one last time."

I wave a hand, indicating the well-appointed room, the top-service alcohol, and the club beyond. From what Linc told me during our consultation, he'd met Ronnie at this club . . . he thought. Maybe. At least he believed it was Ronnie he'd met here.

Again. Fucking. Athletes.

"You're kidding me, right?" Ronnie's grip tightens so hard around her glass that a fissure of concern zigzags through me. It'd be a shame if she got champagne on that stunning white bandage dress. Oh, and blood. That too. "Please tell me you're fucking kidding me."

I shake my head. "Sorry, I can't do that."

Her harsh laughter rings out in the suite, and it reminds me of the Liberty Bell. Loud, clear, but with a jagged crack right up the middle.

4

"I can't believe this. I honestly cannot believe this," she mutters, tipping her head back and staring at the ceiling. I take the opportunity to slip the glass from her fingers. Better safe than sorry. Especially if she intends on returning the dress in the morning. No shade. Those are my plans for my leather jacket. "We meant something to one another." She returns her stunned, angry gaze to me. "I know we did. He told me he cared about me. And then he breaks up with me by proxy? He doesn't even have the nerve to face me and do it himself? Who does that? What kind of person agrees to do it *for* him? Is this fun for you?"

I was expecting this transference of emotion. It makes sense since I'm the only available target. And it's a fair question. Hell, it's one my own parents ask. Over and over . . . and over again. Ad nauseam.

"Look, Ronnie, you strike me as the kind of woman who deserves and wants honesty." I wait for the abrupt jerk of her chin.

Each client requires a different approach, because each one is just that—different. But she seems like a straight shooter to me . . . even if she somehow convinced herself that she had more than a one-night stand and some change with Lincoln Young. Even the smartest women can lose their heads over celebrity and big dick. I should know. I grind my teeth. Yeah. This is so not about me.

"Lincoln is a nice guy, a fun guy," I continue. "But he's not the staying, house-family-picket-fence kind of guy. More like the house-bros-with-hos-in-the-hot-tub-for-an-orgy-it-ain't-no-fun-if-the-homies-can't-have-none kind of guy. I'm sure he did care about you because, like I said, nice guy. But, sis, be honest with yourself. Or be mad at yourself. But don't delude yourself. He was not *your* guy. He is not the one who will walk beside you through this life, sharpening you like iron, making you better even as you do the same for him. He isn't the one who will show you the true meaning of love. He just wasn't that person." I dare to reach and cover her fisted hand with mine. "Chalk this up as a lesson learned and some good sex. At least I hope it was good sex," I grumble, squeezing her hand. "And as for what kind of

5

person breaks up with a person on the behalf of someone else? A person who wants to make sure your feelings are handled with care. Not trashed and discarded. Because they matter. And so do you."

I give her hand one last squeeze and release it, then grab my abandoned drink. After all that love-and-completion nonsense, my throat is parched. Everything else, oh, I definitely meant. She deserves only the best, and Lincoln Young isn't it. But that nasty four-letter word that's worse than any f-bomb I could drop? Not a chance in hell.

Ronnie stares at me for several long moments, then dips her head. "Thank you for that," she murmurs.

I smile, turning back to the table and picking up the glass I'd removed from her earlier death grip. After handing it back to her, I hold up my own. And looking at her, at how, yes, gorgeous she is but also how strong and dignified even in the face of being broken up with by someone else other than the one who dicked her, I see her as stunning. A queen. She's a fucking queen. One with sad eyes and regal bearing. And no one's taking her crown.

"A toast." I wait until Ronnie takes the glass and, though not smiling, holds it up to mine. "When one door closes . . . get a hammer, and nail that bitch shut."

She snickers and taps her glass to mine. "Amen to that."

We both damn near drain the champagne without coming up for air. When the last drop is gone, I grab the bottle, pop the top, and pour more for her.

"Listen, old sayings are old for a good reason. They're true. And since we have the best champagne, the most exclusive VIP room in the hottest club packed full of some seriously fine men, this saying is appropriate. The best way to get over a man is to fuck a finer one with a bigger dick."

She blinks, then barks out a loud crack of laughter. "Yeah, I don't think that's how that goes. Although, I think it should."

"Right?" I shoot up from the couch and hold out my hand. "C'mon, babe. Let's go shake our asses and run up a horrendously expensive bar tab."

She studies my palm for a moment; then, shaking her head, she slaps her palm on top of mine and allows me to tug her to her feet. "I'm game. Let's do it." She downs more champagne and then squeezes my hand. "Miriam."

I arch an eyebrow. "What's up?"

"Thank you. For . . . being kind while dumping me. A lot of women wouldn't have."

The sad part? She's not wrong. And that's why I'm in this business. My sister, Zora? She has her reasons. And they all revolve around our train wreck of a childhood courtesy of our parents. Zora, Levi, and I deserve veteran benefits because of them. Me, though? Everyone deserves to be handled, to be treated with care, with respect . . . with decency. You'd think that was a given, but it's not.

Yeah . . . it's not.

Mentally shaking my head and clearing it of thoughts that should have cobwebs—I wish to God had cobwebs—I pull on her hand and lead her toward the VIP suite exit.

"You're welcome. Now, we have acts on our agenda that will have us waking up tomorrow questioning our morality."

Snickering, she follows me, and the sound blooms in my chest like a bud unfurling its petals before the sun. No, I don't take these jobs often. But this feeling right here. This explains why I do.

"Renae, we're going to hit the—damn, hold on a sec." I frown, popping up a finger, as my cell vibrates against my ass. After sliding my phone free, I glance down at the screen and force my expression to remain clear. "Ronnie, I have to take this. Why don't you go ahead with Renae, and I'll catch up with you two?"

I pin the other woman with a pointed look. Though most people might figure her smooth chestnut skin and sharp cheekbones would be more at home on a supermodel, Renae is one of the most lethal women I know. Which is why BURNED hired her for our security staff to cover the asses of our employees when they're out on jobs. Becoming my best friend is just a side benefit.

Ronnie scans Renae from the top of her dark-red twists pulled into a bun on top of her head to the black lace of her tight tank and the red leather of her pants. As a slow smile curls her mouth, I just manage not to roll my eyes. My best friend elicits that reaction from men and women—and rocks.

"Take your time," Ronnie purrs, then turns and descends the steps to the main part of the club.

"I'm not dancing," Renae snaps, her hand on the doorknob. "It's not in my job description, and you don't pay me enough."

"Fine." I sigh. "Just get her a drink, and I'll be right down."

She jerks her chin. Then one corner of her mouth lifts into a smirk. "Tell Jordan I said hi."

Before I can reply, she shuts the door, cutting off my girl Lizzo and leaving me in silence since the phone stopped ringing. But before I can move toward the door, it starts again.

"Dammit," I growl, not even bothering to glance at the screen. I tap the answer button and press the cell to my ear. "What?"

My newest best friend—three-time NBA champion, all-star power forward of the Nuggets, resident pain in my ass, and onetime one-night stand, Jordan Ransom—laughs in my ear. The dark, filthy baritone rolls over me like sin wrapped in midnight, hiding sweaty secrets and dirty acts. Since no one is in here to witness it, I permit a shiver to ripple through me without hiding it. But that's my only concession. Because friends don't have orgasmic shivers over their friends.

But damn.

Jordan Ransom.

Whether a person is a basketball fan or not, most people recognize the inked, pierced Viking that is number forty-seven on the Mile

High City's professional NBA team. Closer to seven feet than six, broad shouldered, slender hipped, with powerful thighs and calves, and with nearly every inch of him covered in tattoos and piercings. As if that weren't enough, he possesses the face of a northern pagan god who requires sacrifices of mead, raucous celebration, and sex.

He's more.

He's living, electric art. And not just because of the vivid tattoos sprawled over his skin. He's so . . . vibrant. Drawn in broad, bold strokes that demand attention. Painted in screaming slashes of color that refuse to be ignored.

I don't need him before me to picture those beautiful yet almost harshly sculpted features. They could've been carved from the rock of his Nordic ancestors' homeland, the same ones who handed down those brilliant blue eyes, arrogant blade of nose with its thin nostrils, and wide, hard mouth that could be brutal and raw in one moment and hot and wild in another.

Not only does Jordan Ransom look like a pagan deity with his dark-blond mohawk; he also possesses the carnal appetite to match.

And I say that from experience. I know how it is to fuck a god.

"Why hello, my lil harpy-flavored gumdrop. I've missed you too."

Again, since no one is here to witness it, I grin at the ridiculous nickname. And do my best to ignore the pitch and roll of my belly at the ever-present rumble in the low timbre of his voice. Friends. After that crazy, insanely hot night together, we agreed that we would never go there again and remain friends. Yet nothing about that syrupy warm coil and tumble in my stomach is *friendly*.

Even though he's on the phone and not in front of me, I roll my eyes. "You say that like I didn't just see you three hours ago. What do you want?"

His heavy and Oscar-worthy sigh echoes in my ear. "This is what I get for being concerned about you. And women wonder why men are afraid to be emotional creatures. We get slapped down at every turn."

I snort. "Yes, yes. It is our fault that men are emotionally constipated creatures. I accept the blame and apologize on behalf of all womankind. Now, really, Ragnar," I drawl, dropping my own nickname, as he does resemble the Viking character from one of my favorite historical TV shows. Well, except for the whole pillaging, ransacking, and killing thing. According to his reputation, though, he has the whoring thing down. "I'm working; what do you want?"

"I'm checking in on you. Seeing how it's going," he says, all hints of teasing and humor evaporating from his voice. I swear, that ability of his—flipping the switch from laid-back, happy-go-lucky celebrity athlete to the serious man who radiates intensity—can be unnerving. "I know my boys can be fucking high maintenance, especially by insisting only you handle their breakups."

"Yeah, well, fortunately, most of you stay true to form and do your fuck 'n' flees. Because if I had to dump every one-night stand, I would be busy from the time I opened my eyes and had my morning caramel frap."

A beat of silence reverberates down our connection like a staticky heartbeat. It's thick and tangled with so much tension it's almost audible. I frown. "Hey, are—"

"What's this 'most of you' shit?" he asks.

The question is calm, even containing a faint hint of humor. Still, Monica Nelson didn't raise an idiot—an emotionally repressed, socially inappropriate nerd, yes, but not an idiot. And I catch the steel threading through his tone like the finest wire.

My lips pop closed around my question, and that warm coil in my stomach? It tightens . . . and heats. A normal person would heed that hard note and back off. Make excuses; switch the subject.

Me, though?

No one has ever accused me of being normal. Not when I was the only twelve-year-old in my ninth-grade class. Or when I sat in freshmen orientation at the University of Denver at the age of sixteen.

Not at seventeen, when I created my own special stink bomb for a certain campus football house that had the house and its tenants smelling like day-old shit for weeks.

Or when I crashed a matchmaking event and handed out BURNED business cards—y'know, juuuust in case. Almost got arrested for my trouble. And yeah, that was last year.

So no, *normal* usually isn't connected with my name. Which is why I ignore the steel in his voice and forge ahead, convincing myself that the thrilling little tug pulling taut low in my belly isn't anticipation or excitement. Friends don't feel that for each other either . . . not unless tacos are involved.

"Don't get your boxer briefs bunchy, Jordan," I say, scrunching my nose, although he can't see the gesture. "I'm the least judgy person I know." Total lie. For most people, I'm all "live and let live." But for the members of the male population who handle balls of all sizes? I've tried and convicted most athletes as narcissistic manwhores with the emotional IQs of sheep embryos. Present company—on the phone—excluded. Well, except for the manwhore part. Still, sometimes I wonder exactly how I became best friends with one of the country's most famous basketball players. It's still a mystery that only Jessica Fletcher could solve. "And I know none of you have taken vows of chastity. I'm actually thanking you. You and your boys' community peens are bringing BURNED a ton of business."

More silence. And yes, it's ridiculous, but I can *feel* the heat simmering on the other end, sizzling down our connection to singe me. I cup my phone, pressing it harder to my face, as if I can absorb more of those smoldering embers that he never allows anyone to see. Not even when he discovered I'd lied to him about where I worked and what I did for a living to cover for Zora so Cyrus, his best friend and the man my sister loves, didn't find out. No, Jordan never loses control. Never lets go of that fire.

Well, that's not exactly true. I've seen it—been licked by its flames—once.

When he had me under him. Over him. In front of him.

That sweet, almost painful tug in my stomach wrenches harder, blooming into a yawning, empty ache between my thighs. I cover my mouth so he can't catch the short, soft gasp I have no hope of containing. And I have zero doubts he will hear it. I've never had a person more attuned to me, more aware of me. It could be intoxicating, addictive—if I permitted it. If I let myself forget that it's not personal, but that perfect attention to detail, the ability to read the room, is just part of Jordan's personality. It's what makes him such a great power forward on the court and friend off of it. And amazing in b—

Dammit. Not going there. Bad enough the images of that night are flickering at the edges of my mind and my panties are going to be a lost cause. I refuse to willingly go traipsing down that road where only memories of the hottest sex of my life litter the pavement, but so does regret. And my own stupidity.

"You're welcome, Marilyn. Our dicks aim to please," Jordan drawls, and both relief and disappointment wind through me.

Relief, because the heat has abated and his usual laid-back manner and ribald humor have returned.

Disappointment, because the heat has abated and his usual laid-back manner and ribald humor have returned.

"That's the rumor," I mutter, choosing to ignore the quiver in my belly at the nickname he dubbed me with on the day we met on account of my dyed-blonde hair. Glancing toward the VIP entrance, I ask, "What's up, Jordan? You okay? Or are you bored?"

For the last two weeks, he's been laid up with a groin sprain. I have jokes about that as well. But damn, that's too easy. But since his injury has prevented him from practicing or starting in the new basketball season, he's been driving me crazy. Well, more than usual.

He calls it *bonding*.

"I'm fine," he says, the answer short and inviting a whole lot of "Move the fuck along." "Like I said, I'm checking in to see if you're okay. To make sure Linc's girl didn't go for your throat when you broke the news to her."

"You do know I'm a professional, right? I do this for a living. You don't have to worry about me or call me every time I go out on a job. Not to mention it would be a gross breach of confidentiality if I shared with you how the evening is going since this is Lincoln's business. And with the amount he's paying for my discretion, my lips aren't only sealed—they're cemented shut with Gorilla Glue."

"Fine." Pause, and in the background, I detect what sounds like another language. Probably Korean. The man loves his K-dramas. "Just tell me this. Are you okay?"

A totally inappropriate flutter caresses my chest wall. Leftover champagne bubbles. Denial, thy name is Miriam Nelson.

"I'm good. But I really do need to get back to my client." My hand tightens on the cell. "Seriously, though, before I go, are you okay? And don't dodge my question or give me that 'I'm fine' bullshit. Are you in pain? Is Cyrus with you?"

"I'm *fine*, Miriam. It's a groin pull, not a spinal break. And no, Cyrus isn't with me," he growls. "He refuses to sit around, braid my hair, and hold my hand since your sister came along."

"Wow. We're in a mood. You have your afternoon nap today?"

"No, dammit, I didn't," he snaps.

A beat of silence. Then I snicker.

Then he snorts and laughs too.

"You're fucking death to my ego, Marilyn."

This time, I snort. "You'll live. Bye, Ragnar, I have to go. And tell Lincoln not to be such a chickenshit. If he wants to know if Renae wants his balls in a Dixie cup, just call and ask."

He gasps. Honest-to-God gasps. "Linc isn't—"

I hang up on him midlie, grinning. But when I lower the phone and realize I'm still smiling like an idiot at the screen, a sharp knife of alarm slides between my ribs. I force my lips to flatten, sliding my phone back into my rear pocket.

Another thing "only friends" don't do.

Friends don't allow just a phone call and the sound of your buddy's voice to stir a honeyed warmth in your chest. Or to stretch that clenching emptiness inside you wider and deeper.

Shaking my head, I stride toward the suite's exit.

Damn good thing we're only friends.

CHAPTER TWO

JORDAN

"Show me a man with friends, and I'll show you a man with one too many opinions and assholes."

—North the Woodsman, Ravaged Lands

"While there are several things I'd do for you as your attorney—some of those things riding the line of impropriety—braiding your hair isn't one of them."

I arch an eyebrow at Cyrus Hart, one of my best friends and my attorney, who's sprawled out on the couch in my Narnia man cave. And no, I'm not exaggerating. You can access the specially built walkout basement room only through a massive-ass wardrobe in a spare room on the first floor. Yeah, I get a lot of shit about it from my boys. But I don't give a fuck.

When a child whose only means of escape were *The Lion, the Witch and the Wardrobe* and basketball grows up to be a man with more money than he ever dreamed of possessing, he indulges in every fantasy that makes him happy. And that's not just limited to homes with personal movie theaters and basketball courts or dirty sex.

That man builds a secret entrance to his own magical world—or an over-the-top man cave. Same difference. I left nothing out when designing this haven inside my haven. HDTV that takes up nearly one wall. Surround sound that'd put a cinema to shame. A bar fully stocked with everything from local IPAs to top-shelf liquor. A separate TV screen for gaming along with classic arcade machines. A library with its shelves overflowing with books. A private entrance to a walled patio, firepit, and barbecue area. Custom-made leather furniture. The most important feature.

When you're six-foot-nine, average-size couches and recliners won't do. I promised myself when I was a six-foot-plus high schooler trying to squeeze my overlarge frame into those one-size-does-not-fit-all desks that when I made it to the NBA—I never once doubted I would—never again would I have to wear someone's ill-fitting hand-me-downs. Whether it was clothes, tennis shoes, or state-issued desks.

"The hell you say. As much as I pay you, you'll braid my hair, then tell me how pretty I am," I say to Cyrus, jabbing a finger in his direction before rounding the back of the couch and sinking down on the far end, resenting the flash of pain that burns a path up my inner left thigh.

I breathe through it, deliberately stretching my arm along the back of the sofa, forcing my fingers to remain straight while that ache radiates like a homing beacon in my thigh and groin. Anger as hot as the pain beats meaty fists against my rib cage. But I cuff the fists, smothering the rage. When I'm alone, when I don't have an audience, maybe then I'll let it go. Maybe. I swallow a snort.

Who the fuck am I kidding?

Not myself. I haven't "let go" since I was eight and witnessed the harm losing control of my temper, of myself, caused. Not the busted lip and black eye Greg Hanson sported after I got through with him. Naw, that little shit deserved every punch I rained down on him for calling my mother out her name. The harm came when Mom showed up in the vice principal's office to pick me up to start my three-day suspension.

I'll never forget how disappointed, how *tired* she looked. On that day, for the first time in my life, I'd felt like a burden to her. So no, in that small crowded office smelling of Lysol and the french fries Mr. Harrison must've had for lunch, I'd learned to control my temper.

"Well, you can't touch mine." Daniel Granger, my friend and teammate, smooths a hand over his own long, intricately braided hair. "No shade, but I don't trust that you know what to do with it. I will let you call me pretty, though." He grins from his sprawl in my recliner.

And I have to admit it. The motherfucka is pretty.

"That's fair." Cyrus shrugs. But the casual gesture belies his too-intense and penetrative stare. I don't like it. I'm not on the stand or under cross-examination. "Why'd you lie to Miriam about me being here?"

"Right, the famous—or should I say *infamous*—Miriam I've heard so much about but haven't had the pleasure of meeting yet," Daniel adds, lifting his beer bottle up for a sip. Because it's the basketball season, it'll be the only beer he'll allow himself tonight. Daniel's that strict with what goes in his body. "Esquire here asks a good question," he continues. "What's up with not letting her know you have company? Didn't want her to be jealous about our spending so much time with him?"

"Yes, that's it exactly."

Of course that's not it, and judging by the arch of his eyebrow, he knows it. But damn if I'm sharing that my pride wouldn't allow me to admit it to Miriam. I'm well aware what she thinks of me. A good-natured, playful manwhore who never met a party he didn't crash. Part of me resents that as my friend, she hasn't looked deeper, *seen* more. But the other half . . . the other half is relieved because it's content that she believes in that facade rather than perceiving that truth. The humiliating truth that I'm afraid to be alone. That when I am, my thoughts plunge into a freezing dark abyss where I have trouble clawing myself free. I've never liked being by myself—I've always hated the silence. Noise, people, distractions. They beat back the engulfing, dangerous quiet.

"On a scale of one, I could play tomorrow, to ten, I'm barely hanging on, how's your pain?" Daniel murmurs.

I grit my teeth, everything in me snapping at him to "Let it fucking go." But he's more than my friend, a word that's thrown around so loosely in my world but rarely meant. He's my mentor. He took me under his wing when I joined the Nuggets when he could've let me stumble my way through that rookie year. No one would've blamed him. I was an arrogant lil bitch. But he saw past that rough exterior, and he and his wife accepted me like family. And when you've been considered a star athlete since middle school and a commodity even before stepping foot in college, that term takes on more significance. He's one of the few people I can honestly claim to trust. So no, I won't tell him to fuck off.

But damn if I ain't thinking it.

"Four, I don't know what the big deal is and I've played through worse," I answer because again, friend.

But I don't add that it's a four only because I've iced the hell out of my thigh and have it bandaged so tightly King Tut is somewhere out there sporting a hard-on over my wrap game. Not to mention I popped my prescribed naproxen.

My fingers involuntarily curl before my brain can send a signal to stop that tell. Barbed disgust wraps around my stomach, tightening, digging deep. I hate drugs. Of any kind. It makes me feel weak to depend on anything other than my own strength and will to get through this injury.

"The big deal is if you return too soon, you'll cause more harm and end up spending even more time recovering and not playing. Would you rather be out another month or four months? Maybe more? Following the doctor and physical therapist's orders could mean the difference between weeks and half your season." Cyrus jabs a finger at me from the end of the couch, eyes narrowed.

"You think I don't know this? That I haven't heard the exact same thing from Coach and the team doctors? But no one knows my body better than me." I thump a fist on my chest. The chest that's suddenly as tight as the pair of Spanx my mother would climb into whenever she pulled on her "feel-good" dresses for nights out with my aunts. "That makes me the better judge."

"Actually, it makes you the worst judge," Daniel says with a shrug. "Are you missed? Yes, and we'll be damn glad to have you back. But you'll be no good to us if you return too soon only to reinjure yourself and have to be out even longer."

"You being the better judge. That's bullshit, and you know it," Cyrus says, and I want to shove him off my couch for that comeback and the casual tone it's delivered in. The ass even has the nerve to cock an eyebrow. "You're not unbiased when it comes to this, and you have an agenda."

"And the team doesn't have theirs?" I scoff. "You're my attorney, and I've seen you in action, so I know you're not that naive."

"No, I'm not. But their agenda is winning the championship, which means ensuring they have a healthy player for the majority of the season. Yours is shortsighted. Play now regardless that you might be further injured and threaten your playing time. Which means leaving room for another player—and yes, I do mean Royce Carlisle—to use the opportunity to shine and prove himself to be Jordan Ransom two point oh. Is that what you want?"

I don't even bother granting that stupid question an answer. Besides, I'm 97 percent sure he meant it to be rhetorical.

But damn. He's right. I scratch my chest. That other indescribable, uncomfortable feeling that's been tickling the underside of my ribs like an unreachable itch has been anxiety. Worry. Worry that if I don't get my ass back to practice, back out on that court, soon I won't have a position, a team to return to. That I'll lose the organization and players who have become family these past years.

That I'll be abandoned. Again.

Ignoring the groaning pain in my thigh, I stalk over to the bar, hating that my strides aren't as fluid as normal. Scowling, I round the bar and jerk open the refrigerator with undoubtedly more force than necessary. I grab a beer and twist off the cap.

"If you wanted a drink, I could've gotten it for you. Doctor's orders are to keep your leg elevated. A grade-two groin strain can become a grade three if you don't follow instructions." Cyrus parks his nagging ass on one of the barstools. Daniel follows him, and damn if I don't feel fenced in.

"I don't need a nanny or a waiter."

I also don't need either of them to tell me what I already know. This tear has damaged a significant percentage of muscle fibers. And every time I walk or try to pull my thighs together, I'm reminded of that fact. And that if I don't take care, the injury can extend to most of my muscle or tendons. Yeah, their warnings are gratuitous when my too-vivid imagination and wake-me-from-nightmares pounding heart are always on call to do the job.

An image wavers in front of my mind's eye like a flag snapping in an overbright summer sky. From one moment to the next, the picture changes, a mental camera shutter echoing in my head, gifting me with my own private showing. Gifting me . . . or condemning me.

Miriam.

Miriam, standing on my private batting cage, stripping off her shirt and revealing those small perfect breasts with their mouthwatering dark nipples.

Miriam, crouched over me, my hands buried in her thick, roughened-silk blonde curls as she attempts to swallow my cock down her throat.

Miriam, beneath me, back arched tighter than an archer's bow, nails digging in my back and her delectable ass cupped in my hands as I fuck her like the continued existence of all life depends on it.

All of these snapshots are as familiar to me as my own hand—the hand that's become my dick's homie, lover, friend since I've met her— because they're the only things that beat back the nightmares. Instead of jerking awake in fear that I'm a failure, I jerk awake, sweating, body strained tight, cock hard as fuck and staining yet another set of sheets.

The consequences of being in lust with a woman who permanently friend-zones you after sex so goddamn good calculus suddenly makes sense.

That's burning-bush, parting-of-the-Red-Sea sex.

"Jordan?"

Shaking my head, I clear my throat. "You want something?" I gesture to the shelves behind me stocked with liquor bottles and glasses. "Another one of these?" I tip the beer in Daniel's direction, even though I know he's going to turn me down. Which he does with a shake of his head.

Cyrus waves a hand. "Whatever you're drinking."

After retrieving another ice-cold beer from the fridge, I slide it across the bar top toward him. Cyrus twists the cap off, takes a long sip, and then lowers the bottle, all while studying me in that unwavering manner they must teach attorneys in school. But I grew up with a single mother and three aunts with eight children between them. Under that kind of training, there's no way I'm cracking under his stare.

"All right, I'll leave you alone about your injury—for now. But that brings me back to my original question. Why did you lie to Miriam?"

"Oh shit, Cyrus. You're like a dog with a bone. Worse. At least I can distract a dog with another bone," I mutter. "Look, it's not that big a deal. Maybe I just didn't want her to think that I'm so pathetic that I need a constant flow of company because I can't be by myself."

Because I do. And I can't. Well, I don't want to.

Still, she doesn't need to know that.

"Where's the shame in admitting you're in a vulnerable place? You two are friends, right? Isn't this something you'd share with a friend? Unless . . ." He cocks his head, that too-shrewd-for-my-comfort gaze narrowing on me. "Are you just . . . ?"

He doesn't finish the question, but really, we both know it's unnecessary.

I lift the beer to my mouth, forcing myself to meet his human-lie-detector eyes. Fortunately for me, concealing your emotions and the truth were survival skills learned alongside sounding out consonants and how to trade punches at recess without the teachers noticing.

"Remind me again." I tip the mouth of my bottle toward him, squinting. "Not too long ago, wasn't it you who said to me that you didn't believe in relationships or love? Now look at you." I spread my arms wide. "Wanting to ship your friends just 'cause you're booed up. It's so cute."

"First, don't ever say *booed up* in the same sentence as me. On second thought, how about as a thirty-year-old grown-ass man, you just never say it? And two, while I might be in love with Zora, I do not see it everywhere. But since my memory isn't failing me, I clearly remember you telling me not too long ago that you believe in the existence of love."

"I also said I'm not settling for some half-ass shit that passes as it."

And living my own personal unrequited-love rom-com movie isn't on this year's bingo card.

"Hmm."

I scowl, snapping my bottle down on the bar top. "Is *hmm* a legal term?"

"Yes. It's Latin for 'I smell bullshit.'" He holds up his bottle.

"While I hate to interrupt this . . . fascinating cross-examination, I'm going to hit the bathroom. But you two, please." Daniel waves a hand between us. "Carry on."

With a half smile, he stands and heads for the bathroom. As soon as the door closes behind him, Cyrus tips his head back, a grimace pulling his face taut.

"Fuck."

Yeah.

A large, Goliath-size fist squeezes my chest, and I lift a hand, trying to rub away the phantom soreness.

The Nuggets drafted me toward the end of my sophomore year at the University of Denver, and Daniel had already been on the team for four years and married for three. And he hadn't been one of those husbands who was married only when in front of his wife. It wasn't only his great basketball talent and skills that I admired and looked up to but his integrity. He'd loved Jerricka, and everyone had known it. He'd been faithful, never bringing random women to his hotel rooms on the road or partying and clubbing. His wife had been his world. And when she'd died two years ago of a sudden brain aneurysm, he'd been broken. It's just been in the last six months that I've started to see remnants of the old Daniel. And I'm thrilled about it. Him hanging out with us tonight when he's turned down numerous invitations in the past couple of years is just one of the signs he's coming back to us.

But shit, talk of Cyrus's new relationship and his obvious happiness in the face of Daniel losing his love must hurt Daniel like raw salt rubbed in an open wound. Something both Cyrus and I forgot.

"I feel like an utter asshole," Cyrus mutters, tipping his head down, regret darkening his eyes. "How could I forget . . . ?"

"Let it go, bruh." I nudge his bottle closer to him. "He knows you didn't mean anything by it. And frankly, he'd be mad as shit if he knew you were out here beating yourself up for even thinking he'd begrudge you the happiness he had with Jerricka."

"Yeah, I know. Just . . . shit." Cyrus picks up his bottle and takes a long pull from it, then drops it to the bar top again, eyes narrowing on me. "This is your fault." He points the beer at me. "You and your denial over Miriam. You do realize as your lawyer that I'm bound by attorney-client privilege? But if you want me to pretend that I don't notice the way you look at Miriam, then that's fine too. And before you ask, you stare at her like plane-crash victims look at each other on week two of being stranded on a deserted island after they've gone through all the food supplies."

Heat scalds my chest, rolling up my throat and pouring into my face. Dammit. And here I thought I had my "We're only friends" game on lock. If Cyrus guessed even a bit of the truth, has anyone else? Does Zora know? Levi?

Fuck, does *Miriam*?

Shoving aside the panic thrumming through my veins, I jam a finger, growling, "You know what? I'm beginning to appreciate my alone time."

"Touchy." He holds up a hand, palm out, and cocks his head. "Is that due to the injury or the current subject?"

"I think I liked you better when you were an emotional wormhole."

Cyrus snorts, a smirk curling his mouth. He does that more. Smiles and laughs. Especially since he's met Zora Nelson and opened his own entertainment law firm, leaving the toxic environment of his old one behind. It's good to see him . . . happy. Cyrus deserves that.

But even as the thought passes through my head, his smirk disappears, leaving his customary serious expression behind.

"I didn't think I needed to say it, but just in case I do . . ." He folds his arms on the bar top and leans forward. "That confidentiality clause doesn't pertain just to our professional relationship. Whatever you tell me stays here, between us."

"Yeah, I know." I clear my throat, ducking my head. "And no, you didn't need to say it."

Silence beats in the room.

Then I add, "I feel like when Daniel gets back out here, we should go play some *Fortnite* so I can shoot you in the face a couple of times. It's either that or I come over there and put my head on your shoulder while eating my feelings."

"I vote for shots to the face."

"My man."

CHAPTER THREE

MIRIAM

"I can kill you or fuck you. Either one works just fine with me."

—Sarafina Rose to North the Woodsman on their
meeting, Ravaged Lands

"Explain to me again why my presence is required at this shindig?"

Jordan glances over at me, momentarily swinging his attention from the road. A smirk tugs at the corner of his criminally sexy mouth, lifting the hoop piercing the corner of his bottom lip. The order for him to turn his eyes back to the road hovers on my tongue. Not for road safety, although yes, there's that. But also for my vagina's sanity. That heffa has no shame when it comes to this male.

Thirsty bitch.

If it wasn't for her, I wouldn't know how he sounds when he powers inside a woman. Or that the mountain-fresh-and-dark-earth scent rises thicker from his skin when sweat coats it.

Or that he can fuck like he owns the patent and copyright.

For a moment, an image of a slightly older, harder, more battle-worn version of Jordan superimposes itself over his features. But the same sharp, noble features. The same intelligent eyes. Identical mouth with its full, indecently sensual curves.

A shiver works its way down my spine, seizes my lower back, and then travels lower still to echo and throb in my sex. Attempting to not be conspicuous, I shift in the passenger seat of his Hummer. As if my agitation isn't enough of a problem, that same alluring scent—minus the perspiration-dampened heaviness—fills the interior of the vehicle. I can't escape it. When I return home tonight and slide between my sheets, I'll probably smell him on my clothes, in my hair. Why that thought of physically wearing him deepens the ache between my thighs, I choose not to dwell on.

And as Bobby Brown once assured me, it's my prerogative not to.

"Shindig?" He snickers. "I'm sure Linc would love that you've referred to a catered party with one of the most popular DJs in the country at his mansion as a *shindig*." He shakes his head. "And your presence isn't required, but didn't you just break up with Antonio? I'm not about to have you sitting at home brooding over that shit."

I look away from him, staring out the passenger window as the dark scenery of the wealthy Cherry Creek neighborhood passes by. This is light-years from the Park Hill area I call home. And I'm not just talking geography and tax bracket. Mentality, mindset, lifestyle, values . . . this isn't my world. It is Jordan's and his teammates', though.

I don't have many rules, but one of them is "No athletes." Not as lovers, not as friends. Not as anything. Yet in the past couple of months, I've screwed an athlete, become friends with one, and taken on a stable of them as clients.

Part of me feels like I've stepped through that freaky wardrobe man cave entrance of Jordan's and really entered an alternate universe.

One where I go to parties attended by athletes. My fucking origin story.

"Hey." A huge, long-fingered, tatted hand that I'm intimately acquainted with lands on my leather-covered thigh and squeezes. I covertly peer down at my bra-covered nipples, grateful to see the lightly padded black cups concealing the hardened tips. "You okay? If you really don't feel like going tonight, I understand."

Turning to him, I rummage up a bright, cocky smile that has become my signature. How I've learned to face the world.

"I'm good. And for the record, I'm not moping over Antonio." He slides me a look that clearly says "I call bullshit," but I hold my hands, leaning back against my seat. "No, seriously, I'm not. Hell, I'd only been dating him for a few weeks. He was a nice guy. Had that John Legend thing going for him. Y'know, sexy, personable, supercreative. And incredibly smart."

His fingers flex the tiniest amount on my leg, but I don't miss it. Anytime he touches me, no matter how small, how soft, the tremor that ripples through me could initiate an apocalyptic event, leaving my body a dystopian wasteland.

Yep, that deep.

Another reason I had to friend-zone him.

Only one thing is allowed to create that kind of energy, that level of excitement in me. Anything, or anyone else, that stirs that intense of a reaction should be booted from your life. Past experience has taught me that harsh lesson, and I failed it with a flaming bright F. Want too hard, need too much, and you might as well hand-deliver that person your power, your dignity, with a glitter-sprinkled bow.

If I had any common sense, I would've shut this "friendship" thing down as quick and hard as he'd made me come . . . the first time. But for some reason that I still can't understand—or am afraid to analyze too closely—I couldn't. Because even indulging in cataclysmic, albeit horribly misguided, sex doesn't change the fact that Jordan Ransom, with his ridiculously beautiful face, gorgeous body, wicked sense of humor, and magic peen, has never once treated me like a weirdo. Or handled me like I'm a spun-glass figurine on a high shelf, seconds from teetering off, crashing to the floor, and splintering into hundreds of pieces.

Worse . . . worse, he's my muse.

For that alone, I couldn't let him walk away. Even if it means insulating myself with a thick layer of bright-yellow caution tape.

Friends. That's all I can allow and still keep him.

Because more would be disastrous.

For me.

"Then what was the problem?" he asks, his deep, gravel-smoothed-by-sand voice calm. Although that slight flex carried a hint of edge.

I loose a sigh and look out the window, a faint pulse of disappointment echoing in my chest like a shout in a vast cave.

"I dropped my wallet, and he saw my Mensa card."

A beat of silence. Then, "So?"

Warmth surges within me, and my attention switches away from the monuments to wealth and gratuitous abundance outside the window to Jordan. As if feeling my gaze on him, he glances at me.

"What?"

"Nothing." Everything. His response is *everything* to the woman who's always been called a nerd or weirdo or freak because of something I never asked for or have no control over. And those were the kinder names. "I guess Antonio was cool with my job as a breakup specialist, just fine with my lack of filter, and completely okay with my slightly obsessive preoccupation with anime, but my being a card-carrying member of the largest and oldest high-IQ society in the world? That made him squirrely."

I frown, not needing any prodding to remember the new speculative looks slid my way and the inevitable questions threaded with disbelief and resentment. Those particular notes are so familiar, we're frenemies.

"Fuck. Him," Jordan snaps.

"I did. And that was anticlimactic. Literally."

It's late October, and warm air streams out of the vents to combat the dip in temperature outside. But I swear, a blast of arctic air swirls in the interior of the Hummer, skimming my exposed skin. The big hand on my thigh is a leaden weight, and though shadows cling to him, I still catch the hardening of those almost too-full lips and the flicker of a muscle at his jaw.

Heat flares so hot, so suddenly, low and deep inside me I wouldn't be surprised if my ovaries are covered in soot. I recognize signs of annoyance, of anger, when I peep them. I should since I inspire both on a regular basis. Possessing a strong IDGAF gene tends to do that. Yet for the first time, a thrill sprints through me as if chasing a gold medal. My chest rises and falls; my muscles tense. Excited. I'm excited, teetering on the edge of a precipice, eager to see what he's going to say, do.

I'm wrong. I'm a conflicted mess of signals, wants, and intentions. And I don't care.

"Then it's a damn good thing you got rid of him. Bad dick is horrible. Insecure bad dick is all kinds of fucked up."

Disappointment pops inside me, and I deflate like a pricked balloon. Hell, what did I expect? We're strictly friends. I made sure of that. And what the hell am I doing? Stomping into territory that's pocked with land mines that could blow me to emotional pieces.

"I'm sorry," he murmurs, dragging me out of my head.

"What're you apologizing for?" I ask, hating the snap in my voice.

"He hurt you."

"With underwhelming smashing?" I snort. "Please. If I cried every time a man failed to make me orgasm, I'd have my own special raft to sail down the river of my tears."

I wait for a laugh or a smart-ass comeback at the very least.

But . . . nothing.

The fingers on the steering wheel tighten, and he moves his hand from my thigh back to his. Like air hitting a burn after the bandage has been torn off, my leg throbs, branded and aching from the heavy weight of his heated touch. I stare down at my hands, daring them to move.

Stay right where you are, you shameless hussies. Don't you dare grab his hand and put it back.

Thank God they obey, but I swear "selfish bitch" whispers through my head.

And *holy shit*, what was in that spaghetti I ate earlier tonight?

"He hurt you, Miriam," he says again. Softer. And Miriam. Not Blondie. Not Marilyn.

Miriam.

He means business.

Gritting my teeth, I consider not answering. But then refusing to gives his question more importance, more *meaning* than it deserves.

"Yes."

I twist in my seat. Tonight, his long dark-blond hair is pulled up and away from the shaved sides, secured into a loose bun at the back of his head. The style offers an unimpeded view of the sharp lines and angles of his profile. And the flagrantly carnal curves of his mouth. Silver glints at his eyebrow, ear, nose, and lip. My fingertips itch to trace those edges and slopes. Map them out so I can close my eyes, pick up a pencil, and re-create them just from memory. I could do a perfect rendition. With no problem. Because I crave that so badly, I rub my fingers together, reminding myself of the perils of touching what I shouldn't.

"He hurt me. Being treated like a novelty instead of a woman, a damn person, stings just a little bit." I was a sixteen year-old college freshman; God knows I should be used to that feeling by now. He's also aware that I've erected a wall around myself countless times to try and guard my heart, but maintenance on that thing is a motherfucker. "I didn't need a nine hundred number or spirit guide to see where it would go from there. Either one of two places—morbid fascination with fucking the certified genius or suddenly having a condescending competitor in my bed hell bent on proving his manhood. No thank you. So I did us both a favor and dumped him before we could even travel down that road."

"Know it well, do you?" he murmurs.

My mouth twists in spite of my determination to not reveal how another failed potential relationship has left me beating back resentment like a prizefighter.

"I have the hobo stick and blisters on my feet to prove it."

Silence thickens in the car, only the sound of Lizzo telling people about themselves and their rumors emanating from the radio. Already, a prickle of discomfort tingles beneath my skin. I shouldn't have said anything. One of my pet peeves—one of my fears—is revealing weakness. For too many years, I walked around as a living, breathing target. Until I refused to be the butt of anyone else's—of the world's—jokes and told them all to go fuck themselves with a rusty-ass spork.

I'll never be that naive, vulnerable girl again.

I *loathe* that naive, vulnerable girl.

"I hate to break it to you, Marilyn, but it wasn't your gigantic brain that had him acting like a fucking pussy."

"Please don't insult my sex. Its strength and adaptability are incomparable. Now a dick, on the other hand . . ."

He purses his lips, then nods. "Good point. I stand corrected. So it wasn't your beautiful, gigantic brain that had him acting like a raging dick. It was me."

"What?" I bark out a laugh, shifting in my seat and turning my body toward him. And determined to ignore the spurt of warmth at the "beautiful, gigantic brain" compliment. "Oh this is going to be good. Please explain."

"It's simple. Your boy was a ball bunny."

"A ball bunny," I slowly repeat.

He hikes a shoulder, lets it fall. "Yeah. It's not just women who're groupies. And you should be ashamed of yourself for being so sexist and narrow minded." He tsks. "Once you told bruh we were friends, he obviously just used you to get closer to me. Sad but true." He sighs, shooting me a look. "Can you blame him, though?" He sweeps a hand down his torso. "I'm sorry you were caught in the middle."

I stare at him—no, gape.

Casting a glance at me, he pats my hand. "It's okay, Marilyn. We'll get through this together."

I can't help it. The laughter barrels out of me at breakneck speed, rolling into the car and filling it. Jordan's teeth flash in the shadows as he grins wide.

That quick, the ashes of pain, resentment, and bitterness blow away. Leaving behind a golden light that I lean into, tip my head back and bask in.

Yeah, I think I'll keep Jordan Ransom.

JORDAN

Fuck. Him.

I did. And that was anticlimactic. Literally.

Miriam's words loop through my head like a bloopers reel—or a tragic shit show that is some sort of eternal punishment.

Fuck. Him.

I did.

Fuck. Him.

I did.

Goddammit.

My fingers curl around the glass water bottle that no doubt cost more than a rib eye at Shanahan's, and I lift it for a deep drink. Funny. Thirty-dollar water should at least taste like Beyoncé prayed over it, but nope. Tastes like regular old spring water to me. Sighing, I survey the "get-together" that Linc promised me would be low key. Just the team and another fifty or so people to celebrate last night's win before they hit the road for an away game on Friday.

Get-together, my ass.

The bass under the music played by the hired DJ throbs throughout the house but still doesn't manage to drown out the deafening chatter and laughter of the guests pressed wall to wall inside Linc's Cherry Creek mansion. Even more spill out into the back onto the patio and pool area, even though it's too cool outside for a dip. As the alcohol flows, that won't stop anyone, though. As sure as I am that I won't be using any of his bathrooms because of the bodily fluids being swapped there, I'm certain people will end up playing naked volleyball in that Olympic-size pool.

Fuck. Him.

I did.

As I grit my teeth, my grip on the water bottle tightens, and since I don't want an injured hand to go with my groin, I deliberately relax my fingers. And try to focus on the brunette perched on the arm of the chair I'm sitting in instead of those mind-fucking words. Forcing a smile, I aim it at the beautiful woman poured into a gold strapless dress. What is she talking about? A birthmark? A mole? Surgery? The hell? Nothing about me says *doctor.* Why would she think I care—

Well, fuck.

I stare at her naked breast topped by a dark-brown nipple.

And yup. There is most definitely a mole.

A glance upward, and there's no missing the invitation or promise in her green eyes, wide smile, or bare breast.

And . . . nothing.

My cock doesn't harden. My pulse doesn't race. My stomach doesn't tighten. I've felt more anticipation and hunger gazing on a turkey club sandwich than on this woman. And it's not her fault. She's gorgeous, and apparently confident as hell. I mean, she just dropped her dress in a houseful of people. Far be it from me to shame anyone for pursuing what, or who, they want. But . . .

My gaze shifts across the large living room to the far corner. A wide circle of men, more than a few of my teammates, is gathered there. And right smack in the middle stands Miriam, holding court like a debutante at some garden party. Or a vampire queen choosing her snack for the night.

The last one is closest to the truth.

And I want to volunteer as tribute.

Goddamn, how does one woman contain so much earthiness, so much raw sexuality? Her beauty—the graceful bone structure, the oval-shaped cocoa eyes, the elegant slope of nose and wide flare of nostrils, the brazenly sensual mouth—is obvious. But there's so much more to her than that conglomeration of features that can make a person stop, stare, and contemplate violating personal boundaries to touch.

It's the thick, dense wealth of shoulder-length tight curls dyed a honeyed blonde with darker roots that proclaims, "I do what I want, and I don't give a flying fuck what you think." It's the petite, almost dainty frame with the insane curves in the form of sexy, less-than-a-handful breasts; rounded hips; a perfect, worship-worthy ass; and thick, toned legs that shouldn't seem miles long. It's the loud laughter, the in-your-face confidence. The infrequent glimpses of vulnerability.

She's a dirty secret growled in the dead of night.

She's a hallowed supplication whispered on the edge of dawn.

She's beyond me.

Maybe she feels my eyes on her because Miriam swings that wicked, blinding smile from one of the men surrounding her, and it lands on me. Like the brightest ray of sunshine. Like the heaviest boulder on my chest. And I'm left breathless, incapable of moving. Trapped by that warmth, by the weight of it. But that's okay. Because I don't want to move.

And there it is.

What the brunette with the mole couldn't do with an impromptu striptease, Miriam achieves with a mischievous smile.

Lust rushes through my veins, screaming hot, scalding me, branding me. My lungs punch the overtime clock, pumping air to my starving body, my brain, and it echoes like a harsh wind in my head. It's not normal; I've experienced desire, need before. This isn't that. I've had her, tasted her, been buried so deep inside that tight pussy I still bear the bruises. And yet . . . and yet, I'm famished. My cock pounds out a steady beat that translates to "I don't give a fuck. More."

And all I can do is return her smile.

Return her smile and pretend that I don't physically ache for her. So I do.

I smile.

"Is she your girl?"

I jerk my gaze away from Miriam and back to the brunette. Hell, what's her name? I'm such an asshole. Belle? Beth? Benita?

"No. Friend," I say and nod toward her breast that's still just hanging out, saying . . . hi. "You're a gorgeous woman, sweetheart, but cover up, yeah?" And to try and ease the sting of rejection, because I, more than anyone, understand and hate its sting, I grin. "In my opinion, though, leave the mole alone. It adds character."

The pout that had already turned down the corners of her red-painted mouth disappears, and she returns my grin. She slides a glance over in Miriam's direction, proving she hadn't missed where my attention had detoured.

"Friend, huh?" She trails a finger down my chest, bisecting my abs, and I gently cuff her wrist when she reaches my belt. A smirk quirks the corners of her mouth. "Is she the reason you're not interested in my . . . mole?"

I snort. "I don't think there's a person with a working brain stem who wouldn't be interested in you . . ." Bethany? Barbie? Bren? "But

I just came here to hang and relax, not to fuck. Sorry, sweetheart." I release her, lowering my arm to the chair.

Disappointment and maybe just a hint of anger flash in her eyes, and I brace myself for a clapback, maybe a scene. Wouldn't be my first—can't say it'll be my last. While I've found it's best to be honest, my blunt nature isn't always appreciated.

But instead of stabbing me in the chest with one of her long jeweled fingernails, she dips her chin and rises from the chair's arm and saunters off, slim hips swaying and long hair brushing the bare golden skin of her back. For a moment, I still, waiting—*praying*—for regret. Regret means the pleasure/pain hold Miriam has on me has loosened its grip. The power of it has eased, and maybe I can move forward. Maybe I can get over this fever for her that's raging through my body. I wait . . .

Dammit.

I deliberately avoid looking across the room again and tip the bottle of water to my mouth. Instead of cool liquid, the dirty ash of resentment coats my tongue. And I hate myself a little for that. She's a grown, independent, strong-willed woman who knows her own mind and can make her own choices. And she's chosen to have me as a friend, nothing else. I have a choice too. Respect it or walk away.

My ass is here in this chair, isn't it?

Because I'd rather have her in my life as a friend than nothing at all.

That's my burden, not hers.

"Jordan." A large hand claps on my shoulder. "What's up?"

I glance up as Daniel drops down on the couch adjacent to my chair, and smile a welcome.

"What's going on?" I arch an eyebrow as he sprawls his long legs out in front of him. "I'm a little surprised to see you here. I thought you usually avoided these things."

Daniel laughs, shaking his head and making a show of scanning the room. Damn, are there even *more* people packed in here? I lean closer to him; otherwise we'll be shouting to hear one another.

"Yeah, I do. But somehow I must've missed the memo about this being a party straight out of *Love & Hip Hop*." Daniel props his beer on his denim-covered thigh, giving another abrupt shake of his head. "Damn, there's a lot of shit I can't unsee happening here tonight. Including the strip show I didn't ask for just now. Being married for eleven years has left me woefully unprepared for all of . . ." He waves the bottle in the general vicinity of the debauchery around us. "This."

He's not lying; whereas Daniel is all easy grace and coordination on the court as the team's shooting guard, there's an underlying tension in his tall wiry frame that his relaxed position can't hide. He's not completely comfortable here. And I can't blame him. This isn't his scene. It's never been in the ten years I've known him. He was happily married for most of those years, and he and Jerricka much preferred small get-togethers at their house rather than the blowout parties.

Seeing him here is a huge and surprising sign that he's emerging from the self-isolation he'd cocooned himself in except for games since Jerricka's death.

Although, I doubt being flashed or having a front-row seat to the ménage that looks like it's about to go down on the other couch had been on his bingo card when he arrived tonight. Public sex in the day and age of camera phones and TikTok. Yeah, how can you say *poor decisions* without saying *poor decisions*?

"Yeah, I should've expected it, but . . ." I shrug. "Can't blame the guys for wanting to blow off some steam, though. After losing the first four games, it feels good winning the last four in a row. Hopefully, we're turning a corner."

"I hope you're not blaming yourself for our rough start. Because that wouldn't only be a misplaced burden, but it would be unfair," he says, casually lifting his beer for another sip. As if he hadn't just reached into my brain and pilfered my thoughts like a shifty thief.

"I don't know—"

"I suffered an injury, too, a few years back. You remember." I do. A high ankle sprain had benched him for nearly two months. "You might also remember the team experienced one of the worst seasons we'd had in the last decade. And I blamed myself. I was the starting shooting guard. If I hadn't gotten hurt, then we wouldn't have been losing heartbreak games. Ten points. Five points. I shouldered that. Then I remember, one night after I returned to the house from a home game, Jerricka sitting me down and ordering me to stop. Well, her actual words were 'Cut that shit out.'" He chuckles, and I laugh with him because there's no sadness in that sound, only humor and warmth. "No one man wins a game, and he doesn't lose one. This isn't on you. This is on the team."

I nod, clenching my jaw against the sting there. He and Cyrus said pretty much the same thing to me only days earlier, but hearing it from him again, another ballplayer who's been there . . . a man who understands on a visceral level how it burns to the soul to have your ass planted on a chair, helpless, powerless, while your team plays their hearts out feet in front of you on the court . . . it's different.

"Especially, if part of your hurry is fear."

Daniel doesn't say more. But he doesn't need to. He slides a glance toward the floor-to-ceiling windows that encompass one of the walls and offer an unrestricted view of the pool area—and Royce Carlisle, the rookie power forward out of Rutgers University. Also my temporary replacement.

I open my mouth, the words "I'm not scared of anyone, especially a kid with milk on his breath" bouncing on my tongue. But my lips close, trapping the cocky assurance, the lie, inside. And it would be a lie. The pressure that squeezes my ribs like Popeye's tattooed arms hyped on spinach every time I look at him proves it.

I'm fucking terrified.

And since Grace Ransom didn't raise a liar, I don't say anything.

Miriam sinks down onto the recently vacated arm of the chair, nabbing my bottle out of my hand and tipping it up for a long pull as if it's a local IPA instead of overpriced water.

"Okay, you dragged my particularly tight and spectacular ass to this party, not the other way around. So why're you sitting over here looking like someone just plopped a tit in your lap and you're fresh out of dollar bills?"

"Saw that, did you?" I wince and drag my all-too-fascinated stare away from the bob of her elegant throat as she swallows. My mind easily conjures a memory of my teeth grazing a path along that column, and I'm afraid my poker face isn't up to par tonight.

"Oh, I saw," she drawls, retaining hold of my drink. "Not that I'm mad at sis." She peers down at her breasts, beautifully encased in a black bra with a sheer black top molded to her petite frame. "That was a perfect double D. Had me drooling, and I'm strictly dickly. Weeell." She screws her face up in an adorable little moue, tapping a bare fingernail against her pursed lips. "Except for that one time . . ."

A sputtering cough reminds me that we have an audience. I wince again.

"Miriam, let me introduce you to Daniel Granger before you divulge any more of your sexual history." I turn to Daniel, waving a hand toward Miriam. "Daniel, this is my friend Miriam Nelson. And I apologize in advance for whatever the fuck comes out of her mouth."

She slaps my arm, snickering. But not contradicting my words. I fight a grin. We both know I'm not sorry for shit. Her unpredictability and I-don't-give-a-fuck-itis are two of the things that drew me to her.

They're two of the things I . . . adore about her.

"Nice to meet you, Daniel." She leans forward, extending her hand toward him. When he wraps his around hers, she narrows her eyes. "I don't recognize you. Must mean you haven't availed yourself of my services."

Daniel's eyes widen, his head jerking to me, then back to her. "Excuse me?" he rasps.

Laughter barrels up my chest as Miriam nods a little too vigorously. Oh yeah, she's enjoying herself.

"I don't mean to brag, but if you don't believe in yourself and think you're the best, who else will, am I right? And Daniel? I'm the best. Never an unsatisfied customer. And that's really hard in my line of work. But we go all out. Whatever it takes to make the customer happy and have them walking away smiling and feeling good about their experience."

"Uh . . ." Daniel stares at Miriam in what appears to be equal parts horror and enthrallment. Yep. She tends to have that effect on people. I swallow a chuckle. "We?"

Another overly enthusiastic nod. "Yes. My sister and brother. We keep it in the family." How a smile can be equal parts angelic and wicked at the same time boggles the mind. "We're *really* close."

This time, I can't contain the laughter that bursts free.

"All right, Marilyn, let him off the hook," I say.

"What? I tell no lies."

Turning to my friend, I reach over and pat his arm. "No worries, bruh. She's not an escort. She and her family own a breakup-service company. They end relationships with people, not fuck 'em."

He blinks. "Is that a thing?" Blinks again. "And oh thank God."

Miriam tilts her head to the side. "Thank God. Why, Daniel? You think I wouldn't make a great escort?"

His mouth opens. Snaps shut. Pops open again. "There is absolutely no good way to answer that."

She drops her head back, the laughter rolling out of her loud, uninhibited, and free. More than a few heads turn our way, and it's not because of me or Daniel. They're staring at this beautiful, sexy woman with abandoned hilarity and lack of self-consciousness. It's confidence.

It's hot as fuck.

"Smart answer, Daniel Granger. Here." She stands and reaches behind her. A moment later, she hands him a card. "The first breakup is on the house."

"Seriously, Marilyn?" I scoff. "You brought business cards to a party?"

"What?" She shrugs and softly pats my cheek. "First rule of being an entrepreneur. You're always on the clock, and always be prepared."

"That's two rules."

She scowls. "Don't ruin my moment." Holding up my empty bottle, she shakes it. "I'm off to get a refill. You two want something?"

"No, I'll get it; you stay—" I push up from my chair, my thigh groaning a muted protest at the sudden movement.

"I got it." She pops up a hand, palm up and out. "I'm a big girl and can find my way to the bar unmolested. Now, you want something?"

Anger and humiliation flash inside of me like a struck match. She's not fooling me; this isn't about being a "big girl" or some shit like that. It's about her covering for me. Protecting me. But that's my job. Has been since I was old enough to understand what my mother's tears and her latest asshole boyfriend's shouts meant.

It's the only role I know.

"No," I murmur, shame a grimy film coating my throat. No amount of water is going to wash it away.

"You, Daniel?" she asks.

He shakes his head and holds up his still half-full beer. "I'm good, thanks."

"Be right back. Unless I bump into your girl, Jordan. Then, I might be a while." With a frankly lascivious grin, she disappears into the thick crowd.

"So *that's* Miriam." Daniel huffs out a soft laugh. "Would you think less of me if I admit that she scares me?"

I snort. "I would think less of you if she *didn't*."

He chuckles again, still staring in the direction Miriam left. "She's gorgeous," he murmurs.

Everything in me stills, pulls tight, and I try my damnedest not to betray the bright, sharp sensation sliding between my ribs.

"Yeah, she is," I agree, amazed that I sound casual, almost bored instead of all keep-your-fucking-eyes-to-yourself.

More staring, and I lower a hand down beside my thigh and out of sight. That way I don't have to explain the reflexive fisting of my fingers. Not to punch my friend. Never that. Although I can't deny the damn near primal need to stalk through this house, hunt down Miriam, pin her to the nearest wall, and take that fuckable mouth so every person in this house knows she's mine and off limits.

But that's just it.

She's not mine.

And Miriam has made it abundantly clear she never will be. That we will never be that to one another.

So no, the clenching of my hand isn't about violence. At least not toward Daniel. To myself, yes. That blunt bite of pain, the dull ache, the control—they ground me. Place me in the here and now. It's a frigid slap of reality.

Daniel edges forward on the couch cushion, the seemingly forgotten beer bottle dangling from his fingers. "I don't want to get in your business or move wrong. And I remember the interrogation Cyrus put you under a few nights ago. But . . . are you two really just friends or are you . . ."

He trails off, and my gut clenches. Hard. Because part of me realizes where this is going. Why he's probing. And if I tell him "Yes, we've had sex. She's friend-zoned me, but I'm secretly and pathetically in love with her like a goddamn heart-eye emoji," Daniel would back off.

What's the saying? The truth will set you free?

Well, for me, it's a fucking prison. And the scarred, wary heart of one beautiful woman is my jailer.

So as always, I keep the whole truth to myself and give pieces of it. Only the palatable ones.

"Just friends." I force my lips into an amused smirk. "You've met her. If she were my girl, do you really think she would take a half-naked chick propositioning me so easily? Hell, they'd have to put her in witness protection so Miriam couldn't track her down."

Daniel laughs, and I join him, though that sharp knife in my chest twists. Because I'm giving myself further proof that the woman I desire beyond reason doesn't feel the same. Shit, Miriam would've marched over here to compare tit size with Beth/Brenda/Becky rather than demand she back up off me.

That's just depressing as fuck.

"I can see that." Daniel's eyes crinkle at the corners, and in spite of my morose thoughts, it's damn good to see humor on him. "If you're sure you're just friends . . ."

"I'm sure."

Gritting your teeth does not make you sound believable.

Right. I deliberately relax my jaw and wish I had another bottle of *something*. My fingers flex, curl. Flex, curl.

"You know Cyrus dates her sister. That's how we met," I remind him.

"That's right. Then you, uh, wouldn't mind if I, uh . . ." Daniel clears his throat and dips his chin in the direction of the living room exit. *Spit it out, dammit.* "If I ask Miriam out."

That knife twists. Plunges deeper.

Rami Malek doesn't have anything on me. My acting skills rival none. Because nothing in my expression gives away the hot anger and pain contorting me into so many knots Cirque du Soleil should be knocking at my door any minute.

"She has a father, and he's not me. You don't need my blessing," I say. Yeah, definitely missed my Hollywood calling.

"I know, man. I just want to make sure I'm not stepping on any toes. And"—he ducks his head, rubbing a palm back and forth over his thigh, and the nervous gesture nabs my attention—"this would be the first time I'm asking a woman out since Jerricka . . . well, it's the first time I would be asking a woman out in a long time."

"Yeah."

I'm an asshole. An insensitive asshole. I didn't even think . . .

Shame churns in my gut, and I look at him. *Really* look at him. See the glints of attraction, of fear . . . of hope.

Fuck.

This is about more than my rejected feelings. Daniel should move on, should reach for the chance for happiness after so much grief. He, more than anyone I know, deserves the chance to walk into the light.

I can't stand in the way of that for my own selfish reasons. And I can't fool myself. They would be selfish.

"You should do it, Daniel," I murmur. "Some advice, though? She's not . . . a fan of athletes. I'm still not sure why she puts up with my ass. So don't come to her like Linc or one of the other guys. Be real and honest. She'll appreciate that."

He nods, a smile brightening his light-brown eyes. "I appreciate that, man."

"No problem. Whatever I can do to help."

And the sad part?

I mean that.

CHAPTER FOUR

MIRIAM

"Pain created me. Now I'm paying it forward. With interest."

—Sarafina Rose, *Ravaged Lands*

"Granted entrance? No one grants me entrance. I take it."

"No." I groan and rub my stylus over the screen of my pro tablet, removing the dialogue out of the small square in the corner of my panel. "That's not right. Corny," I mutter to myself.

Tapping the cushioned bottom of the technical pen on my desktop, I study the illustration of the dark, hooded figure; the only identifying features visible from the shadows are long dark-red locs and a wide yet menacing grin. But the cloak doesn't conceal the black vest or dark-brown leather pants and boots that conform to large breasts, big hips, long legs, and thick, shapely thighs. Neither does the cloak hide all the knives, swords, or bow and arrows strapped to her body. And that doesn't even start to cover the weapons inside of her.

Oh yeah. My Sarafina Rose is a total badass.

But her dialogue really sucks at the moment.

Still, the story line is shaping up great. My half-human, half-demon heroine contemplates how to infiltrate the huge, dark castle of her mortal enemy, the demonic wizard Razvan—who also happens to be her father.

My readers have been waiting for this moment, and I'm not going to half-ass it.

I shift my gaze to one of my newest characters. A bearded, muscled giant of a man standing just behind and to the left of Sarafina. An intimidating figure with long canary-gold hair shaved on the sides and braided down his back, he stands proud and fierce, his wide torso clad in a fawn jacket, dark runes inscribed in his skin, and leather pants conforming to his powerful thighs. With his booted feet braced far apart and a Mammen axe in each hand, he's a warrior.

He's an outcast, as he only looks human but is a changeling—fae offspring switched out for a human child in infancy—and feared and reviled by men who discover his true identity.

He's honorable, loyal, refusing to leave Sarafina's side in a battle, always having her back.

He's her lover.

He's North the Woodsman.

And he's obviously Jordan. Or rather, Jordan was my inspiration for him.

Sue me. So I'm living vicariously through my characters.

It's a safe place to do so without any emotional fallout or damage; it's a damn near cathartic indulgence that isn't hurting anyone. To the contrary. I like to think, in my own small way, that maybe I'm helping some of my readers. Not just offering them a place of escape into this postapocalyptic, war-ravaged, and brutal land of magic and steel, of man and myth, but also, I hope, showing them that strength isn't just about might, power, or brute force. It's about acting in the face of fear and seemingly overwhelming odds, about finding your voice when it's easier to be and stay silenced.

I'm giving my readers what I didn't have. What I wish someone had been there to offer me.

I inhale, shoving the grime of misplaced guilt and shame aside, and allow the pleasure and bone-deep satisfaction to bloom in my chest as I stare at the screen. At the illustrations that are my original creations, that come from my imagination and hand. At the story line I plotted and wrote. This issue, which will end up in the third Ravaged Lands omnibus by the time I'm done, is shaping up to be my best yet, and my online readers are devouring each installment I post. This—my career as a graphic novelist—brings me joy. It's the accomplishment I'm most proud of, so far.

And it's also a secret.

A knock at my office door sends a pulse of panic tumbling through me, and I fumble to save the progress on the current chapter of my graphic novel and put my tablet to sleep. And just in time for my brother, Levi, buttoned up and proper in his immaculate three-piece suit, to open the door and stride in.

Charge in would be a more accurate description.

My older brother, and Zora's twin, doesn't do anything as casual as *stride*. Actually, he doesn't do anything as casual as breathe. He inhales, circulates air for the function of his brain, organs, and other bodily functions, and then exhales. Everything in his life must have purpose or a reason, or he wants no part of it.

A real charmer and people person, Leviticus is.

He's Zadok. A tall, lean, imposing figure draped in all black—long black coat, black shirt and pants, sword with a black hilt strapped to his back. He's a judge traveling from settlement to settlement handing out justice and punishment. He's the Law in the Ravaged Lands.

My brother would probably pop something irreplaceable if he discovered I'd drawn him into a graphic novel as a righteous executioner of men.

The thought brings a small smile to my lips.

"It's customary for a person to wait until they're invited before barging into another's space. Even vampires understand that rule."

Levi stops in front of my desk, a dark eyebrow raised high. Even with the whole cyborg impersonation thing going on, my brother is, well—shudder—hot. Lawd, that hurt even thinking it. Still, with his striking features; tall, wide-shouldered body; and alpha-hole demeanor, he's not hard on the eyes. But he is a pain in my ass. And I'm sure his visit in my office isn't to check on my welfare.

"It might be customary, but since you would've said you weren't here or not answered at all, I decided to bypass the 'niceties' and let myself in."

That eyebrow arches higher, as if daring me to deny his accusation. I shrug and lean back in my desk chair, lifting my legs and propping my red-and-white high-top Converse up on the desk. To Levi's credit, he doesn't even blink an eye. Not at the footwear he considers inappropriate for the office—I know this because he told me—or the black-and-white plaid skater dress and oversized Gryffindor cardigan. Hey, I represent my house proudly.

I'm a mood dresser. Sometimes I feel sexy and wear leather, stilettoes, and lace. And other times I feel equally badass and don my I'm-about-to-be-up-to-all-kinds-of-wizardry-shenanigans clothes. Both set my brother's jaw a-twitching, so I consider it a win.

"Facts." I give my foot an extra wiggle because I'm mature like that. "What's up, brother dearest?"

"What's *up* is that last month's marketing budget has increased by thirty-five percent. And already, next month's projection is looking to be the same, if not higher." He taps on the tablet he holds in his hand and extends it toward me.

Levi doesn't bother trying to break down the spreadsheet to me. To some people, the rows, columns, and numbers might as well be Greek, but they're a second language to me, and I'm bilingual. It's one of the few things we have in common—an innate understanding of math. Only he loves it, and I'm gifted in it.

And that's one of our many differences.

"There's a question hidden among that statement. I can sense it." I narrow my eyes on him. "C'mon, Levi. You can get it out. I believe in you."

He cocks his head. "How is it that a grown woman with two degrees still possesses the mentality of a fourteen-year-old in need of a grounding?"

"Meh. It's a gift." I flick my hand. "Now, can you tell me why you're here so I can get back to surfing porn on company time?"

"Is it hentai porn? That would explain the outfit."

I snicker. Okay, so that was a good one. "Dammit!" I snap my fingers, giving him an exaggerated wince. "Got to remember to clear my browser."

If my brother did things as *human* as roll his eyes, he would do that right now. Instead, he sets his tablet on my desk and nudges it closer until the edge hits against mine.

"Explain the increase in the budget that we all agreed on at our last meeting." He crosses his arms over his chest.

A hot flash of anger ignites in my chest, a flare in a dark night that warns of an imminent explosion. He never enters Zora's office requiring explanations for her business decisions. It's not just about being the youngest sibling. No, this perpetual "accounting" that both Levi and Zora unconsciously demand stems from the sheltered, awkward little girl they remember and the "crazy" woman she became. Because that's how they see me. Crazy. Eccentric. A step away from joining a league of supervillains and becoming their brilliant, charismatic, evil leader. Which is fucking silly. I mean, I don't mind the custom-made suits, but I refuse to shave my head of these bomb-ass curls for anyone.

Seriously, though. It's a catch-22 with my brother and sister. They respect my intelligence and talent. And they definitely appreciate the money I invested in BURNED. But my personality, my live-out-loud demeanor confuse them . . . scare them.

Neither one has asked me why I changed from the quiet, shy, naive girl I was when I left for college. They haven't asked if someone stepped in the path of who I was and shifted the course to change me into who I am. They haven't asked what happened to make me say, no, *yell*, "Fuck it. I'm going to be who I want, say what I want, and screw who doesn't like it."

Even though Zora knows the *what*, she's still never connected the dots of the *why*.

No, Levi and Zora just assigned each other days to babysit me in the office.

Not that I'm bitter or anything. At least, I try not to be.

"Sure." I lower my legs and scoot my chair closer, clasping my hands together next to my tablet and smiling serenely up at him "This time of year, we're heading into three major US holidays—Halloween, Thanksgiving, and soon Christmas. Parties, big dinners, the perfect gifts, families—most promotional ads running right now would have consumers believe those are the things on most people's minds. But we're forgetting one. And I'm not talking about love and romance. I'm referring to those people who are trying to figure out how to extricate themselves from their relationships in order to be free for the holidays for a variety of reasons. To party single with friends. So they don't have to bring home the other person to meet their family when they're just not that serious. Or maybe that person is just a selfish, cheap asshole and plans to break up with them for the holiday so they don't have to buy a gift. Which, I repeat, cheap asshole move, but still, business for us. All business for us."

I lean forward, pinning my still, silent brother with an unwavering stare.

"I, for one, hate to nitpick, but I didn't approve that marketing budget. Nor was I present at that last meeting. You and Zora rolled the numbers for the marketing and promotions over from the previous months, which were fine for August and September but not for the last three of the year. October, November, and December are markedly different consumer months, and that includes us. So yes, I did increase the spending because the numbers were too low if we want to compete with not just online matchmaking companies but holiday movies, music, as well as the romance industry."

And despite the blood pumping through my veins and the drum of my heart echoing in my throat, I grin and hold out my arms, dipping my head.

"And that, my friend, is how a grown woman with a BA in graphic design, a double minor in marketing and contemporary women's rights, as well as a master's in graphic illustration and digital media who possesses the mentality of a grounded fourteen-year-old handles her business. I hope you were taking notes. There will be an exam at the end of the week."

He stares at me for a long moment, then reaches out and picks up his tablet.

"Thank you for explaining the increase to me. I'll make sure Zora is clear on it as well." Instead of turning toward the door and leaving, he remains standing in front of my desk, continuing to study me in that manner of his that has me sympathizing with a dissected frog. "You're brilliant, Miriam. I don't understand why you try to hide it behind outrageous clothes and an even more outrageous mouth."

He's not being mean; Levi honestly believes I'm a teenager in a woman's body, rebelling against who I am—what I am—and hiding behind sarcasm, wit, and nonconformity. And maybe there's a grain of truth in that. For so long, I existed in a small box of expectations and restrictions people placed on me. I allowed them—my parents—to dictate my education, my career path, even down to what time I ate and slept and rose in the morning. I was in a jail with glass bars. So yes, maybe a small part of me is still pounding against those bars, screaming for my freedom.

But . . .

But the other side that Levi or Zora, for that matter, can't see—refuse to comprehend—is that this *is* my liberation. Being able to live my truth out loud, with my voice, my choice . . . that's not hiding.

Liar.

The word spasms in my chest, and I catch myself just before I rub the spot where that phantom accusation reverberates.

Grinning wider to cover my discomfort, I shrug again. "Same reason you hide behind your cyborg persona to conceal your humanity. Wait." I scrunch up my face. "That *is* a persona, right?"

Before he can reply—and this is Levi, so there will be a reply—another knock vibrates on my door.

"Come in!" I call out. Then I say to Levi, "See how that works?"

"I've heard rumors. Nice to see it in action."

I snort as my office door opens and Jordan strolls in. All glorious six-plus-plus feet of him. Damn. I could really hate him for inciting a rebellion in my reproductive organs if not for the fact that I've decided not to act on that revolution.

Yep. That's what I keep telling myself.

My will is stronger than my vagina.

One of these days, I'm going to believe it.

As it stands, my gaze trails him as he spots my brother, and a huge, genuinely delighted smile stretches his mobile, wide mouth. It lights up his face, lifting those carved-from-marble cheekbones and brightening his vivid blue eyes. Jordan goes in for a hug and pat on the back that would most likely knock a smaller man on his ass. Levi, a frown creasing his forehead, doesn't return the hug, but he does awkwardly return the pat on the shoulder.

Something I refuse to label seizes my chest and squeezes so hard I remain sitting in my chair, half afraid if I stand, I might stumble back from lack of proper oxygen. So I look away from him—or, more specifically, away from Jordan showing open and authentic affection to this man whom I love with all my heart despite him being difficult, prickly, and closed off.

Jordan already possesses too much real estate in my thoughts and life. And I can't afford to offer him more.

That's what I have Ravaged Lands for. To purge this totally inconvenient preoccupation and fascination.

Clearing my throat, I snatch up my tablet, open up my desk drawer, and tuck it safely inside.

"If you'd like me to leave my office and grant you two some privacy, I would . . . well, actually, I wouldn't. So either break it up or take it outside," I mutter.

"Aww." Jordan cocks his head, turning his mouth down at the corners and poking his lower lip out. It should look ridiculous, like a big man-baby. I *definitely* shouldn't want to bite it and flick that silver hoop with my tongue. *God. I have* to stop this. "Is someone hangry? It's a good thing I'm here to take you to dinner before anyone gets hurt." He gives my brother one of those chin lifts that I swear they must take all boys aside in middle school and teach them to do in the boys' bathroom. "You want to come with us, Levi? We're getting sushi, and I know how you adore it."

Jordan grins, and I snort, because my brother abhors sushi. Claims if he was meant to eat raw fish, he'd wade into Chatfield Reservoir, catch one, and eat it there. Which to him made more sense than paying someone to serve it up on a plate.

Did I mention he's a charmer?

"That's a funny way of saying I'd rather you not join us for dinner," Levi says. "I have plans, thank you, but no."

"What plans?" I demand.

Girlfriend? Is he seeing someone? Levi is notoriously private, and it drives me and Zora batty. My mother too. But we understand him not wanting Monica Nelson in his business. That's like calling up the IRS, inviting them over for dinner, and serving up your overdue tax returns for an entrée. Asking for trouble.

But me and Zora? We're used to keeping each other's secrets from our parents.

"Plans that are mine and not yours." He arches that damn eyebrow and nods at Jordan. "How's your groin injury?"

Unlike when the rest of us ask, that initial flash of irritation that Jordan probably believes he conceals so well doesn't make an appearance. Most likely because there's no sympathy in Levi's voice, no hint of softness, just a steady matter-of-factness. And it's not because he doesn't care or isn't capable of compassion. No, he wouldn't know how to play games if they came to him packaged with directions. If he honestly didn't care, he wouldn't ask. But Levi's not asking about Jordan's emotional well-being; he's inquiring about his physical state, about the facts. And that clearly sets Jordan at ease.

"It's coming along. Just got back from PT. The swelling and bruising have gone down, and the pain is easing up. If I keep up the stretching, icing, heating, and elevation at home, then hopefully I'll be back on the court in about three weeks."

"That's good news. But I'm guessing the doctors told you four weeks if you're saying three." When Jordan's chin kicks back in surprise, Levi snorts. "Cyrus texted me about guys' night Thursday. I'll see you then."

With that, he leaves, quietly shutting the door behind him.

"I'm still confused on the story of how you three became such good buddies," I mumble, staring at my closed door.

"Some things weren't meant for you to understand." He crosses the room and lowers into the chair in front of my desk. "They're man things."

"Oh. Man things. So how to hit everywhere but the toilet bowl while peeing, how to piss every woman in creation off by mansplaining, and the finer points of farting in public without giving one single solitary fuck. Which"—I hold up a finger as I stand and round my desk—"I personally think that last one is an underappreciated gift." I lean back against the desk in front of him, crossing my arms and ankles.

And pretend my breath doesn't catch when his gaze momentarily dips to my thighs.

He's a man. And an athlete. It's in his DNA and job description to check out the opposite sex. Case in point, the woman from the other night at Linc's party—the boob flasher. I'm sure that's par for the course for him. And of course, *logically*, I know this, but that was the first time I had a front-row, splash-zone seat to it.

I hadn't liked it.

And by "I hadn't liked it," I mean, it'd taken every bit of my flawed self-control and a rousing pep talk of "chicks before dicks" to keep me from flying over to them and punching ol' girl in her tit.

Anger had flooded me like a biblical punishment, and it'd scared me. I'd never experienced that . . . primal urge to claim someone like a feral alley cat. And wasn't that just demoralizing? Only my shock, my horror, and the crystal clear image of Jordan's humiliating reaction had kept me rooted, locked in place. Other than that night when we'd both lost our minds and clothes, he'd never given me the slightest hint that he viewed me as anything other than a friend. Cyrus with a womb. And that's how I wanted it.

Want it.

Yes, want it.

Titty-punching aside.

"Exactly, Marilyn." He nods, holding up his hands. "See? This is why we're friends. You get it without me having to mansplain."

"Whatever." Uncrossing my ankles, I straighten and push off the desk, then retrace my steps to reclaim my office chair. And ignore the spasm in my belly over that "friends." Because that's what we are. All we can be because I demanded it. "Now, what brings you by? And don't tell me you were in the neighborhood because Castle Pines is nowhere near here," I remind him. While a good many of his teammates live in exclusive Cherry Creek, he has a home in the Castle Pines suburb. It's a wealthy community but has a more rural feel with its beautiful scenery, thick trees, and several parks. It's a good thirty-minute drive from Five Points, where our BURNED offices are located. "And my memory might not be as good as it used to be at my doddering twenty-seven years old, but I would've remembered dinner plans. Which we didn't have. So why are you really here?"

If I'm not mistaken, his full lips flatten for a second, and his eyes darken.

But yes, I *must* be mistaken.

Because in the next instant, the corners of that mouth curl up in a smile, and his eyes reflect nothing back but a clear sky blue.

Still . . .

Why can't I shake the sense that I'm missing something?

Or . . . that he's hiding something?

Now *that* I shrug off as bullshit. Jordan might be a lot of things—a charming, lovable manwhore athlete—but he's not a liar.

"Funny you should ask that, bestie," he drawls.

"Oh fuck." I groan, tipping my head back and blinking at the ceiling. "What?"

"Miriam."

Miriam again. He has my attention. Lowering my gaze to him, I scrutinize him. Notice any traces of humor have fled, leaving behind a rare seriousness that those intrusive reporters' cameras never catch unless he's on the court. *Fine*, sue me. Since we've become friends, I've gone back and watched some online footage of him playing.

The man is *magnificent*. Beauty and animal grace in action. Only to myself—and then in the darkest of hours when just the shadows of my bedroom stare back at me—do I admit watching him on that screen sent heat and smoke spiraling through me. Those same powerfully cut muscles that had flexed under taut skin . . . the same exquisite control that had allowed him to leap in the air, snag basketballs out of the air, and fly down a court . . . the same intensity and concentration tightening his face, narrowing his eyes . . .

That same body, that same strength and domination had covered me, moved against me, been inside me. So fucking deep inside me.

Looking at this man do what he loved most was foreplay.

Dammit, what am I doing? And now I can't glance at him with those images trucking through my head like semis on a long-distance haul. On the pretense of getting ready to shut it down for the day, I start clicking out of programs on my computer. Anything to corral my thoughts and get my face—and vagina—under control.

Besties.

He called us besties. Because that's what we are. Get with the program, and stop campaigning for a repeat that's never happening, you shameless hussies.

And why yes, I am having a conversation with my nipples and pussy.

Sigh. This is what I've been reduced to.

"Miriam." He repeats my name, and because it *is* my name, I stop shutting down my computer and risk looking at him. Hoping, *praying* my face can keep its mouth shut. Or its face shut. Or . . . hell. However that works. "I need a favor."

"Yes."

His big frame stiffens, and he blinks. "You haven't even heard the favor."

"Okay." I shrug. "But yes."

He's never asked me for one before. Ever. So for him to come to me, it must be important. At least to him. So it's a yes. Because he's important to me.

A soft chuckle escapes him, and Jordan shakes his head. "Miriam . . ."

"Oh, just ask it already, and give me the details."

He rubs his hands along the length of his powerful thighs, but that's the only sign of his nerves, his agitation. Yet it's enough. My heart inches toward the base of my throat, mingling with my pulse. A cacophonous rhythm thrums in my head, and I'm nearly rising from my chair.

"Jordan . . . ," I whisper.

"I need you to go out on a date with Daniel Granger."

My ass plops back into my seat, my knees transforming to the consistency of my sister's watery-ass turkey gravy. Relief? Shock? Both?

What. The. Fuck?

"Excuse me?" I rasp.

Exhaling a breath that echoes in the room like a boom, he tunnels his fingers through his long hair, dragging the thick strands away from his face. A couple cling to heavy scruff like a lover reluctant to relinquish their hold, and my fingertips itch to brush them away. To take their place and discover if that hair is coarse, silky, or somewhere in between.

He'd been clean shaven that night we . . .

Focus, bitch.

Right.

Date. Daniel Granger.

I grasp the armrests of my chair and lean forward, pinning Jordan with a glare. "What—and I can't stress this enough—the fuck?"

"Hear me out." He pops a hand up, palm out.

I jerk my chin, but inside my head, a whirlwind of thoughts bangs against my skull, tangling with surprise, resentment, and hurt. Yes, hurt, because he's playing matchmaker between me and his teammate. Okay, he doesn't want me, so he's throwing me at another man?

I'm keeping my mouth shut . . . for now.

But inside? Inside, I'm fuming.

"Since you don't follow sports, I'm going to assume you don't know much about Daniel?" I shake my head, still keeping quiet. His eyes narrow on me, but he says, "Yeah, okay." After rising from the chair, he stalks over to my smallish window, props a forearm on the wall, and stares out onto Welton Street. Several moments pass by in silence before he turns around, inked arms crossed over his chest. "When I first joined the team, I may've been a cocky shit on the outside, but inside? Scared as hell. Professional basketball is as different from high school and college ball as flag football is from the NFL."

I stare at him.

"As the first *Fast & Furious* movie from the last fifty."

I stare some more.

He sighs. "As different from old-school *ThunderCats* to new-school *ThunderCats*."

"Ohhh." I shudder. "Got it."

"Anyway," he continues, "Daniel had already been on the team for four years and saw past the smart-ass mouth and that other bullshit to the terrified rookie beneath. He took me beneath his wing. Showed me how to be not just a better player but a professional and a good teammate." He gives his head a small shake, and a low, short laugh escapes him. "There were times my mouth wrote a check my ass couldn't cash, and he got me out of those tight situations. Didn't berate me or make me feel like the asshole I was, just gave me advice and became that big-brother figure I never had but needed. Especially in this industry. When they turn you into a millionaire at twenty, they don't exactly teach you how to be a morally and fiscally responsible man with it. If I'd been left to my own devices, my whole first check would've been spent on houses and cars I don't have the time to live in or drive, clothes, watches, and all this other bullshit that don't mean a damn thing. I definitely wouldn't have investments, a financial portfolio, or a fucking future after basketball. Hell, he introduced me to Cyrus."

"He sounds like a good guy." He does. But . . . "I still don't see what this has to do with me or why I should go out with him." *You fucking date him if he's so great* bounces on the tip of my tongue, but I swallow it down. There is a line of callousness even I hesitate to cross. Not often, mind you. But it does exist. "Besides, I don't date athletes."

But you fuck them.

The words, unspoken but deafening, vibrate in the abruptly dense silence.

Neither of us moves. At least, I can't. Not with that electric stare like a physical hand pinning me to my seat. No, that's a lie. It doesn't trap me. It *touches* me. Strokes over my face, feathers down my neck, glances over my collarbone.

Grazes the top of my breasts.

Dips lower . . .

I inhale, the overly loud sound cracking the tension like a stone flung against a windshield. I uncurl my numb fingers from around the chair's armrests and lower my hands to my lap, where I flatten them against my thighs. A small movement to that piercing scrutiny across the room, but only I am aware of the truth.

It's either this or press my palms to the suddenly achy breasts that also felt that visual caress.

"I'm hoping you'll make an exception. For me," he murmurs. "You've never explained your rule to me."

And I'm not about to now.

Maybe not ever.

"You were right." I roll back and stand, pressing my palms to my desk. "I should've waited to see what you asked before agreeing to this favor. We're friends, and I appreciate the new flow of clients your teammates have brought to BURNED, but I'm not dating one of them. That's out of the question."

"Miriam . . ."

A match strikes, and anger flickers to life with a metallic *whoosh*. It's irrational to direct my hurt, my pain toward him—my head acknowledges this. But my heart? My heart sweeps me back to that moment when I was at my weakest, my most humiliated and helpless. When I was a victim of not just a mean, harmful, demeaning joke but of my own naivete. My own willful stupidity.

"No," I say, perhaps more vehemently than the situation calls for. But the sticky wisps of the past cling to me like spiderwebs.

He shoves off the wall and crosses the room, stopping just short of my desk. "You promised to hear me out," he gently reminds me.

Dammit. I did. And it's not his fault that he doesn't understand why I have a nearly decade-long moratorium on dating athletes. Especially when I won't tell him.

Only Zora knows, and I told her years later. Not even Renae knows.

"Daniel's a widower."

His blunt statement falls into the room, each word a pebble striking my resolve and sending ripples over it. Sympathy for the handsome man with the beautifully braided cornrows and lovely hazel eyes squeezes my sternum. I can't even imagine . . .

Renae lost her fiancé a year ago. A drunk college student out celebrating her entrance into law school plowed her car into Derrick, killing him instantly. The woman survived with a broken leg, but Renae? She remains broken in places the eye can't see, and yet, at times, it's a physical thing.

"Shit. And I handed him my business card." I pinch the bridge of my nose. Sighing, I meet his steady gaze. "How long was he married?"

"Eleven years. He lost Jerricka two years ago. He's been like a ghost since then, just a shade of the man I'd known. You're the first woman he's shown interest in dating since her death." Jordan slides his hands into the front pockets of his jeans and briefly glances back toward the window before turning to me again. "This is a big ask, but if he hasn't called you already, would you, as a personal favor to me, give him a chance? Just one date, Miriam," he softly pleads. "If he's taking the risk and putting himself out there, I'd hate for him to be hurt."

He moves closer to the desk until his thick thighs press against the edge, and this close, I catch the tiny, almost imperceptible tic of a muscle along his jaw. As if he's holding himself back from . . . what?

A rabid curiosity filters into the dregs of resentment and sorrow still sticking to my chest.

"And you're putting this on me?" I ask, genuinely confused. "I'm the one person you should keep your friend far away from. Not only do I break up with people for a living, but I want nothing to do with athletes—Jordan, you know what I mean," I scramble to cover, to fix that thoughtless remark.

He nods, but the ice that crystallized his expression doesn't thaw. Doesn't melt the deep freeze in his eyes. Dammit.

"Jordan . . ."

"No worries, Miriam. I know what you mean." A smile curves his mouth, and in spite of the circumstances, in spite of the inexplicable tension crowded into the room like a nosy neighbor, my gaze still drops to it. Still notices the beautiful shape of it. Still notices that it doesn't reach his eyes. "And you've made your views about being involved with athletes clear, which is why if I could avoid having this conversation with you, I would. But it's you he's attracted to, not another woman. And so I'm asking."

"What do you get out of this?" Frustration creeps into me, peppering my voice. I fling a hand toward my office door, as if Daniel stands on the other side of it. "Other than warm fuzzies for being the team matchmaker? Which, by the way, technically makes us mortal enemies," I hiss.

"He was there for me when I didn't have anyone," he says. "I owe him."

"So you're fine with just throwing me at your friend? Like I'm payment for some debt?"

The bitterness that coats my question sours my stomach. Stupid. Stupid to feel like . . . traded goods. Like I should mean more to him.

Don't men have a bro code like women? Jordan's been inside me. How can he so easily just hand me over to a friend, no matter how much he believes he *owes* him?

Shit. Why doesn't he just tag my ear and herd me out to Daniel's waiting car?

"What the hell is that supposed to mean?" he snaps, his brown eyebrows slashing down into a dark frown. "I've never disrespected you. Never treated you like you were some nameless random who doesn't matter to me."

You just did.

And I should know. I've been that nameless random before.

The difference between then and now? *This* man I care about. *This* man is my friend.

And dammit, I'm a sucker for a widower.

"Yeah, you're right. Forget I said it. You know me, letting shit just fly out of my mouth." I force a smile that's all teeth and fake as a porn star's moans. "Fine. I'll do it. If Daniel calls, I'll go out with him."

"Miriam . . ."

I shake my head, cutting him off. "Quit while you're ahead, 'kay? But"—I pop a finger up—"I'm promising one date."

Another pall of silence blankets the office, and I suppress the urge to rub my arms as the chill in the room is surely part and parcel of my imagination. But not the rigidity of his huge frame. I'm not imagining that. Tension rides through him, stiffening his shoulders, transforming him into living marble. I'm not even sure he's breathing.

Would he be offended if I stuck my finger under his nose to double-check?

Best not to chance it.

"You'll do it? You'll go out with him?"

"Yes." I huff out a chuckle that's far, far from humorous. "I thought this would make you happy. I gotta say, Jordan, you don't look happy."

For another long moment, he stares at me, and alarm spears through me. And the urge to round the desk, charge over to him, and cup his face is so strong I grip the edge of the desk. In the time we've been friends, I've always been able to read him, tell what he's thinking.

Those amazing sky-blue eyes have hidden nothing from me. I didn't think they—or he—were capable of it.

Now, though? Peering into eyes that have gone shuttered?

I'm rethinking that belief. And it scares me a little.

Is the man I'm closest to—a man I've let inside me—a stranger?

"Of course I'm happy." He returns his attention to me, and it's with a smile. A smile that's so wide, so familiar, it almost dispels the twist of unease in my belly. Almost. "And thank you. Now I owe you."

"Right." Here's where I say I don't need him to be in my debt. But the conciliatory words don't emerge. Because a dark part of me wants him to be beholden to me. In a base way, it links us. And I like that. "Well, mission accomplished. Now if you don't mind, get out. I'm about to leave for the day."

He cocks his head, a smirk riding the corners of his mouth. And that quick, we're back on familiar ground. The teasing, laid-back, harmless player. My bestie.

My sarcasm game is strong tonight.

"I thought we were going to dinner. My treat."

"Sorry, but if you'd called before you dropped by to guilt me into dating your friend, I could've told you I had plans." I add a smile with my lie.

Well, not necessarily a lie. My plans include leftover pizza, Netflix, and more Ravaged Lands.

He nods, taking a step back from my desk, but he stops. Doesn't turn for the door. Instead, he remains so still only his electric-blue gaze moves as it roams my face before meeting my eyes once more.

"Say no," he says, voice low, almost a rumble in his wide chest.

What is he talking about? I frown, shaking my head, confusion swamping me.

"To what? My plans?"

He stares at me for another moment, then pivots and heads for the office door. Hand on the knob, he twists and pulls it open, throwing me his trademark cocky grin over his shoulder.

"Your loss, Marilyn. It was going to be some damn good sushi."

With that, he's gone, and the room seems smaller, the air in here staler.

I'm less . . . charged. Energized.

Giving my head a hard shake, I return my focus to shutting down my computer and gathering my things. I have cold pepperoni-and-onion pizza to get home to and a graphic novel to finish.

Enigmatic basketball players are above my pay grade.

CHAPTER FIVE

JORDAN

"Honor. Integrity. They are not choices. But being a dick?
Well, that's simply a pleasure."

—North the Woodsman, *Ravaged Lands*

I'm sure when those old pastors preached about hell and fire and brimstone, they weren't referring to a three-million-dollar home in a Colorado gated community.

But hey.

Right now, sitting on the couch in the great room with a wall of glass granting a gorgeous view of a star-studded dark sky and acres of wide-open space, I'm definitely in hell.

Because my team is losing, and I'm sitting on my ass on the afore-mentioned couch and can't do a fucking thing about it.

"Rebound, dammit," I snarl under my breath, even though there's no one in the house to hear me. Marlon Lester races back down the court after having allowed the Celtics forward to box him out and recover the ball Linc had shot and missed. "What the fuck are we doing?"

They fall back on a man-to-man defense, and I sit forward, elbows propped on my knees, leg jumping. The score keeps fluctuating. We jump up by three points. They tie, then surpass us by five. We come back, then pull ahead.

Shit. Watching, being on this end . . . my fingers fist on my thighs. Helplessness, fucking powerlessness, sweeps through me, threatening to drag me under. And I fight, but shit, at this point, I'm a swimmer battling against the tide.

I hate it.

Anger whips at me, leaving bloodred lashes behind.

I hate being weak.

I hate . . . *fuck*.

The peal of the doorbell echoing through the house snatches me out of my downward spiral, and I shoot up from the couch. Pain throbs high inside my thigh, and I grit my teeth against it, embracing it. Grateful for the opportunity to focus on something else besides the bitter, acrid taste of failure in my mouth.

Though I live in an exclusive gated community, and given the small list of people allowed to freely visit without security first checking in with me, I still pause in my foyer and check the video monitor beside the front door. Having money hasn't stolen my common sense.

Miriam.

The blast of warmth to the chest should take me by surprise. It doesn't. I've become accustomed to this heat that's a direct hit of sunshine to the veins. The phenomenon hasn't become common—never that—but it's not as shocking as it was the first, second, or eleventh time it happened. I've almost resigned myself to the fact that my body will flip a switch and come alive at just the sight of her.

A lesser man could resent her for that.

Okay, fine. It's me.

I'm that lesser man.

After unlocking the door, I pull it open with a grin and fall into the role I've appointed and accepted for myself—platonic best friend.

"Marilyn." I step back into the foyer, arms crossed over my chest. "What're you doing here? And don't tell me you're just in the neighborhood since Castle Pines is nowhere near Stapleton." I toss back her words from three evenings earlier when I visited BURNED's office.

When I asked her to go out on a date with Daniel.

The curious mix of anger, pain, and resignation rushes back in without warning, swirling and temporarily choking me. Which is dumb as fuck. *I* asked *her* to give Daniel a chance. And then I asked her to say no. I still don't know where the hell that came from. After I'd damn near begged her to see my friend, I'd then turned around and tried to sabotage it? For what?

For me.

For my own selfish needs.

For her to look at me and not want to be with anyone else but me.

But that's not who we are to one another. That's not what she wants from me. Who she sees when she looks at me.

Thank God she'd misunderstood my plea. Because explaining would've been damn hard when I didn't even understand myself.

"Oh, don't worry, I'm not going to blow smoke up that beautiful ass of yours," she says, arching a dark eyebrow. "I knew you would be moping in your wardrobe while watching the game. So I dragged myself all the way over here to distract you."

"Damn that." I scowl down at her. "I don't mope."

She moves forward, passing me by with a pat on the chest. I lock down the deep inhale of breath that feels too much like a gasp at the back of my throat.

"I apologize. Brooding. I knew you would be brooding."

"Thank you," I say, shutting the door behind her. "That sounds much more manly."

She snorts and holds up the brown paper bag I'd noticed she'd carried into the house. "Of course it does. I brought gifts. Where do you want them?"

"What did you bring me? In the great room," I add, dogging her steps.

"What?" she asks, throwing me an exaggerated wide-eyed glance over her shoulder. "No magical man cave?"

"Go 'head, Marilyn. Get in all the shots you want at my Narnia wardrobe. I'm secure in my manhood to take 'em." I pause. "That and I saw you sneak my DVD into your purse. That might have more sting if you weren't stealing my movie to watch."

"Prove it."

She strides into the great room and stops short at the back of the couch, attention snagged by the game still playing on the seventy-inch television mounted above the gas fireplace. For several long moments, she watches the back-and-forth action on the screen, and I join her, halting directly behind her. It strikes me that from the instant her image appeared on that video camera, my frustration and guilt over not being with my team disappeared. That's Miriam's superpower. Making me forget. Causing everything but her to fade into the background.

It's a dangerous gift.

"I knew it," she murmurs, her gaze still fixed on the TV. "That's why I came over. You needed me."

A teasing joke hovers on the tip of my tongue, but it dies a swift death there. My fingers curl into my palm, the tips pushing into the flesh so hard a dull throb of pain flares in protest. A shiver works its way through me, tripping down my spine. The need to touch her, to wrap one hand around the vulnerable column of her neck and the other on the soft curve of her hip, has me damn near vibrating like a tuning fork. And she's the frequency that's calling me. I want to press into her, cover her, bury my face into those thick curls, and . . . inhale.

But I squeeze my eyes closed and settle for "Are you going to tell me what's in the bag or what?"

Maybe she doesn't hear the grit in my voice. Or maybe she pretends not to. Either way . . . I'm grateful.

"When I tell you I braved the crowds of the market on a Saturday and damn near ended up in a catfight right in the middle of the deli just to grab the last tray of . . ." She rounds the couch and, after setting the large paper bag on the glass table, reaches in and pulls free a medium-size tray of Italian pinwheels. "Your favorites. Why, I have no idea. I mean, make a sandwich, and call it a day. But hey! This is about you!"

She sets the black plastic tray on the table and reaches into the bag again, then emerges with a carton of Arnold Palmer. Two more retrievals reveal a family-size pack of vanilla Oreos and an unopened deck of UNO cards.

"Holy shit." I laugh, checking out her haul of all my favorite snack foods and game.

It's funny; my chef left a refrigerator full of prepared food, including appetizers such as these miniquiches, stuffed meatballs, and parmesan bites with marinara. I guess he thought I'd have company over this weekend. But I haven't even thought of touching them, my stomach in knots over this game. But Miriam shows up with discount deli food and cookies that my very expensive chef would probably have an apoplectic fit over just seeing in the house, and I'm suddenly starving.

"I know, right?" She wheels around and pads on sock-covered feet—when did she get rid of her boots?—toward the kitchen. "I'll get the glasses. You start filling your gut with all that processed meat."

She doesn't have to tell me twice.

I grab the tray. Damn. It's plastic and flimsy, but getting it open is like trying to wrestle a bag of wet feral cats.

A huge sigh reaches me from the depths of the house. "I've said it before, and I'll say it again. You know I'm only friends with you because of your house, right?"

Chuckling, I finally pop the lid off the deli tray. Another person wouldn't have the balls to say something like that to me, but it would undoubtedly be the truth. I might have come into this league young and brash with a big mouth, but I've never been naive. Growing up the way I did, experiencing all I did, knocked the rose-colored glasses off early—if I ever owned a pair in the first place. I've never deceived myself into believing it's just my face that lures women or people in general to me. It's all that comes with this lifestyle and what I can do for them. Money. Fame. Perks. Connections. I can recognize a user before they open their lips. And Miriam, despite her words, isn't a user.

Still, I get what she's saying. It's a lot of house. Yeah, I freely admit it. I was the typical athlete who bought his mama a new house after his first contract and then himself one. And after living in one trailer park after another, one shitty apartment after another, I ensured both of us lived in houses with so much space we wouldn't have to see our neighbors if we didn't want to, much less hear their arguments—and other shit they were doing—through the walls. And to make sure we had views other than concrete parking lots and other mobile homes. And my six-bedroom, five-bathroom home that backs up to a wildlife preserve definitely fits that bill.

I should be at least a little ashamed over the excess. But yeah, I'm not. Only people who have never had to sleep on a thin mattress that should be too embarrassed to call itself a bed while their mother slept on a nest of blankets because she couldn't afford another frame or a place with another bedroom would feel anything close to shame.

After nabbing a pinwheel in triumph, I bite into it. Pepperoni, salami, prosciutto, and provolone cheese with the sweetness of red peppers and honey-dijon mustard explode in my mouth, and I groan. Yes, I've dined in Michelin-starred restaurants in the last ten years, have been served food by the most celebrated chefs. But in this moment, this supermarket pinwheel ranks right up there with the best of their food.

"I hope you saved some for me," Miriam says, voice as dry as the bottle of wine she carries in one hand.

"All I'm going to say is you're lucky you returned when you did." I accept the wineglass she extends to me. And snort. The Arnold Palmer half-lemonade, half-tea drink in wineglasses. Classy. "Here."

I trade her the glass for a pinwheel. She pops it whole into her mouth, and I valiantly try not to stare at her lips and the slender column of her throat as she swallows. Try not to let my mind wander.

Try and fail.

If her goal in showing up here today was to distract me from the game, mission accomplished. Hell, all Miriam has to do is breathe.

While she's distracted with demolishing the deli food, I gently take her flute and the bottle of merlot she helped herself to from my wine closet and pour wine into the glass. She takes it with a hum of thanks and sips. This time her hum is of pleasure, and it strokes over my chest, trails down my abdomen. My stomach clenches so hard against the sensation that my teeth grind together, imprisoning the growl clawing up my throat.

I swear to fuck, everything this woman does is intended to seduce. It's not intentional, but that doesn't make it any less agonizing.

"The wine must be extra fabulous because these things can't be this good," she says, snatching another one off the tray.

"Oh, just admit it, Marilyn. I'm right; you're wrong. And you secretly love my . . . pinwheel."

She eyes me over the rim of her glass. "Yes, your pinwheel is like no others."

We stare at each other, then start snickering. With a sigh, she sinks to the couch, cradling her wine. I follow, a little slower, legs spread wide. Thank God my mother's not here, because she would've had something to say about the way we fell on the deli tray, wine, lemonade-tea, and cookies like rabid wolves.

And I only glance at the TV screen a handful of times. On the last one, Miriam tosses the plastic wrap to the deck of UNO cards at me and demands we play. Now, as I slap down a draw-four card on top of hers, she throws back her head and howls—literally—in fury.

"The hell you say!" She jabs a finger at the pile of cards and then at me from her seat on the floor across the coffee table. "What kind of friend does that? I don't even recognize you right now!"

I fake a yawn. "So are we going to pretend you weren't just about to make me pick up eight?" I wave toward the steadily dwindling deck. "Stop stalling, and get your twelve cards."

"Monster!" she hisses. Then she snatches up twelve cards, grumbling about revenge and retribution the whole time.

Grinning, we continue the game, and minutes later, she tosses down a skip, a reverse, another skip, and then a draw four in quick succession. I calmly plunk down another draw four. And she loses her shit.

"What the fuck, man? What have I ever done to you? You're no gentleman! You'd let Tara burn, wouldn't you?" she leans forward and accuses with a hot glare.

"I have no clue who this Tara person is, but I probably wouldn't let her become a victim of arson. But I am going to make you draw eight."

She growls, and for a moment, my laughter becomes strained. Because that sound vibrates over my cock that's always in a semihard state around her. But even that simmering heat takes a back seat to the simple joy of having her here. The tender warmth of her concern for me.

It's friendship; that can't be any clearer. But I'll take it. Because it's all I can have of her. And I'm pathetic enough to be grateful for whatever scraps she offers me.

I want nothing to do with athletes.

Yeah, when I allow it, those words still possess the power to burn like a thousand beestings. Even though I realize what Miriam meant, that knowledge doesn't erase the kick to the gut. That kick being truth. This—hanging out with food and card games on a Saturday night—is all I'll ever have of her. The one night we shared—fucking hot and goddamn gloriously dirty night—was a mistake. To her. And I have no choice but to respect it.

And I have to move on.

For my sanity, for my eventual peace, I have to let her go.

Another reason I asked her to give Daniel a chance. Maybe if I see with my own eyes that she's happy, that she's with a good man who is deserving of her, then as painful as it will be, I can let go of the fantasy of her. Of us.

Fuck if I know if it'll work. But I'm a desperate man, and it's worth a shot.

Still muttering to herself, she snatches the cards up. Ten minutes later, the game ends, and I win. Surprise, surprise.

"I want a rematch," she demands, shuffling the cards.

"Nah." I recline against the couch cushions, stretching my arms above my head. "I prefer to go out on top. What'd you tell me before? Quit while I'm ahead."

I meant to tease her, but the joke falls between us like an anvil tossed from a cliff. The gleeful light in her dark-brown eyes dims, and her hands hesitate over the deck of cards. She ducks her head, paying undue attention to stacking them neatly and packing them into their box.

Damn. Regret kicks me in the ribs, and I lower my arms, flattening my hands on the cushions beside me. Resisting the need to rub the pang just under my heart. Why had I said that? Why had I brought that day, that conversation, into this space?

As I study her bent head, the thick honey-blonde curls brushing her cheeks, her shoulders, the answer snaps clear in my head. Unease. Guilt. My own.

Did I push too hard? Did I steal her choice? Put her in a position where she felt she couldn't say no? Those questions, the possibility of any of them being answered with a *yes* has kept me up these last few nights. How many times I've reached for my cell to call, to ask, I can't even count. But fear of the answer kept me from dialing.

Yet now, with her here . . .

I can't avoid it. At least my subconscious refuses to.

Part of me longs to rescind the comment or swiftly change the subject, but I remain silent. Let my words hang in the air like an acrid scent from singed food.

"I did advise you to do that, didn't I?" she murmurs, setting the game on the edge of the table. The movement seems restless, as if she needs something to do with her hands.

"I was surprised to see you here today," I say just as softly. "Thank you, Miriam."

She tilts her head, studying me, and I don't flinch under that too-perceptive inspection. No matter how uncomfortable it makes me. No matter how much fear crawls inside me at what she might see, what I might accidentally betray.

"I don't need your thanks, but you're welcome," she says. "It doesn't take a genius or psychic to figure out that you were sitting up here watching your team play and beating yourself up all to hell. Especially when Zora called and mentioned you wouldn't let Cyrus hang out with you. It's why I didn't call ahead. I wasn't going to give you the chance to tell me no." She shakes her head, her gaze soft like melted toffee, sweet and stirring the need for more inside me. More of her looking at me like that. More of that sweetness. "I knew what you were doing, Jordan. Sitting here, watching the game, and tearing yourself to pieces because you couldn't be there with them. Blaming yourself. Not granting yourself any grace, any compassion."

I don't have a reply to that, as she's not wrong.

Common sense dictates, *You're injured. You have no control over that, and no one's condemning you for it.* But my heart—fuck it—that little boy who carried the weight of his family on his thin shoulders too soon, who understood only the principle of "You don't work, you don't eat," can't accept not being in control of this.

She rises from the floor, effortlessly fluid and still elegant in ripped skinny jeans and a tight gray long-sleeve T-shirt boasting across her breasts a jacked golden-haired anime figure in orange pants and a blue belt. I adore this about her. Whether she's dressed in leather and a corset or one of her beloved anime shirts and jeans, she's confident, comfortable in her skin, in her innate sexiness. Hell, Miriam *is* sex.

And as she crosses the short space that separates us, stopping in front of me, then kneeling between my spread thighs, my breath snags in my throat.

Fuck.

I curl my fingers into the cushion next to my legs, scrambling for the physical purchase that has eluded my mind. Heat pumps through my veins, so hot the air in my lungs transforms into steam. Unbidden, images of another time, another night when she knelt in front of me, flash across my mind. Then, I'd been allowed to tunnel my fingers through the coarse but soft strands of her hair, to scratch my nails over her scalp. To cradle her in the V of my body. My thighs tense, the dull echo of pain pulsing down my right leg . . .

Don't you dare move, I silently order my body. More specifically, my dick.

Miraculously, I remain still. But goddamn. What is she doing?

She answers my question. Not with words, though.

Miriam presses closer, closer still until her breasts press against my abdomen . . . and her arms wind around my back.

I exhale.

And wrap mine around her.

Closing my eyes, I nuzzle her curls; the earthy, sultry scent of cinnamon with a sweet hint of vanilla teases me. And for a self-indulgent moment, I permit myself to get lost in it as well as in the crush of her flesh to my body, in the gentle yet strong clasp of her embrace. I ignore the protest of pain in my thigh, and I shift my legs closer, returning that hold.

"What's this?" I murmur.

"Growing up, Zora, Levi and I didn't know what it meant to have a safe space to express ourselves. To voice how you felt—especially for Levi—meant ridicule. And with my father, a side dish of scripture and an unsolicited definition of 'being a man.'" Her arms squeeze me, once, before loosening but not letting go. Nor does she remove her ear from my chest; she doesn't tip her head back, instead seeming content to speak without our gazes connecting. "I want to be your safe space, Jordan," she whispers. "Now, without having to look at me, tell me the truth. What are you afraid of? Truly afraid of."

I swallow, burying my face deeper into her curls. Hiding. From that question. From the truth.

From the persistent need to purge myself.

A need I surrender to because this is Miriam. And though what she incites in me is too unfamiliar, too terrifying for her ever to be *safe*, I can deny her nothing.

"This—basketball—isn't just about me. When I first started playing, yeah, it was. It, along with my books, provided an escape from the loneliness when my mom worked one of her many jobs or the fear and anger when she dated one of her asshole boyfriends . . . or broke up with them. Basketball offered me the dream, the hope of one day leaving the shit places we lived, of being able to give my mom more. To take care of her like my bastard of a father could never be bothered to do." I clear my throat. "But when I got to college, it hit me that ball could no longer be about what I needed. It had to be the way I took care of my mother, of her future. She sacrificed so much, being both parents, working herself to the point that she was too tired to cry. Now it was my turn to provide for her so she didn't have to take on one more job that took and took from her and didn't pay nearly enough back. Failure, Miriam, is not an option. And every time I'm on this couch, watching my team instead of playing with them . . . every time I can do nothing but sit here with my thumb up my ass as someone else takes my place on that court, I'm letting her down."

"Bullshit."

"Excuse me?"

She loosens her hold on me and leans back, and I'm stunned by the anger tightening her lush mouth and tautening the skin across her high, sharp cheekbones. That same fury glitters in her narrowed eyes, and I'm caught between shock and an inappropriate, misplaced amusement.

Informing her that she looks like a pissed-off fairy right now would probably put my nuts in jeopardy.

"That's bullshit. And I refuse to accept that you believe it."

Again . . . "Excuse me?"

"There's not a damn thing about you that says *failure*."

She pushes off me, jackknifing to her feet, and I immediately miss her warmth. If I hold still, I can savor the imprint of those perfect firm breasts like a brand. Flattening my palms against my thighs, I trap the heat of her in my skin.

So consumed with soaking in and entrapping that sensory memory, I almost don't catch the rant happening just in front of me.

"One, you, a boy raised in a single-parent home in an economically depressed environment, graduated high school, entered college, and then beat the odds and made it into the NBA. Do you understand how incredible and statistically difficult that is? Only three in ten thousand, or point zero three percent."

Pacing, she pops up a second finger, clearly on a roll because she's breaking out the statistics.

"Two. You're a three-time NBA champion. Most players can't even claim one championship, much less *three*. And three. You're one of the rare few to win NBA MVP, All-Star Game MVP, and Finals MVP awards all in the same year."

"You have no idea what any of that means, do you?" I interrupt to ask.

She draws to an abrupt halt and scowls at me. Her lips part, then snap closed. Then open again to admit, "No, but it must be impressive since it's on your Wikipedia page."

My snort of laughter hurts my nose, but damn, that's hilarious.

Throwing me another glare, she resumes her pacing. And ranting.

"And I've met your mother." *That* sobers me up quickly. "Grace would be appalled and hurt to know that you're using her welfare, her happiness, as some sort of screwed-up whipping post. Because in her eyes, you're perfect. You were perfect before you ever even picked up a basketball. And if you decided today to never touch one again, you'd still be."

That isn't true. It's a beautiful thought and sounds nice, but I've been in this league too long. You're only as good as your stats. Only as worthy as your next endorsement. Only as legendary as your next championship.

Hell, even my own father nailed that lesson home. The man who couldn't be bothered to stick around long enough to teach his son how to hit the toilet bowl had somehow found his way back years later when I was drafted into the NBA. Only when I had something to offer him.

Only when I was worthy.

So no, that shit doesn't fly with me.

"You're not a failure, Jordan Ransom," she says, stopping again, and though her frown is just as fierce, her voice is gentler. "It's not in your DNA. And this game doesn't define you. Not the *you* who matters."

I don't agree with her, so I just nod and give her the words she needs to hear. "Thank you, Marilyn." I cock my head, squinting up at her. "That delivery needs a little work, though."

She huffs out a laugh and crosses back over to the couch, then drops down next to me and curls up against my side. For a moment, a pounding wave of tenderness and lust grips me, tugs me under, and I can't move. All I can do is experience.

Feel the thrust of her breasts against my side. The press of her knees to my outer thigh.

Glimpse the dense fringe of her lashes on the arc of her cheekbones, the sensual bow of her top lip, and the impudent, fuller curve of her bottom one.

Inhale the earthy and sweet scent of cinnamon and vanilla from her hair and skin.

Moving, touching her, especially when all my senses are so sharply attuned to her, might be the thing that breaks me. But in this moment, I can't give a solitary fuck.

I'm going to be selfish and indulge myself with this one small thing.

Slowly, I lift my arm and slide my fingers into her hair. The strands slide over my skin, and I lock down a moan at the caress. But I don't stop, don't remove my hand. Not when I'm finally caressing her in a way that's even faintly similar to that night. And she's allowing it.

Dragging my fingertips over her scalp, I don't miss the little shudder that runs through her. An answering one ripples down my spine, the tiny electric currents pulsing along my veins. Because I'm like an addict when it comes to her, I do it again, hungry to glimpse that reaction again. To see if I can have more.

More. More. I always want more when it comes to Miriam. I'm never satisfied.

And it's that relentless craving that will ruin our friendship if I am not careful or don't protect it. From myself.

Dropping my arm, I curl it around her shoulders and squeeze. But my fingers still tingle, and I flex them, trying to banish the phantom sensation of curls stroking over them.

She shifts her head a little, presses it closer, so her breath skates over my nipple. Only cotton separates that puff of air from my naked flesh, but it might as well have disintegrated. My body has transformed into one sensitive, exposed nerve, and anything she does is pleasure edged with pain.

"Why'd you stop?" she asks, her voice low, almost quiet.

"Because I didn't ask if it was okay." Not a lie. I got wrapped up in my greed and neglected to ask her permission to touch her.

But it's not the whole truth about why I stopped.

Yet in the immortal words of dear old Jack, she can't handle the truth.

"You're not fooling me, y'know," she says against my chest.

I stiffen, my arm involuntarily tightening around her. What is she saying?

"You're just patronizing me. Everything I said to you went in one ear and right out the other," she continues.

Relief so strong rushes through me it's a damn good thing I'm already sitting down. For a minute there, I thought . . .

"It didn't." When she snorts, I squeeze her shoulders. "I heard you. I promise."

"No," she objects. "You listened, but you didn't *hear* me."

Again, I don't answer because she won't like it. Hell, I don't like it. Instead, I pose a question of my own that has been nagging at me since I walked out of her office days earlier.

"Miriam," I rasp. Stop. Clear my throat. And try again. "Miriam, when I asked you to give Daniel a chance, did I . . ."

When my voice trails off, she flattens a palm on my abs and pushes away, tipping her head back to meet my gaze. Concern darkens those expressive eyes as they roam my face.

"Did you what?"

"Did I force you into something you didn't want? Did I impose what I needed on you and steal your choice?"

There. It was out there. My fear. The one that had run in my head at night like a rat in a cage.

Too many times over the years I'd witnessed men commit the same sin against my mother and aunts. Whether it was something as small as them insisting on meat loaf for dinner when my mom had talked all afternoon about having a taste for spaghetti and had even gone to the store and bought the ingredients for it. But in the end, she'd submitted, her desires taking second place to his. Or if it was as huge—as damaging—as demanding she ship me off to my aunt's house for a month so they could have alone time without her kid underfoot. She'd done that only once. And it'd been only a few days before she'd come and picked me up and kicked him out. But even at eight, I'd been old enough to understand the asshole move her ex had made. And promised I'd never place a girl—and later, a woman—in that position. Never bend her will to mine.

God, I pray I didn't do that to Miriam.

The shame over possibly being that man eats at me like acid.

For every second she remains silent, that guilt becomes more corrosive, burrowing deeper.

"Would going out on a date with Daniel have been an idea I came up with on my own? No. Would I have done it if you hadn't asked? Probably not. I honestly can't say for certain. When I met him, there was a . . . maturity about him that was different from your other teammates. And a calmness. Then discovering he was a widower? In retrospect, I might've just because of that last fact alone because of Renae and knowing the hell she's gone through. And seeing that he's being brave enough to take this step back into what has to be the most difficult arena of his life after losing his partner, his wife?" She shakes her head. "Certainly you had influence, but I can't say for certain if that influence was enough."

She lifts a hand, and it hovers between us. My heart kicks at my sternum during that hesitation, like SWAT ramming in a door. As if she makes a decision, she grasps a few loose strands of hair that escaped the band at the back of my head. She twists them around her finger, seemingly engrossed in the action. It's a gentle grip, barely a tug on my scalp, and yet I'm captivated, trapped. Because not only is she touching me, but she's *willingly* touching me. If she resented me, she wouldn't be anywhere near me.

The knowledge slams into me, followed by a nearly crushing relief. For the second time in just minutes, I'm thankful to be sitting because my legs wouldn't be able to support me. Why hadn't I realized that the moment she showed up on my doorstep?

There's nothing fake about Miriam. The only games she plays are the ones we just enjoyed this evening. It's one of the reasons I trust her, so willingly and easily invited her into my small inner circle. That never happens with me.

And I've come to find out that doesn't happen with her either.

"We may not have been friends as long as you and Cyrus or Daniel," she murmurs, "but I think you know me well enough to understand who I am. And you can't force me to do anything I don't want to, Jordan. And we're friends; I care for you. A lot. Because of that, what concerns you concerns me. That carries weight with me. But that said, I've had my voice stolen before. And I'll never go back to that period in my life. Not even for you." She releases my hair, and it requires every bit of restraint I've learned on and off the court to not grab her hand and wrap her fingers back around those strands. Order her to reclaim them. Reclaim me. Just for a little while. "So no, Jordan, you can lay that particular worry to rest if that's what has been bothering you. We're good."

"Thank you." This time I don't try and clear the rasp from my voice.

"You're welcome."

The low drone of the television provides a muted soundtrack for the thick silence that falls between us. *Don't ask it,* an insistent, fucking *wise* voice advises in my head. So of course I don't listen.

Because I'm a goddamn glutton for punishment.

"Did he call you?"

No need to clarify the *he.* We both know who I'm referring to.

She nods, her gaze locked with mine, so I don't miss the elusive emotion that flares in her eyes. It's there and gone before I can decipher it, and I'm 2.5 seconds from opening up a question-and-answer period about its origin. But apparently, I do have some restraint left.

Or self-preservation.

"He did. Yesterday."

"And he asked you out?"

"Yes."

"You said yes?" I press.

"I did. Isn't that what you wanted?"

"I'm sure Daniel was happy about that." I rummage up a smile, turning up the wattage to cover the howl of pain echoing in my head. "I hope you have a good time too. You just might surprise yourself."

No, I didn't answer her question. I evaded it like a fucking dodgeball.

But none of us want the truth.

Not her.

Not Daniel.

I don't even want it.

So I'll go along as I have been. The best friend. The confidant.

The man secretly in lust and love with the one woman he can't have.

Yeah, no one wants that.

CHAPTER SIX

MIRIAM

"They want to use me for my blood. Little do they know, I'm out for theirs."

—Sarafina Rose, Ravaged Lands

"I swear 'fore Black Jesus if that DJ plays the 'Cha-Cha Slide' one more time and I have to see another grandma get funky with it, Dad's next altar call is going to be quite busy lifting my name in prayer."

I stare at the dance floor as the wedding reception guests bum-rush it like the DJ just announced a going-out-of-business sale at Gucci instead of spinning the opening notes of the *still* popular song. I mean, don't get me wrong. I love a good "Cha-Cha Slide." But *three times*? Kill me now. But I promise I'll take DJ Casper with me.

"What are we even doing at this wedding anyway?" I continue to gripe. "Dad and Mom have never mentioned these people. I'm sure they're very lovely, but I don't need to be here celebrating their connubial bliss. Do you know what I could be doing on a Saturday afternoon? Nothing. Absolutely *nothing*. And enjoying every bit of it."

"Here." Zora shoves a clear plastic plate of chicken fingers, coleslaw, meatballs, and deviled eggs into my hands. "You're hangry. Follow my lead, and stuff your face. If you eat, it's less painful, and the time goes by quicker."

I accept the plate from my sister with an arched eyebrow. "Did you just make that up? Because one doesn't sound like it correlates to the other."

She shrugs and grabs a sauce-covered, toothpick-speared meatball off Cyrus's plate. "You're the genius. You'd know."

There was a time when comments like that from her and Levi would aggravate me. But back then, it'd been my sensitivity that had made the comments sound mocking and unkind instead of the regular sibling teasing it was. I'd had to grow into that understanding, though. And it hadn't been easy.

I guess some people could say I could thank Robert Sampson for that revelation.

Well, "some people" could go fuck themselves right along with Robert Sampson.

"Do you want me to get you your own plate?" Cyrus asks Zora as she forages on his plate again and retrieves another meatball.

"Why? You have a problem sharing?" My sister pops the appetizer in her mouth, then slowly withdraws the toothpick, and the way Cyrus studies her mouth is positively pornographic.

Yech.

"Excuse me, but never let me see you eye-fucking my sister in front of me again. Please and thank you." Levi doesn't glance up from tapping on his phone as he delivers that blunt gem.

Food lodges in my throat, and I cough, eyes watering. Note to self. Laughing and swallowing may result in death by coleslaw.

"Really?" Zora glares at Levi. Not that he notices. Whatever's on his phone has captured all his attention. No, wait. Correction. Not that he cares. Because Levi notices *everything*. "You have no problem saying *eye-fucking* to your sister?"

"Not if my sister has no problem allowing her man to do it in front of God and country. And me."

Cyrus, Lord love him, pats me on the back, helping to dislodge that pesky mayonnaised-for-life cabbage. And I do love him. And not just because he's a genuinely good guy, but for one main reason—how he adores my sister. Zora's dated some real douche canoes in the past. Men who didn't appreciate her for the beautiful, intelligent, curvy woman she is. They tried to change her, bully her into losing weight or scaling back on her dreams. But not Cyrus. He fully supports BURNED and, as evidenced by the visual-screwing incident of seconds ago, can't keep his hands off her. Figuratively and literally. I love him for her. And though they had a bit of a rocky start, they're each other's heroes.

A twinge of loneliness pings inside me.

But I snuff it out, and if wisps of it persist in hanging around like tendrils of soot, well, I can ignore those. I'm damn good at ignoring shit I'd rather not acknowledge. Sooner or later, they evaporate as if they never existed.

Now that's some bullshit.

Yeah, if only people followed that logic so easily.

Still, I don't need anyone to be my hero. I'm my own damn heroine. I've assigned myself an alter ego and a costume, and saved my own life.

Because that's what women who have been beaten down one too many times do. They face the choice of either staying down on the ground, breathing dirt, or clawing their way to their knees, then to their feet, and telling the world to get fucked. And then we get on with the business of surviving.

That's what Ravaged Lands is for me. My business of survival.

But if there are moments when I look at Zora and Cyrus and that loneliness is edged by a jagged rim of envy?

Well, there's sex to ease that.

Jordan's face wavers in my mind.

Dammit.

No, sex with him didn't ease a thing. It made the itch, the loneliness, fucking *everything* worse. Now I can admit that the demise of my relationship with Antonio didn't all fall on his shoulders. Jordan was right—some of it rests on him.

If his dick hadn't spoiled me for all men, then maybe, just maybe, I wouldn't have been unimpressed with Antonio's.

But Antonio, and men like him, are safe.

Jordan is the very definition of *not safe*.

"Are you okay?" Cyrus gives my back another pat, frowning down at me.

I nod, discreetly shifting away from him. Just in case there's a Heimlich maneuver in my immediate future.

"I'm good," I wheeze, reaching for the plastic cup of wine in Zora's hand.

"I was drinking that." She switches her scowl from Levi to me. That's fair. Plastic picnic cup notwithstanding, the white wine isn't bad.

"But I was choking, and you don't want my death on your hands." After another healthy sip, I pass it back to her and dig in to the plate, avoiding the killer coleslaw.

"There you are." My mother sweeps over, beautiful in a royal-blue wrap dress that embraces the curves we inherited. Her thick dark-gray curls frame her lovely face, and I'm not surprised to see several heads turn and follow her. Confident in her body and person, Mom owns any room she walks into. That and her passion for history and education are the reasons why she's such a brilliant social studies teacher. "I thought I told you to mingle. Instead I find you over where I left you. Lemetria is your second cousin to my great-aunt. You should be getting to know your family. There's plenty of history in this room."

"History because everyone here's old as Methuselah and Moses put together," my father mutters, coming up behind her.

Mom whips around, and I swallow a sigh. Shit. We're at a wedding. A place where love is supposed to be the theme of the day. Yet my parents can't control themselves for one day. Hell, hours.

Not for the first time *this week*, forget in my life, I silently ask why they're still together. My parents' union more resembles that of the United States between 1861 to 1865 than a happy marriage. I'm sure at some point they loved one another. Zora, Levi, and I are standing here. But that's the only empirical evidence I've ever had. And even then . . .

Well, I've indulged in hate sex before.

And frankly, it would've been kinder to the three of us if they had divorced. Then we wouldn't feel like hostage negotiators every time we're in the same room with them. Us being the hostages *and* the negotiators.

Although, to be honest, that role has fallen on Zora more often than not. Levi seemed to become desensitized to it like a phobia, and I . . . well, I turned to the thing that labeled me as different. My brain. I got lost in my head, tuning out the world. It was my safe space when home wasn't.

I'd like to claim that I've broken that habit.

Yeah, I'd like to claim that . . .

"If I recall, no one asked you to come, Reggie," Mom snaps at Dad. "But with so many of your church members here, you couldn't pass up the chance of being here. Don't act like you're here for us."

Us? We don't want to be here either. But our choices were either attend this wedding and reception or face Monica Nelson's cold and eternal wrath for the next month of Sundays. The woman can hold a grudge like nobody's business.

"Please. If you didn't want me here, you wouldn't have mentioned it in front of me. Besides, you couldn't have your family believing you were divorced. We have pretenses to keep." He scoffs.

"Can we . . . not?" Zora asks, a weariness in her voice. Cyrus slides his arm around her waist, tucking her into his side. "Especially with an audience?"

She's not referring to Cyrus; I don't need to be inside her head to know that. He's well acquainted with our parents and the dysfunction that is their marriage and aware of the home we grew up in. Zora's talking about the other guests. Being a spectacle at today's wedding wasn't on my bingo card today. But with our parents . . .

Giving my father one last glare, Mom jerks her chin up. "Fine. Giving my aunt gossip isn't something I'm looking forward to anyway. Speaking of"—she turns back to us—"I've told your aunt and cousins that the three of you own a marketing business together. Please don't give any more details than that. God knows I wouldn't begin to know how to explain what you really do." Her voice drops to a whisper, and she glances around, as if checking to see if anyone had crowded close to eavesdrop on our conversation.

Because heaven forbid anyone discover her children owned and operated a legitimate, successful business that helped people in toxic relationships not end up like *them*.

"Too bad," Levi drawls. "I'd planned on handing the bride our card if she asked. Especially given how the groom keeps eying the maid of honor's breasts. They're clearly having sex."

"Levi! Quiet!" my mother whisper-yells.

He shrugs. "The marriage is doomed. We would be doing her a favor."

Tact. The tact is strong with that one.

But he's not wrong.

"I have to agree with your mother," Dad adds, resting his gaze on each of us but resting extralong on Levi. My brother returns it without flinching. That relationship . . . *whew*. "Let's keep your sordid little company outside of here."

Anger flashes inside of me, hard and bright. Almost as if he senses that burst of hot emotion, Dad's attention shifts from Levi to me, and that quick, the rage curls up like a match that's burned itself out.

It's not extinguished; no, from one instant to the next—and without my permission—I'm reverting to that little girl who hated the fighting, the acrid, scalding taste of fury in the air, the noise. I tuck myself into my head, wrapping myself in facts, in numbers. They're not tumultuous. They don't fluctuate and pitch with chaotic emotions and tempers.

$x = -b \pm \sqrt{b^2 - 4ac}/2a$. *The quadratic formula. Used to determine the x-intercepts of a quadratic or parabolic equation.*

$d = \sqrt{(x_1 - x_2)^2 + (y_1 - y_2)^2}$. *The distance formula. Calculates the distance between two points on a coordinate plane.*

Slope $= y_2 - y_1 / x_2 - x_1$. *Slope formula. It determines the angle of a line that connects two points on a plane.*

The equations and formulas roll through my mind, greeting me, comforting me like old friends. They go on and on until the tension in my shoulders eases, and I distance myself from my parents, from the weight of their emotional turmoil.

"Excuse me. I need a drink," I say, edging away from our dysfunctional little circle.

"Not yet." Mom steps forward and loops her arm through mine, locking me into her side before I can move toward the open bar. "Your aunt and uncle are dying to meet you. The wine can wait a couple of minutes."

I'm not so sure about that.

I throw Levi and Zora a glance over my shoulder, and my sister winces. Levi and Dad remain engaged in their silent visual war.

Again. That relationship. *Whew.* Daddy issues, for real.

Forcing my lips into a smile that my mom is way too smart a woman to believe is real, I follow her across the room. Not that I have a choice since she still has me hooked like a fish.

I'm the storyteller of Ravaged Lands, always the one in control. There's . . . safety in that. In knowing the story, the correct decisions, and the potential consequences ahead of time. For instance, I know when Sarafina is faced with those out to use her for her demon side—just a drop of her blood imbues one warrior with the strength of ten men—then vilify her for it, she doesn't cower, doesn't break. She fights, dares them to try and take anything from her that she hasn't consented to, whether it be blood, her body, or her autonomy.

As the storyteller, I can momentarily live through that strength, craft it, and steal some of hers for my own.

But now, as I allow Mom to drag me over to a group of people and introduce them as various aunts, uncles, and cousins, I don't have any to hoard. Instead, I paste a smile on my face and greet them, nodding and responding when appropriate. All the while wondering—again—why I'm here.

"Miriam, I remember when you were just a little girl," one of my aunts says. Henrietta, I think? "Your mom couldn't stop bragging enough about you. A real genius in our family. Can you imagine?"

My smile stiffens until it feels like it could crack right down the middle and tumble off my face.

"We're so proud of her. It's not every day a child enters college at sixteen and graduates with not one but two degrees with honors," Mom practically crows, squeezing my arm and beaming down at me.

My stomach pitches, bile scrambling for the back of my throat.

"What are you doing now, Miriam? With all those smarts, changing the world, no doubt," an uncle chimes in with a chuckle that grates over my sensitized skin. Over the exposed, aggravated nerves under it.

"I—"

"She runs a marketing company with her brother and sister," Mom interrupts, answering for me, probably afraid I will spill the beans about our unseemly breakup-service company.

Because apparently my brain can be trusted to grapple with the Collatz conjecture but not remember that less than five minutes ago, she told me to keep my mouth shut about BURNED.

Typical.

Even though I'm twenty-seven years old, my mother still treats me like a fragile specimen that needs to be coddled and handled with care. Was it any wonder I went to college and—

No, dammit. That's not fair.

But in this moment, when she still refuses to let me be *me*, I struggle to give two fucks about fair.

"For a while there, I thought she would follow me into teaching. Can you imagine sharing her love and knowledge of mathematics with all these younger minds?" She shakes her head, as if the waste of my potential, my career path, just saddens her. "But what can you do? As parents, we support our children and their decisions."

"Oh." My uncle frowns down at me. "That's too bad. We need more women, especially Black women, in education. And in STEM."

And I've officially had enough.

It's one thing to have my mother offer her unsolicited and uninformed opinion on my life. But it's a completely different thing to have the peanut gallery of the unknown-until-today distant relatives weigh in with their not-so-subtle disapproval.

"It was wonderful reminiscing and seeing you again." I untangle my arm from Mom's and sweep a general smile around the circle. "If you'll excuse me."

I turn and walk away, not offering an explanation to Mom or them about where I need to go or why. Yes, it's borderline rude. But if their manners don't extend to not criticizing me as if I'm not standing there in front of them, then my etiquette has limits too.

And I need a drink.

Desperately.

Five minutes later, plastic cup of champagne in hand, I take a long sip, but the anger and, yes, sense of betrayal still bubble like golden wine teasing my nose.

"Love of mathematics," I scoff. "She doesn't know me at all."

"Is this a private conversation, or do I need to be concerned that it's a private conversation?"

I glance up, meeting Cyrus's blue gaze. It's on the tip of my tongue to give him a flippant comment about being in talks with the most intelligent person in the room. Instead I say, "I'm fucking brilliant at math. Like, scary brilliant. But it's never been my passion. I've never loved it. How does she not know that? She's my mother, for God's sake."

To his credit, he doesn't blink or back away from the crazy person who just emotionally and verbally vomited all over him like a drunken coed.

Lifting a hand, he signals the bartender behind me. In seconds, he has another plastic cup in his hand, and he gently trades my champagne for his drink. One sniff, and the smoky aroma of whiskey teases my nose.

"Go on," he softly urges. "Sip it. I'll carry you out of here if I have to, but I'd rather not."

"Such a gentleman," I mutter, then do as he orders.

The whiskey burns a path down my throat, exploding in a ball of warmth in my chest and stomach. *Wow.* The bride and groom might've gone cheap with the flatware and cups, but they didn't hold back on the alcohol. So good to see their priorities are in order. Maybe there's hope for their marriage yet.

"It's been my experience with people that they perceive what and who is most comfortable for them to see. Especially with their children or other family members. If anything threatens that perception—maturity, growth, even a death—they would rather be willfully blind and in denial than admit to that change." He slides his hands into the front pockets of his pants and leans an elbow against the bar. "I admire your mother. She's a strong, intelligent, caring woman who is passionate about her family and her job. She's also a perfect example of what I'm talking about. I believe in my heart she doesn't mean harm, but unfortunately, I think we both know intentions don't mean shit when in the line of fire."

Air grates against my lungs, and for a horrifying second, I consider throwing my arms around him and burying my face against his chest.

Goddamn, that's some good brown liquor.

Clearing my throat, I glance away from him on the pretense of surveying the room. Anything so he can't glimpse how his words touch me.

"Where's Zora?"

"She had to go to the bathroom. And it was either me escort her and your brother come over there and rescue you or vice versa. Since I was less likely to offend everyone within a mile radius, Zora appointed me as your emissary." He jerks his chin in the direction I just escaped from. "Not that you needed my help." Pause. "You okay?"

"Yes." I exhale. "Just . . . family." Shame and dismay slam into me like a brick to the face, and I jerk my head back in his direction. "Oh shit, Cyrus. I'm sorry. I didn't think—"

How could I have forgotten that he'd lost his parents years earlier? And here I am complaining about mine . . .

He waves a hand, cutting off my apology. "Stop, no need for that, Miriam. Zora, Levi, you, Jordan . . . all of you are my family. I've been blessed to have one of blood and one of choice. Speaking of Jordan, though." He cocks his head. "I'm kind of surprised you didn't invite him as your plus-one. I thought you two were connected at the hip. And bonus—he would've shut down whatever that"—he nods toward where my mother still gabs it up with my relatives—"was."

Yes, he would've. And done it with so much charm and such a big grin they wouldn't have known they were being put in their places.

God, I miss him.

It's been a week since I visited his house with my impromptu snacks and card game. This might be the longest we've gone without seeing one another since becoming friends. Of course, we've talked on the phone, but . . . something's off. If I didn't know any better, I'd think he was avoiding me.

But that's ridiculous.

"He's been busy with physical therapy, practice, and home games. You know he's been faithfully going to the last two, even if they won't let him play," I say.

"Yeah, I know." He studies me, and I lift the glass of whiskey to give myself something—anything—else to do to avoid his unwavering scrutiny. Freaking attorneys. Make you feel like everything that comes out of your mouth is a lie. Especially if it *isn't* the whole truth. "But if you'd have asked him, he would've been here with you."

I shrug. "This isn't a big deal. Hell, *I* don't want to be here. And besides, that's all I need is my mother assuming there's more between us than friendship."

Monica Nelson meddling even in my theoretical love life. Shudder.

"Is there?"

The plastic cup pauses halfway to my mouth. "What?" I blink. "No. *No*." Am I protesting too much? Does he know about *that* night? Did Jordan flap his gums? I mean, I did to Zora, but that's beside the point. "We're just friends. That's all. And why are you looking at me like you're about to go Jack McCoy on my ass?"

He snorts, pushing off the bar. "Sometimes you and your sister are so much alike it's scary. You want another one?" He arches an eyebrow, glancing down at my nearly empty cup.

After throwing back the little bit of alcohol left, I hand him the empty one, and he tosses it. "No. Thanks, though."

"I'm not sure what 'going Jack McCoy' looks like, but if it's an expression of skepticism touched with amusement and a dash of exasperation, then yes, that's it." He settles his palm on the middle of my back and guides me across the room.

"What is that supposed to mean?"

"It means now I'm understanding why your brother wanted to stomp a hole in me not too long ago."

I draw to an abrupt halt and scowl up at him. "Is it me, or did you just threaten me with bodily harm?"

"Listen, I have my life insurance premiums paid up, but I'm still not taking my life in my hands." A smirk quirks the corners of his mouth. "And you know damn well I'd never do that. What I'm saying is I now get your brother's frustration with me having my head up my ass when it came to your sister."

Yeah, I'm still not getting it. And I tell him so. "Still not getting it."

His smirk deepens. "You will."

"Now who's the frustrat—"

"Just one thing, Miriam," he says, interrupting my incoming grumble about enigmatic lawyers.

His words don't necessarily stop me, but his tone does. The humor has vanished, leaving behind a seriousness that demands my attention and sends a note of trepidation skating down my spine.

"Don't hurt him." His gaze locks with mine, and the intensity there coupled with his words strangles the breath in my throat.

My lips part, and my throat works, but no words emerge. I can only stare at him, stunned, frozen. And when Zora and Levi approach us, my chance to ask him for an explanation slips away. But even as my sister leads her man toward the dance floor and the rest of the evening passes by, his murmured request haunts me.

Don't hurt him.

Hurt him? That would mean Jordan's heart was at risk. That he opened himself to the pain of rejection, of betrayal, and is terrified of facing that pain again.

Not Denver's irresistible charmer. Not basketball's affable playboy.

No, in this scenario, I'm the one in danger.

CHAPTER SEVEN

JORDAN

"Yes, I'm immortal. Which means I have forever to hate you or love you."

—North the Woodsman, *Ravaged Lands*

"Hey, man. What's going on?"

A hand slaps me on the back, and I look up from pulling on a pair of socks in my locker room chair. Daniel smiles down at me. In spite of the ugly, dirty knot tightening my stomach and twisting it until my gut hardens to the consistency of concrete, I return my friend's smile.

After all, he *is* my friend.

And it's not his fault he can have what—who—I can't.

"Nothing much," I say, bending my head to drag on the other sock and grab my tennis shoe. "You look ready for tomorrow's game."

"The Heat." Daniel nods, sliding his hands in the front pockets of his team sweats. "It's going to be a tough one, but I'm confident we'll pull it out."

"At least the next three games are at home, and I get to be there for you guys." I finish with my other tennis shoe and shake my head. "I hate watching from home. It's the worst fucking feeling."

"You mean the helplessness?" Daniel's mouth twists into a wry smile as he sinks into the chair next to me.

I stare at the picture behind the seat. Just last year, another stand with another image stood behind that chair. It's a sharp and all-too-real reminder that anyone can be traded. Anyone can be gone. Even me. I resist glancing over my shoulder at my own picture. Reason scoffs at my inane fear that it won't be there as it'd been minutes ago when I'd returned from the showers. Still . . . I don't turn around.

"I remember that well," he continues. "Watching from the bench isn't that much better, but at least you're with the team. Can offer advice or encouragement. Sitting on that couch, unable to do anything? The powerlessness . . . yeah, I get it." He dips his chin, shooting a look down at my leg. "You had physical therapy today, right?"

"Yeah." Without my permission, my hand goes to my thigh, and I absently rub the sore muscle. A good sore, though. One that means I'm that much closer to fully being healed and getting back on the court. "Three more weeks. I'm trying to get it down to two."

Daniel laughs. "I would be wasting my breath telling you to listen to the professionals since they're the ones with the degrees."

"And you'd be a bit of a hypocrite too," I drawl.

"That too." He smirks. Glancing around the empty locker room, he drums his fingers on his thighs and heaves a sigh. "I wanted to hit you up about something. You got a few minutes before you head out?"

That knot in my gut returns, unease crawling through my veins. Because I don't need closed captions to clue me in on what this is about or where it's headed. And coward that I am, I'm itching to leap from this chair and run out of this locker room—hell, Ball Arena—like flames are licking at my balls.

But instead, I remain in my seat and say, "Of course."

Relief flickers across Daniel's face, and the shame over my first inclination to bolt and avoid this conversation damn near eats me alive.

"I don't know if you've talked to Miriam . . ."

When he doesn't finish his sentence, I battle back the urge to curl my fingers on my thighs in a futile and stupid attempt to fight off this topic. "No," I reply, voice low. And hopefully containing some semblance of normality. "I haven't spoken with her in a couple of days."

My fault. Ever since she dropped by my house over a week ago, we haven't seen each other, and the days since we've spoken have stretched longer and longer. I've texted with excuses—busy with practice, physical therapy, watching tape. All true but bullshit. And she's too smart not to eventually guess it, if she hasn't already.

It's selfish; I freely admit it. But I need space. Her admission that she'd accepted Daniel's invitation to go out on a date had delivered a reality check I needed.

Miriam doesn't want me—doesn't see me—how I want her. Our night together hasn't stopped her from dating other men . . . being with other men. And I'm not judging her for that. Far from it. We have no commitment; hell, we're not even in a relationship. Still . . .

Would she find it hilarious that I haven't fucked a woman since her? It's like my cock has rebelled at just the thought of being inside another woman when it's been buried deep inside her.

But I can't live my life as a monk waiting on a fairy-tale ending.

I might believe in love and finding that special person to spend the rest of your life with, but it doesn't mean shit if you're in it alone. And unrequited love makes for good theater, but in real life? It just goddamn sucks.

No, I have to move on. Let the hope of her go. And part of that involves placing some distance between us. Even if she might not understand why. And I can't explain it to her.

"So she hasn't told you about our date?" Daniel asks.

"I know she was going out with you, but no. I didn't know it was a done deal."

He exhales a heavy breath, the sigh ending on a rough and somewhat grim laugh. Well, that's not good.

"There's that, I guess." He drags a hand over his head. "It was . . . bad, man."

I straighten in my chair, tension zigzagging through me like a jagged lightning bolt.

"Define *bad*."

Another one of those awful laughs escapes him, and he shoots me a dry look. "I know I'm out of practice with dating, but damn. It was awkward as hell. Not on her part; believe me." He holds up his hands, palms out. "This was all on me. Miriam was as funny, smart, and witty as she'd been at Linc's. Me, though." Rubbing a hand over his mouth, he closes his eyes. "It's like every thought just disappeared from my head, because I had no clue what to say to her. Suddenly, I forgot how to hold an intelligent conversation. Shit. It was never this hard with Jerricka. It was just so . . . easy."

Jesus.

The tension seeps from my body, leaving me a heavy bag of bones and muscle. And regret. And pain. For my friend. I can't even imagine how he's treading this unfamiliar and scary path. Daniel's always been a private man, and now that he's opening up to me? He must be confused and more than a little overwhelmed. I mean, what the fuck do I know about losing a wife and jumping into dating after being with a woman for over a decade?

Trust. He trusts me.

That's never been clearer to me than in this moment. And what do I do with it? I can't mishandle it. Can't damage it or this fledgling attempt to step onto the other side of his grief, his healing.

"From what you told me about you and Jerricka, you two were high school sweethearts, right?"

Daniel nods. "Yes. We met freshman year and were together ever since."

"You grew up together, were each other's best friends. There were no secrets between you. Not many people share that kind of bond or love. So yeah, having to actually get to know someone and starting conversations and icebreakers and getting past those awkward silences—it's harder. Especially when you haven't had to do it in twenty years. Stop kicking yourself in the ass over it."

"Thanks, man." He stares straight ahead at the monitor on the far wall. "I needed to hear that. Just like I'm telling you to cut yourself some grace, I guess I need to remember that. Not that it's doing me any good with Miriam. I blew that. Horribly."

"Just call and ask her out again." Shit. Even given my newfound conviction of moving on, I can't believe those words just came out of my mouth. But I don't take them back—I can't. Not with the misery etched on Daniel's face.

He falls forward, propping his elbows on his thighs. "Yeah, I don't see that happening," he scoffs. "She was polite about it, but Miriam couldn't get out of that restaurant fast enough. There wasn't even one of those 'We should do this again' moments. Because she wasn't going to. I messed up my chance with her."

"Daniel, you're selling Miriam short. She's not heartless."

"So you're saying she'll go out with me again?"

I hesitate. Damn. "I can't speak for her. But we've been friends awhile, and I know her pretty well. She's a big fan of honesty. Have you tried being truthful with her about what happened?"

"What?" He huffs out a chuckle, arching an eyebrow. "Call her and say, 'Hey, Miriam, I know I was a selective mute on our date. But it was my first since my wife died, and I was severely out of practice, nervous as hell, and had no clue what to say to you. But if you give me another chance, I promise to actually talk this time'?"

He shakes his head and is still laughing when I say, "Yeah. That'd be perfect."

His humor cuts off, and he stares at me like I just announced I'm quitting the team to go find myself on a spiritual hike through the Himalayas.

"Excuse me?"

"Call her and tell her that."

"You're fucking with me."

"You're a handsome guy 'n' all . . ." I snort. "I'm serious, though. Like I said, Miriam is big on honesty. Probably because she's blunt to a fault, and she appreciates it in return. If you hit her up, tell her what you just told me, and be sincere about it, chances are she'll give you another shot at a date. I mean, I can't promise anything." Because I won't. And I'm not interfering. Not again. I won't do that to her—or myself—again. "But she would understand. And besides, I think you'd rather have her know you froze than believe you're a boring-ass date who couldn't string two sentences together."

"Yeah, you're right about that." He pinches the bridge of his nose and studies me for a long moment. "You know what? That actually makes a weird kind of sense."

"And if she does give you another opportunity, forget the fancy-restaurant shit. That was fine for a first date, but do something different to show her you don't see her as one of many. That you're thinking outside the box. She does graphic design for a living, and she loves art. I've seen her sit on her phone and stare at a painting for minutes at a time because it captured her attention. She's also a huge fantasy and paranormal fan. Anything with magic or mythical creatures. Huge *Supernatural* superfan. So think about taking her to the art museum or Monster World. There are haunted houses now that're open for just a few more days. She loves to be scared."

I'm throwing him all the ideas of the places I'd planned on taking her.

"Haunted house, huh?" One corner of his mouth twitches.

"Yeah," I rasp.

Slapping his hands down on the arms of the chair, he announces, "What the hell? I'll do it. What do I have to lose, right?"

"Your pride. Dignity. Reputation," I supply.

"Asshole." He grins, and the fact that he looks more relaxed, happier than he did minutes ago eases the vise grip around my ribs. After a moment, a small frown wrinkles his forehead. "You know her really well, don't you?"

Yeah, I might've spoken too soon. That binding on my chest tightens, and I'm back to watchful and uncomfortable. Back to deliberately quelling the desire to escape.

"We've gotten close. Why?"

"I *like* her, man," he murmurs. His gaze drops from mine to the floor, as if he can't meet my eyes when he admits that. As if he's ashamed to say those words aloud. "Just from the little time I've spent with her, I can tell she's different from the other women I've been with since Jerricka . . . *shit*." He scrubs a hand down his face. "Is it bad that I sometimes still can't say the word?" He doesn't seem to expect an answer because he sighs and continues. "I've been with women, but I can't tell you their names, can't even remember their faces. And I know that makes me sound like the worst kind of bastard. But it's true. I was only with them when the loneliness became too damn unbearable and I just needed to alleviate it. But Miriam . . . for the first time, I want to *know* the woman. Her likes, dislikes. What makes her tick. Hear her laughter. Hell, be the one to make her laugh. And at night, that's made me feel like shit. Like I'm cheating on Jerricka. But I keep telling myself this is what I need to do to *live*. That she, more than anyone, would want me to live."

Silence resonates like an arena's roar in the locker room. And underneath it throbs my guilt like an open wound. I might want Miriam—such a pallid, weak description of the clawing, desperate thing that beats at me with relentless, battering fists—but Daniel? He *needs* her.

"What do you need from me?" I ask.

"Help me. If she gives me another chance, I don't want to screw up like I did on our first date. Just like you did with telling me how she loves art and all things *Supernatural*, help me out with things like that. Let me know if I'm fucking up. Let me know if I should buy roses instead of lilies. I just don't want to mess this up."

Oh God.

Ask me for anything else. Didn't I do my part as a friend? What more can be expected from me? She's not just my friend, but she's the woman I'm fucking in love with. It takes everything in me not to tip my head back, look at the ceiling, and ask God, "What have I done? Let me know so I can get off the hook, please?"

I'll make whatever sacrifice is necessary.

But there's no answer coming. Not that I expected one.

Because there are times I believe he gave me Miriam as an answer to my prayers.

And others—as punishment for my sins.

In this moment, I'm on the verge of falling to my knees and begging for penance.

The fact is Miriam isn't mine, was never mine, regardless of what I let one hot-as-hell night try to deceive me into believing. Into hoping. And I have a choice here. I can say no to Daniel because, shit, just the thought of her with another man—much less one I know and will possibly have to see her on the arm of, smiling into the face of—has my gut churning and heart twisting.

Or I can agree to Daniel's request. He seems to be really into Miriam, and who knows? Though she claims not to date athletes, once she gets to know the real him, maybe he could be the one to change her mind. To be the man for her that I couldn't be. Both of them deserve that. Deserve happiness.

And so do I.

At this point, it's almost self-preservation.

"No," I say, studying him, my heart lodging in the base of my throat.

"No?" He frowns.

"No flowers. She doesn't like them. Says they're a waste of money when all they do is die after a few days. Surprise her with her favorite drink, a chai latte. Or a gift card to her favorite bookstore. Something like that."

"Got it." Daniel smiles, and I glance away on the pretense of standing. I've made my decision, but damn, I'm going to need some good fucking alcohol to live with it. "Jordan." He claps a hand on my shoulder, offering me no choice but to stop. "Thanks, man. I appreciate everything you've done. You've been a great friend."

"Yeah, you don't need to thank me. That's what we do." Desperate to go now, to put space between me and this decision I can't come back from, I return Daniel's pound on the shoulder and head for the locker room exit. "We'll talk later."

And I walk out, feeling like I just committed a prison break.

But it's just a fantasy, a trick of the mind.

Because I can't break free of myself.

CHAPTER EIGHT

MIRIAM

"I trust two things in this world—me and my sword. Everything and everyone else are suspect."

—Sarafina Rose, *Ravaged Lands*

"Cyrus is being really cagey about this party," I mutter to Daniel as he grasps my hand in his and guides me out of his car.

A valet in black pants, a white shirt, and a red vest accepts the keys to Daniel's Lexus to park it who knows where as we step on the curb outside of Cyrus's gorgeous Washington Park home. Since he and Zora started dating, I've visited the upscale residential neighborhood and his luxurious house several times, but it still never fails to amaze me that my sister is damn near glued at the hip to a man who lives *here*. When did we—her, Levi, and me—start moving in these circles? And I haven't decided if I want to be pinched or not.

Light pours from the windows of the home as well as the wall nearly encompassed by glass. As usual, I'm totally enamored by the beautiful winding staircase on the side of the house that leads to the upper level. It's fanciful and dainty, a bit of unexpected whimsy, and a perfect contrast to the limestone exterior with its slopes, angles, and arches. I love this place. My favorite detail, though? The love and unconditional welcome inside of it.

"Yes," Daniel says, settling a palm on the middle of my back. The touch is light, polite. Friendly. The very definition of our interactions as of yet. "He's kept the purpose of the get-together close to his chest so far."

I hum in agreement, although I have my suspicions as to why. When I asked Zora, she said something about this being a party for his clients—thanking them for coming over with him in his new firm. I could go with that if his clients—Daniel being one of them—knew they were being honored.

Yeah. Suspect.

Cyrus is lucky I adore him.

I have an issue of Ravaged Lands due to be uploaded in the next few days, and I still have a couple of panels to finish. I'm not worried about getting it done. Everything is falling into place, and I've hit what I call that "magical space" where the story and character arc are in sync and the illustrations are flowing from my head to my fingers in a flood. Not only are Sarafina and North on the cusp of another battle, but their cautious and tumultuous dance of a relationship is approaching critical mass. I couldn't sketch fast enough to keep up with the images. Excitement sparks inside me, and for a second, I glance over my shoulder with a little bit of longing. But the valet has already disappeared down the street. I'm committed to attending this party.

Still, as much as I love Cyrus, I'm giving him two hours before I'm ditching and heading back home and returning to my work.

Sadness pinches my chest, temporarily dimming my pleasure. This is when I wish others knew about Sarafina Rose, North, Ravaged Lands, and my second career. About my joy in the creating of this world so I can share these moments of delight or even doubt.

Correction. I wish I possessed the courage to open up to them and reveal this part of me.

Swallowing a sigh, I climb the front steps to the house. As soon as we approach the door, a man in a black suit opens it. With a smile, he greets us, takes our coats, and guides us toward the formal dining room, where about twenty or so guests have gathered.

Zora and Cyrus stand in the middle, his arm wrapped around her waist even as they're surrounded by a small group of people. It's as if he needs that connection to her, and she to him.

Dark, murky vines coil in and around my ribs like an oil spill, ugly and corruptive.

Envy.

I don't try to pretend not to acknowledge the emotion. And I'm not proud of it. Envy for that intimacy my sister has with her man. We grew up in a house where we never witnessed it; how amazing that she should find it. How astounding that I should recognize it when I've never really experienced it.

Lie. I did. Once. And ran from it. Shut it down.

Because as much as I stand here, staring at the epitome of trust, acceptance, and vulnerability, as an ache of longing pulses in my chest, I'm terrified of it. I'm scared shitless for Zora. Because I know—God, do I know—that people like us, people who grew up in war zones, yearn for that connection too much. And we can lose ourselves in the yearning.

We become easy pickings for those who aren't careful with our hearts. Those whose intentions aren't good. Those who want to use us for their own selfish reasons and pleasure.

I don't believe Cyrus falls into those categories; he's a good man.

But it doesn't erase my fear.

Doesn't absolve me of shame.

"Would you like a drink? Wine? I'm sure the bartender has merlot," Daniel offers, waving a hand toward the full-service bar set up against the far wall specifically for the party.

I smile, a burst of pleasure blooming inside me. This is the fourth time we've been out together, counting that first disastrous date, and his attentiveness still surprises me. It's as if he keeps this little journal in his head, and it's all about me. It's flattering and thoughtful. And kind.

I'm coming to believe it's Daniel.

"That would be great, thank you."

"Be right back."

More than my gaze follows Daniel as he cuts a path across the room. And not just because he's tall as hell. Or a beautiful man. Given Cyrus is an entertainment attorney, Daniel isn't the only athlete in the room. So no, it isn't his height or handsome face. The man carries a sense of utter confidence and calm around him—like an indomitable shelter in the midst of a raging storm—that draws people to him. I almost missed that given how bad our first date went. And whew. It was *bad*. While I sat at that restaurant table, a tingling had started at the back of my eyes as I'd wondered if I'd been set up for humiliation with another athlete.

Again.

But then Daniel had called a couple of days later and explained why he'd been so stiff and painfully awkward. His willingness to be so open and vulnerable with me, little more than a stranger to him, had dented the shields I'd reinforced. How could I *not* have agreed to go out on another date with him after that?

"Please tell me his dick isn't underwhelming like the last guy."

Well, thank God I didn't have wine already, or I would've been choking on it. On it and my mortification.

"Could you say that just a teensy bit louder? I'm not sure Cyrus's geriatric neighbor heard you," I snap at Renae.

"A shame." She tips a dark-green beer bottle to her mouth, arching an eyebrow. "I'm sure she wants to know too. Now spill. Because if he has whiskey dick sans the whiskey, I think I'm going to cry for the fate of all men."

I return her arched eyebrow, taking a step back and scanning her from the top of her crown of dark-red twists, down her tightly toned body draped in a sleeveless floor-length dress with an empire waist, and back up again.

"You look gorgeous."

"Don't try and change the subject."

"I don't think I am."

She snorts. "What I look like has nothing to do with whether that guy has granted you answers to whether or not alien life forms exist. With orgasms."

"Ma'am," I growl. "Keep it down. And I have no idea what intergalactic mysteries Daniel can solve with his penis because we haven't had sex. And of course alien life forms exist," I scoff. "Leave it to humans to assume they are the only race on the sole life-sustaining planet in this huge universe. We're so arrogant. No wonder we're always being probed."

"Focus." Renae snaps her fingers in front of my face. "Say what now? You two haven't fucked? What is this? Date five?"

"Four."

"Four? And he looks like that? *And* he's a basketball player? What's wrong with him?" she demands, voice flat. "Forget it. I'll find out."

"Nothing's wrong with him, sheesh. And could you dial back your secret-agent crazy?" I shake my head, caught between wanting to laugh and wanting to dash across the room to urge Daniel to run to the nearest safe house. "He's a widower," I murmur, and the pain that flashes across Renae's face pulses inside me like a hot brand. "I don't think he's looking for sex from me. Just companionship. I think he's . . . lonely."

"I get that," she murmurs back. "But, babe. Have you seen yourself?" She waves a hand up and down in front of me. I don't need to peer down at myself to take in the long-sleeve emerald-green dress with the plunging neckline and flared skirt that hits me midthigh. "Widower, yes; eunuch, no. He wants to hit it. So that must mean you're the holdup."

Friends are beautiful, priceless blessings.

And other times, like now, they're complete pains in the ass.

Especially when they refuse to let you avoid shit.

"Spill it, chick," Renae presses.

"I—" I frown, wrestle with what to say. What not to say.

"Just say it, Mir. No judgment here. You know that," she says, voice gentle.

I shift my gaze from her to Daniel, who stands by the bar, wineglass in one hand and a tumbler in the other. An older man, face lit up, hands gesturing, talks animatedly to him, and Daniel nods, wearing a patient smile.

Sighing, I glance at Renae's beer and wonder if she'd risk a scene and pin me to the floor if I made a grab for her drink. Who am I kidding? She totally would.

"He's a genuinely nice guy, Renae. Respectful, funny, nice, sensitive. And . . ." I pause, finger the pendant resting between my breasts. "And I am not attracted to him like that. I like him. God knows I do. In some ways, he seems to know me better in four dates than men I've been with for months. If I let it, that kind of attentiveness could be . . . intoxicating."

"Why not let it be, then?"

"Because . . ."

The *because* chooses that moment to walk through the living room entrance. As fanciful and inane as it sounds, a shiver of tension preceded him, alerting me to his presence before I actually spotted him. Call it intuition, a sixth sense, or the fucking Force, I don't care. But by the time he enters the room, my gaze is already locked on him.

Heat coalesces low in my belly, a molten, liquid burn settling there, swirling, expanding. It takes every last scrap of my pride not to press my palms to that spot just below my navel. Not to squeeze my thighs together in this dress and telegraph to everyone in this room that my sex just lit up like the aurora borealis.

Oh, this is concerning.

But then again, I dare anyone to take one look at Jordan Ransom in a black suit perfectly tailored to his big, wide-shouldered, lithe frame and not hover on the verge of a spectacular eruption.

It's been almost two weeks since I've laid eyes on him. Even our calls have dwindled to texts. And seeing him again after so long is like staring directly into the sun after emerging from days in a dark cave.

Blinding. Painful.

Gorgeous.

Even the civility of the slim-fitting suit and white shirt can't contain the pervasive sexuality that emanates from him like a damn life force. All that dark-golden hair flows to his shoulders, hiding the shaved sides and framing the stark beauty of his face. The ball piercings in his eyebrow, nose, and mouth and the tattoos climbing up his neck from the open collar of his shirt don't detract from that beauty—they add to the vitality, the edginess of it.

He's a warrior wrapped in the trappings of civility. Raw power temporarily tethered by the bounds of decorum.

He's walking savage art.

He's . . . not alone.

The jab of pain catches me by surprise, snatches my breath. And the grimy residue claiming space inside my chest damn near chokes off what little air I have left.

"Y'know, I joked with you about Jordan Ransom, but I didn't think you'd gone and done something as idiotic as fall for him."

My chin jerks back, punched by her verbal blow. "The hell? I haven't fallen for *anything* with Jordan." Well, other than fallen on his dick. "We're just friends."

But the idea of . . . *being in love* with him is fucking ludicrous.

"Friends." She twirls the beer bottle in her hands. "I've looked at exactly one friend in my life before how you just stared that man down. And I ended up almost marrying him. Would have if not for the fuckery of life. So you want to try that *friends* line again?"

"Is he a good-looking man? Yes. Am I dead? No. So of course I've noticed. But that has nothing to do with love, for God's sake. At least not how you make it out to be. I love him as a friend."

Which sounds better than *I think he broke my cooch.*

Which sounds a helluva lot better than *I think he broke something inside me.* Something visceral and necessary that seems to respond to only him. And that's unfortunate since I can't have him. No, I won't *allow* myself to have him.

He's not safe.

He's the most dangerous man in this room for me.

Because no other tempts me to forget what I know to be more certain than any math equation.

Trust equals vulnerability. Vulnerability means exposure.

And exposure . . . well, exposure means getting what you deserve when you allow yourself to be weak.

I'll never be weak for anyone again. Including myself.

But *fuck.* He makes me want to be.

"Yep. Keep telling yourself that," Renae murmurs. With a gentle bump of her shoulder to mine, she walks away before I can toss out my comeback.

If I had one. Which I don't.

"Sorry it took me so long." Daniel appears at my elbow, jerking my attention away from my departing friend. "I got held up by a basketball fan. Nice guy, but damn could he talk." He chuckles, handing me my forgotten-until-now glass of wine.

"Thanks." I sip, suddenly in desperate need of it. Part of me wishes he would've just brought the bottle.

That same part refuses to glance in the direction of the living room entrance.

"Everything okay?" Whereas with other people, that would be a throwaway question, with Daniel, that thread of concern in his voice turns it into a genuine inquiry.

Dammit. Why can't I be into him?

"I'm fine," I assure him, even rummaging up a smile. "Just a little nervous for Zora. My sister is not a fan of surprises."

As far as excuses and misdirection, it's not a bad one—and still the truth.

Daniel nods, lifting the squat glass of amber liquid to his mouth. After a sip, he says, "I wouldn't worry too much. I don't think I've seen a man as enamored with a woman as Cyrus is with your sister. I don't think he'd do anything to embarrass or hurt her. Even inadvertently."

That's true. Still . . .

"I have something for you." Daniel switches his glass to his other hand and reaches inside his jacket pocket.

A wisp of alarm trips through me. "Oh, Daniel, you didn't have to—"

"Here." He hands me a folded piece of paper.

The objection dies on my lips, quieted by surprise. "What's this?" I frown down at the note.

"Take it and find out." He laughs softly. "I apologize in advance that it's not the number to Harvelle's Roadhouse."

"I should hope not," I scoff, accepting the paper from him. "Demons burned it to the ground. But extra points for the *Supernatural* reference." After unfolding the note, I scan the writing on it. There are three website names and, underneath each one, a username and password. "What . . . ?"

"You've been working some long nights," he says. And I have. Not on BURNED matters, though. On finishing the current Ravaged Lands issues. Uploading a new chapter each month on top of keeping a full-time job isn't easy. A lot of times, I'm up late, completing my illustrations, writing dialogue, or concentrating on marketing for myself—or my pen name—instead of my family's company. "I know you enjoy anime. I figure while you're up, these sites might keep you company. They're supposed to have all the best shows on them."

I blink. "They do," I whisper. Then clear my throat. "I can't believe . . . thank you. This is one of the most thoughtful things anyone has ever done for me."

"You're welcome, Miriam," he murmurs.

I glance down at the paper in my hand again. One of the sites, I already have a subscription to, but not the other two. And I'm not hurting for money—BURNED is successful, and the royalties I earn from Ravaged Lands sometimes exceed my day job's salary—but it isn't about that. He thought of what would make life easier for me, what would make me happy . . .

Once more, I keep my eyes fixed on the note and don't seek out the Viking in the room.

Why, dammit? Why can't my body set on fire for Daniel? Life would just be simpler. I have a feeling it would be amazing.

But the warmth that fills me isn't from desire; it's friendship. Admiration.

And it's not fair to him if I allow him to think it's anything different.

"Daniel—"

"Excuse me." Cyrus's voice rings out in the room, interrupting me. "Can I have everyone's attention, please?"

Swallowing the words that will probably hurt the pride, if not the heart, of a good man, I turn toward Cyrus, who stands in front of the massive fireplace that nearly dominates one wall.

"I want to thank all of you for being here for our belated celebration of the opening of Hart Entertainment LLC. Tonight is about more than the firm, though. It's about you. Because without each and every one of you here—whether as a client, staff, family, or friend—none of it would've been possible. So thank you. And I'm looking forward to a long and prosperous future with all of you."

He lifts a tumbler of golden-brown alcohol, toasting the room. A series of whistles, applause, and cheers erupt, including from me. Cyrus left a firm with an environment that contained an ozone layer of toxic masculinity, but it'd paid. Brilliantly. It'd cost Cyrus to walk away. But he had, and I'm proud of him.

"I would be completely remiss if I didn't recognize the woman who inspired me to take this huge step. Zora . . ." He turns to my sister and takes her hand. After setting his glass on the fireplace mantel behind him, he cups her cheek with the other hand. "You came into my life and upended every plan, and I've never been so grateful. Building something new that doesn't look like only me, but us, has been not just my pleasure but my honor. You've changed me, Zora. You changed my world. And every morning I wake up excited about where our journey is going to lead us that day. So, baby . . ."

He kneels before her, and though a small voice in my head had whispered this might be on the agenda, my heart still soars for the back of my throat. My hands rise of their own accord and clasp in front of my chest like some romance damsel, and I stare at my sister. At the shock that widens her eyes and parts her lips.

At the dawning joy on her face.

"Zora Neale Nelson, I want to continue on this adventure with you and begin it every morning waking up to you. I love you, Zora. Will you do me the great honor of becoming my wife?"

"Yes."

The word erupts from her mouth even before he finishes proposing the question. Cyrus's grin is so "un-Cyrus" and absolutely beautiful. We all burst into deafening cheers, and tears burn my eyes. Well, shit. I unclasp my clutch, but wouldn't you know it? Not a freakin' tissue to be found. Because the last time I cried would've been my junior year of college.

Leave it to Zora to break my streak.

"Here you go."

Daniel presses a handkerchief into my hand, and I accept it, dabbing at my eyes and attempting not to ruin my makeup.

"Thank you," I mutter. "Allergies are hell this time of year."

"Sure." The corners of his mouth quirk.

The next hour passes in a blur of champagne, hugs, and laughter as I celebrate with Zora and Cyrus. Even Levi nearly cracks a smile. In all the revelry, I almost manage to forget that Jordan is there—with a date.

Almost.

Okay, no, I don't.

But I do carry off the pretense that I've forgotten about him.

I mean, I do contain a flair for the dramatic. After all, I did play Dancer Number Three on the *Corny Collins Show* in my high school's production of *Hairspray*. It was my one and only attempt at extracurricular activities, but hey, I slayed.

Because I'm more at home here than other guests, I harbor no discomfort in slinking away for a second into the kitchen for a breather. And because Cyrus's amazing glass-encased wine closet stands in there. Oh, it's a work of art. And the wine in there would have a sommelier weeping in joy.

Humming, I bypass the Lafite Rothschild 1900 and grab the Dom Pérignon Rosé Vintage champagne. I'm not an asshole. I'll drown out this shameful, ugly stain of jealousy with the four-hundred-dollar bottle of alcohol rather than the ninety-five-hundred-dollar one.

Someone had the foresight to crack a window in the kitchen, and the slightly chilly October night air filters in, cooling my overheated skin. The heels of my stilettos click-clack over the tiled floor as I cross the room to the cabinets and grab a glass. Within moments, I have the pink liquid poured and lifted to my mouth.

"Does Cyrus know you're in here raiding his wine closet?"

I pause, and since my back is to him, I indulge in the luxury of closing my eyes. It was only a matter of time, right? I couldn't avoid him all night. And that wasn't even my intention. My plan had been to stay in here just long enough to understand *why* I'm avoiding him.

Needless to say, I'm not ready.

But it doesn't matter. Jordan is in my space. The low, sexy timbre of his voice reverberating through me, caressing me from the inside out. His earth-and-sky scent reaches out to me with nebulous fingers, teasing and taunting. All night, I've snacked on the delicious spread Cyrus spared no expense on for his guests, but in this moment, my stomach gurgles as if it hasn't been fed a morsel in months.

Because one concentrated hit of *him*, and I'm *starving*.

And I'm angry. And hurt.

And jealous.

Wine. Give me all the wine now.

I lift the glass to my mouth and down a large gulp, and somewhere a sommelier is swooning in horror over how I'm disrespecting this champagne. Inhaling a breath, I finally turn and face Jordan.

"Since he stared me down as I headed in here, I'm guessing he has an idea what I'm up to. But just in case, snitches don't just get stitches but an incurable case of jock itch." Oh thank you, God, for at least letting me give him Angela Bassett *Gunpowder Milkshake* vibes when inside I'm much closer to Scooby—*ruh roh*. "What are you doing in here? I thought you were perfecting the art of avoidance with me."

Yes, kettle, I'm calling you black. Suck it up.

"That was the plan."

Well . . . damn. Jordan has never been one to beat around the bush, but I did expect him to hedge just a little.

"Great. Fine." I toast him with a smile so fake the feds should be busting through Cyrus's door any second to arrest me for counterfeiting. "Thanks for that clarification. Now if you don't mind, I'd like to continue robbing Cyrus in peace."

"I said that was the plan." He edges closer, leans a hip against the marble island, and crosses his arms over his chest. "I didn't say it's been working."

"Seems like it's been working swimmingly from where I'm standing."

Drink, bitch. Shut up and drink.

For once, I listen to that small voice in my head. If my mouth is filled with wine, I can't talk. Stupid, too-revealing words can't tumble from my lips.

Silence blankets the room, the muted sounds of laughter and chatter from the formal dining room only emphasizing the strain that didn't exist between us before.

How did this happen? How did we get here?

I hate it. Hate that I'm scared to ask him those very questions because the answers might wound me more than his admission of avoiding me.

"Your sister and Cyrus. Engaged. Did you have any idea?" he murmurs.

I let out a short harsh laugh that scratches my throat. "Is this the small-talk portion of the program? Okay, I'll go with it. No, I didn't know. And yes, I'm thrilled for them. They deserve all the happiness, and if Zora doesn't ask me to be maid of honor, I'll shave her eyebrows while she sleeps."

Yikes. Maaaybe I've had a little too much celebratory wine.

I set my glass down on the counter.

He doesn't move, and his facial expression doesn't change. Yet a sharpness enters his eyes, and I stifle a telling flinch. Too many people underestimate his pretty face and laid-back manner. There's nothing silly or unobservant about him. He possesses a dangerously sharp intellect, and a cop on stakeout and hopped up on coffee couldn't beat his perception skills.

The man sees too much. Like right now.

Full of liquid courage, I hike up my chin and meet that ice-blue gaze.

"What's wrong?"

The blunt demand—not question—seems to echo in the room, bouncing off the pristine kitchen walls. What's wrong? Really?

Let's start with, Why have you treated me like I have the clap for the last two weeks?

Why have you dropped me like a bad habit after bulldozing your way into my life with your easy smile and easier promises of friendship?

Who's the gorgeous woman in the black minidress?

I don't voice any of that. Instead, I mimic his pose, crossing my arms and cocking my hip against the counter.

"Is this what we're going to do now?" I ask, deliberately infusing my voice with a calm that evacuated the building about three glasses ago. "Since when did we become the people who pretend with each other? Who don't acknowledge the elephant in the room and wrestle that bitch to the ground? Just let me know so I can adjust my expectations of this relationship." I wave a hand back and forth in the wide space between us. "But do me a favor. Don't gaslight me. Don't ignore me for days, then walk in here acting like nothing's happened and we're good. Because news flash, Jordan. We're. Not. Good."

My breath seesaws in my chest, my fingers fisting under my arms. Regret tries to barrel in, and for a second, the urge to cringe away from the flood of accusations, of emotions, overwhelms me. But I don't backpedal from them; I don't leave the kitchen.

No, I want an answer. Even if we leave this house tonight with our relationship redefined, at least I'll know it.

I won't be left in the dark, left wondering, made the fool . . . again.

"I miss you."

No fair. He's not playing fucking fair.

Now, I retreat, physically and emotionally. One step. Two. And another one. Until my ass hits the opposite cabinet and the counter edge digs into my lower back. And all along, I stare at him, at the chiseled lines and indecent curves of his face, at the broad, big perfection of his body, and I curl in on myself. Protecting myself from anything else that will slip out of his mouth.

From one instant to the next, I'm transported to another time when a man I wanted to believe in, when a beautiful man who held me in his thrall, used pretty words. Used lies. And then betrayed me in the most brutal way with them.

For the first time since meeting Jordan, I don't trust him.

His electric-blue gaze narrows, tracking each of my movements, and he shifts forward, but I shove a hand out, silently ordering him to stop.

"I don't know what the fuck this is, but I don't play games. If I didn't inform you of that in the beginning, then let me make it crystal clear now."

"Games?" He frowns, and though my hand is still up, he edges forward again. Not close enough to touch me but nearer so I catch the flash of confusion and embers of fire in his eyes. He's angry? Good. That makes two of us. "What the hell are you talking about, Miriam?"

"I miss you?" I repeat, throwing his words back at him on a low hiss. "When did that revelation hit you? When you were sending me to voice mail for the fifth, tenth time? When you texted me yet another excuse about being too busy? Or when you walked in here tonight and realized since your best friend is marrying my sister, ghosting me might not be as simple as you thought?" Curling my fingers around the counter rim, I shake my head, another caustic chuckle escaping me, even though I try to trap it. "Bullshit wrapped up in a pretty bow doesn't make it stink any less. And that *I miss you*? Utter bullshit."

"I'm sorry," he murmurs. And this time, when he moves forward, he doesn't stop. Not until the wide wall of his chest presses against my palm.

"Jordan—" My fingers involuntarily curl against that dense muscle, and I grind my teeth together, fighting the heat of battle and lust. He's armed with not just that voice, face, and body but his scent, his dominance.

My fucking weakness.

"Sweetheart, look at me. Please."

I reluctantly drag my gaze from over his shoulder at some distant, blurry point to meet his. Not because he asked, but pride insists I do. Especially when my heart does this humiliating, fluttery thing in my chest at his low, silken *sweetheart*. The fickle organ shouldn't get too excited. I've heard him call women who served him beers the same thing. It's not unique. It's not special.

"I'm sorry," he says again. More insistent. With a fervor that tugs on an achy place low inside me. "I thought I was doing the right thing by stepping back, giving you space. Giving you and . . . Daniel space to get to know one another."

Shock rips through my hurt and anger like a fissure, and frozen, I stare up at him, temporarily uncomprehending.

Maybe he reads my bemusement, because he shakes his head. "Sweetheart, no man—no matter how good friends they are—is down with another one hanging around the woman he wants for himself. If you two were going to have an honest, strong chance, you didn't need to be splitting your time with me. And you would've never seen it that way. So I decided to place some distance there myself. So you wouldn't have to."

"Let me get this straight." The anger rushes back, burning the shock and confusion to ashes. Good. Anger's good. "You believed I couldn't manage my time between a potentially new relationship and a friendship, regardless that I've been managing my whole life for some years now." He winces, but I don't give a fuck. "You also took it upon yourself to make a decision for the both of us instead of talking to me. Ignoring the fact that I wouldn't want anything to do with a man so insecure he would be threatened by my friendship with another guy. A friendship that predated him. Do I have all that right?"

He sighs, tunneling a hand through his hair and tugging the strands away from his face. "Fuck. It sounds so much worse when you say it."

"You're lying," I state flatly. Baldly. "There's something else you're hiding from me, because the man I've been friends with, the man I've known, is not that stupid or disrespectful. You're the same person who worried over stealing my voice, my choices. Either you're flat-out lying to me, or there's more to this."

His mouth thins, and he glances away. Sorrow threads through my anger, and in that moment, the heaviness of it sits on my chest. Because he's not going to be truthful with me. Lie, evade, refuse . . . he's preparing to do one of those, and I won't be able to deal with that. Not from him.

"Maybe you're not the only one who fears being left, rejected," he almost snarls at me. The air snags in my lungs at the embers that have struck to flames in his eyes. "Because that's what's behind this, isn't it, Miriam? Abandonment issues? I get your past, your childhood. Being who you are wasn't easy. People who probably lied and called themselves friends, then proved they weren't when it came time to claim the school genius as their buddy. That wouldn't earn them any cool points. And kids can be little shits when it comes to being popular over integrity. And then your parents. Good people, but when it comes to insight and unconditional acceptance of their children . . . well, let's just say if insight were lard, they wouldn't have enough between them to grease a pan." He edges forward, crowding me even though he still doesn't touch me. But his words—his too-incisive, too-truthful words—accomplish what his big frame doesn't. "But that's not it, is it? Why do I still get the feeling there's more, as you put it? And right now, I'm the one paying for that *more*?"

"We're not talking about me," I rasp.

"Aren't we?" he presses.

He's too close. Too . . . much. I can't breathe.

"Move back." I shove against his chest. "Move."

But before I say the second *move*, he's backing away, granting me space. I claw the air like a drowning woman whose head just broke water. I whirl around, flattening my palms on the counter. Blindly staring straight ahead at the marbled backsplash, I force my breathing to slow. To even.

I'm not that lonely, broken, lied-to girl anymore. The one he so accurately described. The little girl who'd hungered for friends only to be rejected and bullied for daring to try to be . . . normal. The child and woman who treaded the precarious line of being too perfect and terrified of fucking up and marring that perfection, of losing her parents' esteem and affection.

And then there was the young woman who'd been so desperate for love, for acceptance, to belong that she'd given herself to the first guy who'd shown interest in her. And been betrayed in the cruelest way for that trust.

They're not me, and I'm not them.

Not anymore.

Not anymore, dammit.

"I was afraid," comes his velvet-and-gravel voice. "I was afraid, and I panicked. The ugly, dirty truth is I was protecting myself. What I said before? True. If I had a woman and the relationship was brand new, I would want her time for myself to find out if there was something there without another man's interference. Especially if she spends a lot of time with that other man. I'd want her to divert some of that attention to me, let me know I mattered. Insecure, needy? Maybe. But again, the truth."

Two large inked hands bracket mine, and I stare at the differences in size, in complexion, in strength. For an instant, I'm damn near entranced by them. Fingers and palms almost twice the length and width. Light to dark. He could easily enclose my hands in his, covering them, squeezing them, pressing them together. Now, he does none of those. Just braces me.

The heat from his body warms mine even though he grants me the space I demanded.

Well, his version of it.

"I'm sorry, Miriam," he apologizes again. "I . . ." He pauses, and his forehead presses into the back of my head. His breath grazes the nape of my neck, and I sink my teeth into my bottom lip, imprisoning the whimper climbing up my throat. "I was jealous." The admission is low, soft, and growled. With effort I smother the shudder attempting to work its way up my spine, but I can't assure myself of my success. "I was a jealous bitch. What kind of man does that make me? What kind of friend? I didn't want to hear about your date with him, even though I asked you to give it a chance. I didn't want to know you were giving him that smile, your time, your heart that I've come to depend on. I didn't want it taken away from me." He stops, and his breath breaks against my skin like waves against a rocky shore. "So I distanced myself, pushed you away. But I missed you. No games, sweetheart, no lies. I missed you. And walking in here tonight and seeing you . . ." He presses his forehead harder against me. "It was a fucking fist to the chest. If you don't believe anything else I'm saying, please accept that. I *miss* you."

Jealous.

My body lights up, fire pouring through my veins as if my blood suddenly transformed to gasoline and that one word is the struck match. I should have my feminist card snatched and cut up in my face. Because his confession infuses me with a glowing, heady power. This big, sex-on-a-stick Viking wanted to hoard my time, my damn *smiles* for himself. God, yes, I know, pushing me away was shitty. And if he dares to do it again, his nuts will end up on an FBI's most-wanted poster. Yet—

What kind of man does that make me? What kind of friend?

Right. That part. And cold reality snuffs out the liquid flames in my body.

Friend. His friend.

That's who he's missed. Nothing else. Nothing more.

And that's perfect because that's all we are. All I want. Yes, yes. All I want.

Fuck, I'm so confused.

Dipping my head, I stare at our hands again. Imagine them intertwined, grasping, grabbing, clawing . . . *this*. This is why my brain and heart are like two toddlers battling it out over the last Tonka truck in the toy box. Lust. The unerring knowledge that he can master my body like no one else. Give me such pleasure that just the memory of it has heat rolling through me like a sunburned tumbleweed.

Relief courses over me, and I almost sag against the counter with it. Yes, this makes sense. I'm confused about my feelings for Jordan . . . I just want to fuck him.

My body is craving the escape of that ecstasy like a hit.

That I understand. *That* I can deal with.

That I can put myself in dick detox for.

But anything more, anything deeper?

No. I can't. As certain as I am that Zack Snyder's *Justice League* should've been the only one made, I know Jordan Ransom will leave only ashes of me if I allow it. Ashes that will disappear with one gentle breeze, and nothing will remain.

It's simple. I can't allow it.

Good thing it's not an issue.

Desire. Lust. A physical, chemical reaction that can be ignored. I got this.

Turning, I face Jordan. And when my breasts touch his chest, the nipples drawing into tight, beaded points behind my bra, I question my resolve and sanity. My belly spasms so hard it resonates between my legs, setting off a yawning, empty complaint in my sex.

Holy shit.

"Miriam."

"I miss you too," I blurt out. Then, with a shaky chuckle, I dip down and rest my forehead on his chest. "I miss you too," I repeat, softer, calmer.

Strong yet tender fingers slide between us and pinch my chin. He tips my head back so I have no choice but to meet his gaze.

"Am I forgiven?"

"Don't do it again."

"Never."

I squint up at him. "If insight was lard, they don't have enough between them to grease a pan?"

He shrugs. "I think my mother heard it on *Dr. Phil* or somewhere."

I snicker, then shake my head. "Forgiven," I murmur.

"Thank you."

We remain standing there, his hand still cupping my chin, those eyes still holding me captive.

"Jordan," I whisper.

His gaze drops to my mouth, and *oh God*, it's almost physical, that visual stroke. Without my permission, my tongue peeks out and swipes over my bottom lip, savoring that caress, imprinting it.

A sound rumbles out of him, and it's somewhere between a moan and a growl. Maybe an utterly sexual combination of both. Instinct tells me that he didn't mean to release it, but it's too late. That hungry, needy noise reverberates between us, and though space separates our bodies, I swear it vibrates over my breasts, my nipples. And I bite my lip, containing a matching sound inside.

"Don't." The order—dark, hot, and abrupt—sends a jolt through me.

A sizzling jolt that has my nerve endings dancing. My breath catching. My sex quivering.

I don't need to ask what he's referring to; since we've met, Jordan and I have been on a wavelength that should be impossible for two strangers. But it's there, that connection. And so, now, I slowly release my lip from the clasp of my teeth.

And whimper.

Those beautiful eyes light up like a flash of dry heat, searing me. And, in spite of the speech I just delivered to myself on resisting this, I turn my face up to it. Hungering for its burn.

What would Sarafina do?

Easy.

She'd jump into the fucking flames.

"Has anyone seen my sister? I swear, she's probably face first into Cyrus's wine closet." Zora's voice drifts into the kitchen, and I stiffen. "Miriam, where are you?"

Panic claws at me, and I push at Jordan's chest, but I shove against air since he's already moved. Later, I'll analyze what his quick actions could mean—leaping away like I'm patient zero for the zombie apocalypse could play hell with a girl's confidence—but for right now, the last thing I need is for someone to walk in here and misconstrue seeing us together.

Hell, I don't know what they would be seeing.

I'll analyze that later too. When my heartbeat isn't between my legs.

"Miriam."

I draw to a halt at the voice that's lower, gravellier than usual, but I don't glance over my shoulder. Looking at him might be the very thing that tips my precarious resolve over the edge, and I desperately need to regroup first.

"Yes?"

"You and Daniel . . . you're good?"

Were we? Before I came into this kitchen, I'd already decided we needed a conversation about being just friends. Now? When my body hums with pleasure for another man? Hell yes, we must have that conversation.

"Yes, we're good."

Call me a liar. I'll accept it. But I need Daniel as a barrier.

"Good."

And that shouldn't hurt. But fuck if it doesn't.

Zora sweeps into the kitchen. Thank God.

"I knew you were in here," she crows, a wide grin lighting her face. It doesn't dip when she spies Jordan over my shoulder, but I note the glint of curiosity in her gaze as it shifts back to me. "And I shouldn't be shocked that your partner in crime is right here along with you. Or that there's an open bottle in here too."

"What can I say?" I shrug, grappling for and finding an answering smile. "Cyrus should've known better than to hold out on the good stuff with me."

I swipe my glass of wine from the counter and hook my arm through Zora's and guide her out of the kitchen.

"So like I was telling Jordan here, I don't like to resort to violence, but I think it's only fair to warn you that your eyebrows are in danger if that maid-of-honor spot isn't mine . . ."

She throws back her head and laughs. "Honest to God, though? I believe you."

"Oh, Zora." I pat her hand. "You should."

And we head back into her engagement party.

And I escape the brooding Viking in the kitchen.

I'm not proud.

CHAPTER NINE

JORDAN

"I'm a changeling. Shit happens."

—North the Woodsman, Ravaged Lands

I ring the doorbell and stare at the double front doors of the Castle Pines home and wait for it. And she doesn't keep me waiting for long. My grin stretches wide by the time my mom throws the door open.

"Boy, I told you don't ever ring my doorbell. Not ever again." Grace Ransom props her fists on her slim hips and glares at me. "I gave you a key for a reason. No son of mine rings or knocks to come into my house. The door is always open."

"Yes, ma'am. Although to be fair, I am your only son, so there's that."

"Mouthy as always." Her scowl melts into a huge smile, and she holds out her arms to me.

And as always, I walk into them.

Her familiar lavender scent envelops me as securely, as warmly as her embrace, and I sink into it. No matter where we've laid our heads over the years—and there have been several places—this right here will always be home.

"Get in here." She releases me and jerks a thumb over her shoulder. Leaving me to follow, she pads away, and I close the door behind me. "Your aunts are headed over in a couple of hours. They'll be happy to see you since it's been a while."

"Wow, that was subtle." I laugh. "Point taken."

"Oh, no, no," Mom says, holding up a finger and wagging it at me without turning around. "The point won't be taken until your aunts get their say in. And trust me, Jordy, it's not going to be as gentle as mine."

"Has it ever?" I mutter, then huff out a laugh.

The Ransom sisters. Grace, Maggie, and Delilah. As long as I can remember, they've been inseparable, thicker than any thieves. Unfortunately, they've also shared the same shitty taste in men over the years too. God knows we love them, but my cousins and I have endured their string of bad choices like good little soldiers.

"What're you three up to? And should we all be scared?" I drawl, entering the kitchen behind her.

Though Mom worked hard as hell when I was growing up—sometimes two jobs—she always found time to cook me meals. Always. For her, it was a way of showing her love. And when I bought this home for her, not ten minutes away from me, the huge gourmet-style kitchen had been one of the main features. Top-of-the-line appliances, a butler's pantry, custom cabinetry, and a dine-in area that opens up to a beautiful outdoor covered patio encompass a gorgeous room that is my mother's favorite. More often than not, I can find her here rather than any of the other rooms in this five-bedroom, five-bathroom house. And like today, the most delicious smells usually emanate from it.

Glancing up from the pot she's stirring, she arches an eyebrow.

"I'm sorry, did I wake up one instead of fifty-one and suddenly have to answer to you?"

I hold up my hands, warding off the "You're not too old to get told off" lecture that's 2.3 seconds away. "I'm asking just in case I need to scrape up some bail money."

She snorts, shifting her attention back to whatever she's cooking. "I'm sure you can swing it."

"What're you cooking?" I cross over to her, peeping over her shoulder into the pot.

"Vegetable stew."

"Is this a bad time to mention that vegetable stew usually doesn't include chicken?" I jerk my chin toward the package of chicken sitting on the counter next to the stove.

"Is this a bad time to tell you to mind your business?"

"Nope."

"Didn't think so." She snickers. "How's the leg?"

It must've been killing her to wait this long to ask about it. Knowing her, she probably wanted to pounce on me about it as soon as she opened the door. The first week after my injury, I could barely get her out of my house. Don't get me wrong. I adore my mother. But having her trying to ice and wrap my upper thigh so close to my dick hadn't been a happy experience.

"Almost healed. Hopefully, I should be back playing in another two weeks."

She side-eyes me. "Is that what your physical therapist says, or is that what you're saying?"

Sighing, I lean a shoulder against the refrigerator. "Of course, he has to clear me, but two weeks."

"I'm happy for you, Jordy." She reaches over and squeezes my bicep. "I know you've been worried, and I've hated to see you like that. I'll be there for your first game back."

"Mom, you're there for every home game," I remind her, proud of that fact. She hasn't missed a professional home game of mine since I started in the league.

"But even if it's an away game, I'll be there. That's a promise. I've already given Laura a heads-up that she might have to find someone to cover my shifts if I need to fly to Boston at the drop of a hat on a Thursday or Saturday."

It still amazes me that even though she lives in a huge McMansion in Castle Pines and I cover most of her expenses, Mom still insists on going to work. It's my honor and pleasure to provide for her when she's sacrificed over and over again for me. Yet she clocks in at that retail store in downtown Denver four to five days a week. I get it. She's spent too many years being independent and busy, and rattling around doing nothing wouldn't sit well with her.

"Thanks. I appreciate it." I bend down and brush a kiss over her cheek. "But you called me over here for a reason, yeah? Not just to see the pretty face you gave me?"

Truthfully, I'm a replica of my father, although she did share her eyes with me. Another reason I love and will do anything for her. I was—am—a living reminder of the man she once loved who abandoned her with a three-year-old and never looked back. Yet she never punished me for that reminder. Never took her pain, her bitterness, out on me. She's only loved me.

After twisting the burner to low, she covers the pot with a lid and turns to me. There's no trace of humor in her eyes and zero sign of her customary wry smile. Dread drops into my chest like a stone, lodging there.

"What's wrong?"

"Why don't we go sit down?" She waves a hand toward the oak kitchen table and chairs, but I resist, shaking my head. Not only do I want her to just say it—stop prolonging the suspense—but this unease has my feet glued to the floor. "Jordan . . ."

"Mom, just say it," I rasp. "Is it Aunt Maggie? Aunt Delilah? Are they sick? Is that why they're coming over?"

She flinches, pales. "God, no! No, Jordan." Grasping my hand, she squeezes. "They're fine. Your cousins, the family—everyone's fine. I just have some . . . news that I think you should sit down for. It's probably going to come as a shock."

"Shit, okay. That's good." The boulder pressing against my sternum shifts a little, and I can breathe a little easier. A little. Because that cautious watchfulness still hasn't disappeared from Mom's expression. "Christ, Mom, just tell me."

"Watch your mouth," she admonishes, but it lacks heat. "Fine. God, I don't know where to start."

She stalks over to the wooden butcher-block island in the middle of the kitchen and flattens her palms on it, staring down at the top. I wrangle the urge to press her, to growl at her to just say whatever it is. One, I'd never disrespect her. Two, it wouldn't do me any good. Grace Ransom doesn't do anything until she's damn good and ready.

Seconds later, she lifts her head and meets my gaze.

"Your father called me."

Ice stretches through me like frost spreading and crackling over a windshield. I'm cold. So fucking cold. Mom didn't need to worry about me having to sit down. I can't move.

At least, my body can't.

But my mind . . . my mind is whirling like a ballerina on speed. Questions, so many questions, bombard me. What is he doing here? What does he want? Has he asked her for money? Is she going to fall for his bullshit and let him back in?

That last one—that last one has me fucking terrified.

And angry. At him. At her. And she hasn't even told me what he wants yet.

"So he knew how to contact you."

She blinks at me, as if my flat statement and even flatter voice have taken her aback. What did she expect? Me to start smashing dishes or windows? I mean, yeah. She should've. My father hasn't been an easy subject in the past. As a matter of fact, when she's tried to bring him up, I've shut it down with a "Fuck him" and left it at that.

The best thing he did was orgasm and walk away. I don't need him. And neither does she.

"Yes," she says, tone wary. "My phone number hasn't changed in all these years."

"My point exactly. He knew from the time he walked out that door how to contact you, how to call and get money to you to, I don't know, help you survive. But he *chose* not to. So why now? What does he want?"

"He wants to get to know you," she murmurs. "And he asked if I would talk to you about it."

I laugh, and there's nothing humorous about it. The sound is shards of glass abrading my throat. "I'm sure he did. And the answer is no."

"Jordan."

"*No,*" I repeat harder, harsher. And I never, *ever* take that tone with her. But then again, she's never gone to bat for a deadbeat, selfish asshole before. "I don't owe him a damn thing. And that he would go through you rather than come to me shows what kind of ball-less dick he was. Correction. Still is."

"Jordan—no." She slashes a hand through the air, eyes narrowed on me when my lips part. "Don't interrupt me again. I'm still your mother, and you're going to listen to me. You don't have to agree or obey, but you will listen *without* interruption." When I keep quiet, she continues with a heavy sigh. "I get it, Jordan. I do. And you have every right to say no. He wasn't there for you. Has never been there for you. I'm not asking you to forgive him or even talk to him. I'm only telling you you have an opportunity that a lot of people don't. To sit down with your father and ask him all the questions you've had your entire life. To tell him the effect his absence had on you. To get everything off your chest regarding him. This is *not* for him. I want you to understand that. This is for *you.*"

Sounds nice. And for a second, for a quick second, I'm tempted. So fucking tempted.

But then I remember ten years ago.

"When he asked you to arrange this meeting, did he happen to mention he approached me a decade ago?" She frowns, straightens, and I nod. "Yeah, right after I was drafted. He tracked me down to congratulate me. I thought the timing had been a little suspect. After not hearing a word from him for seventeen years, he manages to find me when I'm about to enter the NBA. It could be a coincidence, but I doubt it."

"You never said anything," she says, her gaze roaming my face.

"No, I didn't." Guilt tries to worm its way through me, but fuck that. I'm not ashamed of protecting her from that bastard. "Because I told him I didn't want anything to do with him. And that if he came near me again or you, I'd fuck him up. Apparently, ten years has dimmed his memory."

"Jordan, I'm so sorry."

"It doesn't matter."

I wave away her sympathy; I don't want it.

I don't want any part of the pressure that's ballooning behind my ribs, seeming to bow them out. Not because of *that* man.

"It *does* matter. You should've told me. Why didn't you, sweetie?" she asks.

"Because *he* doesn't matter. He never has. *He* left *us*. And because he decides to waltz back in like nothing happened? He doesn't get to upend our lives. No, fuck that."

"In other words, you were afraid I would go running after him," she whispers.

"No, Mom," I lie.

Because, yes, goddammit. Yes. I was afraid of that.

I still am.

"Yes, you are," she says, her blue eyes sad and so filled with shadows, with shame, that they appear nearly black. "And there's no need to feel bad for believing that, Jordan. It's not as if I haven't given you just cause to fear that's exactly what I would do." She sighs, turning away, her hand stroking over her dark hair. "My choices in men over the years have sucked. Your father being no different. Only that he's the one I actually loved."

"Mom . . ."

"But while I wouldn't be upset with you for forgiving him because he's your father, and you should have a relationship with him if that's what you wanted, I can't do that." She pivots, faces me again. Pain and that remorse still darken her gaze, but a hardness I haven't witnessed on her before tautens the skin across her strong facial bones, sets her mouth in a grim line. "I know we're supposed to forgive, let bygones be bygones, but he doesn't get that from me. If it'd just been me, that'd be one thing. But he abandoned you. He deprived you of a father, of a different life. He hurt you. That's unforgiveable. So no, I cannot go back to him."

I can't speak. But I can move.

Covering the short space that separates us, I pull her into a hug and hold tight.

"I love you, Mom."

"I love you too, sweetie."

An hour later, I jog up the four concrete steps to the lower-level Stapleton condo. An urgency that pumps through my veins pushes me across the porch to the front door. I pull open the storm door, mentally reminding myself to get on her for leaving it unlocked. After knocking on her front door, I wait. But the sense of need rides me, and I damn near vibrate with it.

Shit, I should've called. Texted. Something. It's—I turn my wrist over, glance down at my watch—7:46 on a Monday night. She might still be at the office but not out with Daniel. He's on the road for the first of two back-to-back road games. But she could still be anywhere—

The door opens, and Miriam stands in the entrance.

For a long moment, all I can do is stare.

Then I'm moving.

Then I'm on her. Gathering her in my arms. Holding her close. Tight. So fucking tight.

I didn't know until she opened that door how much I needed her. Needed her arms around me. That curvy body pressed to mine. That cinnamon-and-vanilla scent in my nose. The sound of her breath in my ear. The beat of her pulse under my mouth.

She doesn't ask any questions, just holds me. And when I straighten, lifting her in my arms and pressing her to the nearest wall of her small foyer, she still doesn't utter a word of protest. She just winds her legs around my hips and clings to me, granting me the comfort of her body, her silence, her unconditional support.

Seconds, minutes—hell, hours—pass as we stand there, joined together. After a while, the urgency that chased me from my mom's house, pursued me to Stapleton, and propelled me through her front door starts to ease, and the tension ebbs from my frame.

But as I calm, another, different need starts to sneak in. A darker, edgier one.

That sultry, provocative musk calls to me, and I answer, burying my face in that nook where her neck and shoulder meet. I inhale, closing my eyes, remembering in vivid, technicolor detail just where the fragrance is heavier, more condensed . . . headier. The valley between her breasts. The indentation of her waist. The back of her knee.

The wet, hot depths of her pussy.

The small perfect mounds of her breasts swell against my chest, and, *fuck*, the peaks of her nipples graze me, torture me. And though

139

it's impossible, the sweet heat of her burns me through her thin joggers and my jeans.

With a Herculean effort, I slowly lower her to the ground and back away.

My mind congratulates me, but my arms, my cock, yells, "What. The. Fuck?"

Hauling in a breath, I turn away from her on the pretense of closing the door I left standing wide open. Taking those precious few moments to get my shit together, I grip the knob, nearly strangling the hell out of it.

"Jordan?"

"Yeah?" Tunneling both hands through my hair, I grip the loose strands, fisting them at the back of my head. "I'm sorry." I finally spin around, facing her, the apology spilling from me.

"You have nothing to apologize for," she says.

I smirk, but it feels fake on my mouth, and from her solemn expression and her watchful, steady gaze, I'm guessing it looks that way too.

"Nothing, yeah? Not even jumping on you like a *National Geographic* special as soon as you opened the door?"

"I'm not complaining, am I?"

I drag my gaze over her, savoring everything from the tight blonde curls down to the black tank top stretched over her pretty little tits and on to the gray-and-pink polka-dot joggers molded to her gorgeous hips and ass and thick, toned thighs. My fingers itch to dig into those hips, mark them, bruise them like I did once before. She hadn't seemed to mind them. On the contrary. She'd given me some of her own . . .

"No, you're not."

After pushing off the wall, she approaches me and, with no hesitation, wraps her fingers around mine. If she could only glimpse the thoughts charging through my head, she might grant me a wide berth.

Unaware, she leads me out of her foyer into the living room that flows into her dining room and kitchen. The open floor plan provides an unobstructed view of the main floor and up to the loft that she uses for a home office. I love my house and the one I bought Mom. Yet Miriam's, with her cozy two bedrooms with balconies off of each one, two bathrooms, and a small family room downstairs is *her*. Quirky and beautiful with its eclectic yet classy decor, her townhome has been my haven before. A place where I can escape the oftentimes sticky trappings and expectations of the fame and celebrity that come with my career.

Miriam has become my safe space.

Her house. Her house has become my safe space.

It's amazing how I can still cling to denial when moments ago I clung to her.

She guides me to the couch and, after we sit facing each other, waits. And it's that patient silence that allows me to talk. Miriam doesn't interrupt, just listens as I tell her about my visit with Mom and the phone call from my father. This is my friend, the woman who slept on the other end of my bed when I was first injured in case I needed something in the middle of the night or just to . . . be there. So I wouldn't be alone. Or afraid. I hadn't even needed to say anything; she just stayed.

That's Miriam.

And without conscious thought, that's why I drove over here to her. For this.

"What're you going to do?" she quietly asks when I finish talking, and a silence settles between us. "Or have you decided yet?"

I prop my elbows on my thighs and, head bowed, stare at my hands. "I don't know. Mom—she's leaving the decision up to me. But she wants me to meet up with him, to at least find closure with him. She believes I need it."

"And you?" Miriam murmurs. "Do you believe you need it?"

I laugh, shaking my head. "What is fucking closure? To me, when he left and didn't come back the first time Mom had to take on a second job to make rent, that was the door closing. Or when she pawned my grandfather's coin collection—the only thing she had left of his—so I could pay all of my class dues my senior year of high school. That's a buzzword that doesn't mean much to me. But Mom . . ."

"She feels guilty that you missed out. Even though it wasn't her fault; she didn't make your father abandon his family. But she chose him as your father, and she feels responsibility for that. And that because she made that wrong choice, your life was affected. You went without. So she wants to give you this."

"Yeah," I rasp. "And if I don't want it?"

"Then don't take it. But . . ." Her hand slides into my line of vision, and it rests on my thigh. The slight weight of it singes me, and I wouldn't be surprised to find a scorch mark there. "What're you afraid of, Jordan?"

The question jerks my attention from the brand of her palm, and I go still, meeting her gaze. The denial loiters on my tongue, but looking into those eyes is akin to being hooked up to a lie detector.

"What if . . ." I pause, lick my suddenly dry lips. "What if I sit down and talk to him and he admits why he left? And it's me. I'm the reason. Or he comes clean about why he tracked me down ten years ago? Because I was drafted, and I finally had something to offer him. I was finally worth something."

Her fingers curl, the tips digging into the muscle of my thigh. After a few seconds, they slowly straighten, as if she deliberately relaxed them.

"What?" I murmur. "No 'That's bullshit'?"

"No, because you don't need me to tell you that. You know it."

I shove to my feet, restless. Needing to burn off the frenetic energy crackling through me, I pace across her living room to the dining room, then retrace my steps to the window behind her couch. Pressing a fist to the wall above it, I stare out at the sidewalk separating her unit from the one across the common area, not really seeing it.

Instead, a reel of the last few years of my life runs past my eyes. The games, the press, the parties, the women, the fans . . . all of it. And I can't agree with her. It's not bullshit.

"I know what I look like," I say to the window, to the streetlamp that casts shadows over the walkway and her neighbor's dark porch. "And even if I'd never picked up a ball, I might've still been popular or had my share of women because of this." I flick a hand in front of my face. "But the fact is I did pick up a basketball. I did become one of the highest-rated players in high school and one of the most watched in college. I did enter the NBA. And all that money, celebrity, and connections make you hotter, more wanted, in demand. Not in spite of it, though. Because of it. And not just with strangers. With fathers too."

A small hand settles on the middle of my back.

"I may not know what it is to have a fat NBA contract or women waiting outside my hotel or how it is to pop bottles in the VIP section—oh, wait. I am well acquainted with that last one, actually." When I snort, she presses closer and aligns her side to mine, wedging under my arm and giving me no choice but to wrap it around her shoulders. "I do know about challenging parents, though. You've met 'em. They weren't deadbeats by any stretch of the imagination; one can argue my mother was a little too overinvolved, but there were times I've wondered . . . when I still wonder if maybe I wouldn't have all of their attention if I didn't have this IQ. Sometimes I don't know if I would've been unconditionally loved for who I am instead of what I'm capable of." She sighs. "I get it, Jordan. Or at least some of it. And I don't have the answers, but one thing my parents have taught me? You can't take on other people's shit. We have enough of our own. If we carry theirs, too, we'll buckle under the weight."

The shadows creep a little farther along the sidewalk as we stand at the window, lost in our own thoughts but leaning on one another.

"How about coffee? Or water? I have wine, but I'm out of beer," she says, shifting to the side and tipping her head back.

"Water." I reach behind me and pull my phone out of my back pocket. "And I'll order some food for dinner. That is, if you haven't eaten yet."

"Nope." She wheels around and heads for her kitchen. "You know what I like."

I do. "Sesame chicken. Got it."

I head to the couch and lower to it, swiping my thumb over the screen. Just as I get ready to pull up the search engine, the corner of a tablet underneath a pillow catches my attention. Frowning, I edge it out from underneath, aware that I'm snooping but unable to stop myself.

And when I get a glimpse at the screen, pretending I'm not prying is out the window.

Holy shit.

An illustration of a barren, charred land with a gray sky dominates the screen. And in the distance, an almost medieval-looking city rises in front of a desolate, dark mountain. But it's the lone figure in the foreground that captures and holds most of my attention. Hooded, the woman with the long twists exudes mystery, power, and strength. The detail and color . . . I can't tear my gaze away. I have no idea what this drawing depicts, but I'm drawn to it, want to discover more about this strange and lonely yet beautiful land and its gorgeous, obviously deadly defender.

"Here you—what're you doing?"

I somehow tear my gaze away from the tablet and find Miriam standing at the edge of the sofa, a bottle of water in one hand and a coffee cup in the other.

Though I have no right, I lift the tablet and ask, "What's this?"

Frowning, she sets the water and coffee on the table and reaches for the device. "Mine."

"Miriam. It's . . . fucking phenomenal."

Her hand pauses midair, fingertips grazing the edge. Slowly, her arm drops back to her side, those brown eyes staring into mine, seeking . . . what?

"Miriam," I say again. "Is this yours?"

"Yes." She thrusts her hands into the pockets of her joggers, hiking her chin up. But the gesture strikes me as bravado. As if she expects a blow to that chin. At least a verbal one. "It's mine."

"Sweetheart." I peer down at the drawing again, shaking my head. "This . . . I didn't know. I knew you loved anime, but I had no idea you could do *this*." I keep repeating myself, but goddamn, she's floored me. Miriam Nelson is an onion. Every time I think I know her, another layer is peeled back, revealing a new, startling side. "Why haven't you said anything?"

Especially to me?

I don't add that, but it's there.

"Because it's mine," she repeats. "It's me. And no one in my family is ready to meet me."

"Miriam," I whisper. Her parents—she might have something there. But Zora, Levi . . . "That's not true . . ."

A small rueful smile twists her lips. "Oh, but it is. Even you aren't."

"Then show me," I plead, a desperate note entering my voice, and I don't care. I *am* fucking desperate. We're friends. Even though I've been inside her, we're just friends. And yet the thought of her holding back from me, of not sharing all of herself with me, drives me a little bit fucking crazy. "Give me a chance to prove I am."

She removes her hands from her pockets and folds them in front of her, locking and twisting them together. That nervous tell is new, and I almost launch myself from the couch to cover those hands with one of mine to stop the frantic gesture. That she's anxious—with *me*—has hurt and bile churning in my gut. It's offensive.

"When Zora and Levi asked me to join BURNED, it was because of my degrees in marketing, graphic design, and digital media. But they either forgot or dismissed my master's in graphic illustration. Same with my parents. Because I was so good with math as a child, they all forgot that I would fill pad after pad with drawings to escape the war zone that was my house. To create the friends I didn't have. To build the world

I wished I lived in instead of the one I inhabited. They all believed it was a hobby. A harmless hobby that passed the time. None of them ever understood that math, numbers, equations—they . . ." Her face scrunches up, and she peers up at the ceiling, her hands twirling as if she could conjure the words she seeks out of thin air. "They ground me. But art? Art makes me fly."

I blink.

Desire kindles inside me, her passion a bellow that blows on mine. Only shock holds me to the couch cushion. Shock and the hunger to hear more about this secret-until-now side of her. More. I want more of her. And it's not just physical. It's emotional, spiritual, fucking visceral.

If I could crawl inside her and touch the mystical part that created that illustration, I would already be on top of her, searching for a secret opening like she's my own personal Narnia.

"Mom and Dad"—she flicks her fingers—"I'll never expect them to get it. And I disappointed Mom by not becoming a teacher. There's always been some distance between me and Zora and Levi, and it all didn't have to do with age. They didn't know how to deal with me either. I was younger than them but ahead in school. And then, in their eyes, I went 'crazy' in college. Finding this out—that I'm a graphic novelist— would just be one more item for them to jot down on their 'That's just Miriam being Miriam' list. I couldn't stand to watch them relegate it to something small or inconsequential. Not when it means everything to me. So no, I haven't shared this part of me with them. With anyone. Until now."

Until me.

Clearing my throat, I switch my gaze back to her tablet and study the illustration again. I lift a hand to the screen and glance at her, eyebrow arched, the unspoken request still loud and clear between us. There's a moment of slight hesitation, but then she dips her head.

With her consent, I brush the screen and bring up another panel. In this one, a giant, ripped, Viking-looking male with blazing-blue eyes and a braided blond mohawk fights an emaciated, rotting figure, his axes slicing through gray flesh, gore splattering. In the background, two children in tattered clothing huddle together, fear drawing their faces. But also, awe shines in their dark eyes as they stare at the blond warrior who's obviously protecting them.

The Viking character is dressed in leather and boots with dark tattoos scrawled over his muscled arms and thick neck, but I recognize the shape of the face and mouth, the color of the eyes, the mohawk.

He's . . . me.

My heart thunders against my rib cage, and the roar is deafening in my head. A vise tightens around my chest, and my breath wheezes out of my lungs. A slight tremble vibrates down my arms, and the tablet quivers in my hands as I stare at the next panel. The children run to him and throw their arms around his thick legs. They burrow their faces against him, clinging. As if he's their safe haven, their savior.

Their safe haven. Their savior.

"Is this how you see me?" I rasp. I would've loved for the question to emerge strong, even. But that's beyond me now. Fuck, I can barely drag in air.

I glimpse it in her eyes—the instant she contemplates denying the truth about the connection between the character in the illustration and me. But then she drops her gaze to the screen.

"Yes," she says softly. "His name is North. He's a loner, a warrior, but he feels set apart from people because he's also a changeling, and most fear and hate him for the circumstances of his birth that he had no control over. But he's a protector, honorable. He's good."

Emotion surges within me, a maelstrom of shock, disbelief, hope, joy, and . . . and so much fucking love I don't understand how she can't feel it, *see* it. Right now, I'm probably doing a piss-poor job of hiding it.

Dipping my head, I point at the illustration.

"Tell me," I demand . . . beg. "And leave nothing out."

Her arms drop to her sides, and she freezes, a fine tension entering her body. My breath catches in my lungs, and I match her in stillness. Waiting. But inside my head? I'm pleading, yelling.

Take a chance on me.

"Okay."

Moving forward, she takes the tablet from me and lowers to the couch beside me. In moments, she pulls up a website with different thumbnails. They appear to be comic books with varying illustration styles.

"This is Gen Comics. It's a downloadable app where people can go online and read comic series. It's like Kindle Unlimited for graphic novels. They pay a monthly subscription fee and have unlimited access to every book on the app." She taps on the screen and brings up another tab. "This is Ravaged Lands, and it's one of the highest-rated and most popular series on the app."

She turns the tablet toward me, and I recognize the hooded character in the illustration, though here, there are two additional squares on the screen, and in one the cloak is gone and she's covered in blood and gore.

"This says the author is Rayland Penn," I say.

"That's my pen name." She dips her chin. "This is my latest issue. I release them monthly. So far I have two omnibuses of Ravaged Lands—"

"Omnibus?" I interrupt.

"An entire graphic novel. An issue is like a chapter in a book, and think of an omnibus like a collection of issues. A book. Right now, I'm in talks of possibly having book one put on the shelves in indie bookstores right here in Denver," she says, the pride in her voice unmistakable.

"Miriam." I wait for her to glance up from the tablet and meet my gaze. "You're the shit."

A smile quirks the corners of her mouth; then it slowly spreads into a wide grin across her face. And she's beautiful as fuck.

"I still use my marketing degree to promote and advertise Rayland Penn and Ravaged Lands. I'm much more invested financially and personally with this than I am with BURNED, even though I enjoy the work there. But the business has more to do with Zora and Levi than my love of it. Our motivations behind joining the company are different. Zora wanted to prevent anyone from ending up like our parents. And I"—she strokes the screen—"I wanted to do something with my brother and sister and support their dreams. And Levi . . . well, Levi is complicated."

"But if you could do this"—I nod toward the tablet—"full time, you would."

"In a heartbeat."

"Then do it."

She snorts, setting the device on the table and picking up her forgotten cup of coffee. "Easier said than done."

"Are you afraid you can't earn a living as a graphic novelist? That you can't support yourself?"

"It's not that," she says, frowning. But not exactly at me. "I make good money now, and working full time instead of at night, weekends, and the hours I can snatch during the day, I could probably produce more issues faster. Which means uploading content more often and, in turn, bringing in more royalties."

"Then what is it?" I edge closer.

It's as if a silken web draws me nearer, and I'm helpless to resist. This vulnerable, almost hesitant side of Miriam . . . it's so unfamiliar, so unexpected, that I'm fascinated and caught between needing to study her, never remove my gaze from her, and touch her. Put my hands all over her.

"Yes, Zora and Levi have assigned themselves different babysitting days for me, and yes, sometimes their mistrust in my abilities and decisions chafe, but BURNED is stability. *They're* stability. I've never had it, and I don't want to lose it. I don't want to lose them."

"Peace at any cost is no peace at all."

She cocks her head. "*Dr. Phil* again?"

I shrug. "Mom couldn't afford a therapist. No insurance."

"I should not laugh at that," she says, rolling her lips inward and widening her eyes.

"Yeah, that'd be a little inappropriate."

"*Dr. Phil*, though?" she whispers.

We both snicker. Moments later, our laughter ebbs, and I loose a low sigh, letting my gaze roam over her lovely face.

"My childhood was noisy. Mom worked a lot, so before I was old enough to stay home by myself, I stayed with aunts while she was gone. Never a dull moment at their houses. Between my cousins and the assholes they dated, it was always loud, chaotic. And even at home . . . yes, my mother loved me enough for two parents, but her track record with men was fucked."

I briefly glance at the tablet before returning my attention to her. Curiosity brightens her eyes. Curiosity and a sympathy that should sear like acid against my senses, my pride. But it doesn't. It's a soothing balm.

"I told you basketball saved me when I was a kid. And that's true but not the whole of it. Aslan, Lucy, and Edmund. Peter, Caspian, Reepicheep. They all offered me a place of escape. Gave me a land to travel to where I could get away from the noise, the fighting, the loneliness. I read the Chronicles of Narnia—all seven books—countless times. But it was *The Lion, the Witch and the Wardrobe* that I connected with most. Here were these ordinary kids who people looked at and saw nothing special, but all it took was stepping through a wardrobe to unlock their destiny as kings and queens. I desperately wanted to believe I was destined for more than what was around me, what I saw. That I could *be* more. I saw myself in Edmund. The lonely, scared fuck-up becoming great. Narnia not only was my safe space; it challenged me to dream big." I swallow past the fist of emotion lodged in my throat. "I get your reasons for hesitating about going into this"—I sweep a hand toward the tablet—"full time. But, sweetheart, you're someone's Narnia."

You're mine.

I don't voice those words, but they echo in my head, my chest.

Silence falls between us—and with it, a tissue-fine tension. My palm tingles with the need to stroke that smooth, beautiful skin. To relish all that soft contrast against my hard.

It's a bad idea. Especially given how pulled tight my flesh is over my bones. How raw and exposed I feel, like a nerve bent on snapping. Given how much I crave it.

So I surrender to it.

Of course I do.

She doesn't flinch away from me as I trail my fingertips over her temple, tickle the dark, short strands there. Doesn't move as I cup her cheek or run my thumb across that sharp-as-glass cheekbone.

"You should have everything you want," I murmur. "I'd give it to you if I could."

A bolt of—*fuck*, I refuse to name it—*something* flashes in her eyes. And that *something* fists my dick and squeezes. Electrical currents sizzle up my spine, transforming me into a living conduit of desire, of need. A jagged, ravenous growl rolls up out of my gut, climbs up my chest, and claws up my throat. I lock it down; I have to. This inconvenient lust for my friend is my problem, my issue, not Miriam's. But goddamn, for a second . . . in those eyes . . .

Time to back away.

To retreat, regroup—

She bites my palm.

And I snap.

One second, I'm on the couch, and in the next, I'm on her.

My mouth crushes hers, and the small part of my brain not yet drowning in a lust-induced haze warns me to gentle, to ease back just a little. That I might be hurting her. But then her hands tunnel into my hair and grip the strands, jerking on them, sending tiny nips of pain skittering along my scalp, and that small part shuts the fuck up with an "As you were."

Fuck, her taste. It explodes on my tongue. Her own unique scent mixed with coffee and a hint of peppermint, as if she'd been sucking on the candy before I'd arrived. Now, I try to suck that flavor from her, my tongue, lips, and teeth taking, conquering.

I let that growl that I'd contained only moments earlier loose, directly into her mouth, letting her swallow it. And she does; she claims it and gives me one in return. Releasing her, I slam one hand on the couch arm and the other on the cushion behind her head. I shift, lifting, and press one knee next to her hip and set a foot on the floor, effectively caging her with my body, arching over her.

Angling my head, I dive deeper, take more, silently demanding she open wider. Give me more. I'm so fucking hungry for her. I'm beginning to suspect that even if she surrendered everything, it still wouldn't be enough. I can't ever be satisfied.

Not until I'm buried inside her in every way possible.

Still, she opens for me. Arches up into me. Whines for me.

For me.

I'm not going to survive a fucking kiss.

And there's no other place I'd rather die.

Letting go of the couch arm, I circle her throat, cradling the strong yet elegant column. I lift my head and study her mouth, swollen from this marauding that we'll call a kiss because we don't have anything else to label it. With a groan, I dive back for another taste. She arches into my hand, and I bend my head lower, grazing my teeth across the delicate line of her jaw, down the side of her neck. Releasing my hold on her throat, I tongue her pulse, satisfaction at its rapid beat a fiery blaze in my veins.

I part my lips to tell her how beautiful she is, how goddamn hard I am for her. But I shut up, afraid saying anything will shatter this moment. And selfish bastard that I am, I just want one more minute, one more second, with her. From personal experience, I know how fleeting time with her, like this, can be. In another instant, this will be smoke, another memory for me to fuck my fist to. So I have to drown in her while I can.

Shifting my hand away from the back of the couch to just above her head, I raise the other to her slightly rounded, soft stomach, trailing my fingers over the trembling muscles.

"Fuck, Jordan. Do it," she groans. "Please."

I almost shush her. *Don't break the moment. Don't break the moment.*

But I keep it inside. Because I'm too busy giving her what she wants. What we both want.

I cup her breast.

We both moan. She bows tight. I curse.

It's been only months since we've had sex, but goddamn, if it doesn't feel like years since I've touched her like this. Since my fingers have squeezed and molded this perfect tit, plucked and twisted her beaded nipple.

Since they've slid through the slick, tight heat of her pussy.

God, I need more. I need more of *her.*

Jerking my head up, I take her mouth again, my fingers continuing to plump her flesh, reacquaint myself. Make new memories.

The jarring ring of my cell phone reverberates in the room like the discordant blast of a fire alarm.

Fuck.

Reality crashes over me, a frigid, unwanted flood. I freeze, and Miriam goes still underneath me. Closing my eyes, I press my forehead to hers, and our breaths break like cannon fire in the silence of the room. My body throbs, and I shift my hand from her to the couch arm so both hands grip it. And grip it tight. So I don't put a stranglehold on my dick.

My phone peals again, and it's a special ringtone, or I might be tempted to ignore it.

Still, I snarl a little as I shove myself off Miriam and snatch up the cell. Stalking away from her, I swipe my thumb across the screen.

"Hey, Mom."

"Hey, Jordy. I'm just checking on you." Her sigh echoes in my ear. "You weren't in a great place when you left here."

"I'm good." If frustrated, aching, and guilty as fuck are good. Then yeah, dandy. "No worries, yeah?"

"I'm your mother. Worrying is in my job description," she drawls. "But I want you to know, sweetie, whatever you decide is fine with me. I'll support you either way, okay?"

"Yeah, Mom," I murmur. "Thank you for that."

"You're welcome. All right, I'll let you go. Don't make me have to chase you down to get you over here," she adds.

I huff out a laugh at that subtle reminder. Subtle as a bat to the side of the head. "I won't, Mom."

After ending the call, I slip the phone into my front pocket and slowly turn back around to Miriam. She's off the couch, standing behind it. Probably doesn't want anything to do with the scene of the crime. A grim resolve sinks inside me, a boulder dropping to the bottom of a dark lake.

"I take it that was Grace making sure you're okay," she murmurs.

"Yeah." I stare at her, tunneling my fingers through my hair. "Should I apologize?"

No point in fucking around with pretending that . . . apocalypse of a kiss didn't just happen.

"Apologize for what? If I remember correctly, I was right there on the couch with my tongue in your mouth."

God, wasn't it.

"Yeah," I repeat. Unbidden, my gaze drops to her mouth, still damp, still swollen from my lips, tongue, and teeth. I shake my head and shove my hands into the back pockets of my jeans, fisting them. "Listen, I'm going to leave."

"Okay."

No trying to convince me to stay. To talk about what just happened. Just *okay*.

Because I'm as much of a mistake now as I was months ago.

Got it.

You'd think I would be used to being someone's blunder, their regret. Look at my father. Or the women who fucked me for the money or the fame but wouldn't dare bring the tattooed, rough-around-the-edges ballplayer with trailer park mud still stuck to his shoes home to their parents. Yeah, I'm no stranger to being looked at as a mistake.

But I'm fucking tired of being hers.

And goddammit, I'm wrong. I went into this eyes wide open with full consent. She didn't friend-zone me against my will. I decided to stick around, knowing friendship was all I could have, all she'd ever accept of me. But with her taste still heavy on my tongue, and guilt over what I just did behind Daniel's back a grimy oil slick in my chest, I'm not rational.

So yeah, I need out of here.

"I'll call you later," I say, intending to leave it there and walk out the door. But I can't. Because I can't purge from my mind what she showed me tonight, what she shared with me. "And think on what I said about Zora and Levi. About taking a chance. You deserve it, Miriam."

She doesn't reply, but her pretty brown eyes soften.

I turn and head for the door and let myself out.

And it doesn't escape me that I came here with one burden but leave with another.

CHAPTER TEN

MIRIAM

"Contrary to rumor, I don't enjoy hurting people. Much."

—Sarafina Rose, *Ravaged Lands*

It's official. Daniel Granger is some sort of mind reader or mentalist. Almost from the beginning of our relationship, he's seemed to know all my likes and anticipated my dislikes. Tonight has been no different. It's been the perfect date.

And I've been completely miserable.

I hide my guilt and hurt as he finishes helping me into my seat and rounds the restaurant table and lowers into his own. That's been my only saving grace tonight—I'm apparently a consummate actress because he hasn't seemed to notice. Thank God. My one fear is hurting him. He is such a nice, wonderful guy and doesn't deserve it.

Doesn't deserve me.

Don't you dare think of why you're so awful. Don't you dare go there.

But it's too late. All it takes is a tiny opening, and my thoughts fly through that crack with a dirty, gleeful abandon that floods me with shame—and heat. Soooo much heat.

That kiss. It's been two days since that kiss, and my vagina hasn't let me off the hook yet. It's steadily punished me for not getting relief—a.k.a. an orgasm. And the one . . . or two . . . or four I self-administered don't count.

Foolish. It'd been so damn foolish of me to go there again. And it'd been my fault, not Jordan's. I'd been the instigator. He'd been nothing but sweet and supportive after I'd opened up and shared with him about Rayland Penn and Ravaged Lands. And when he'd touched me, cradled my face, I'd bit him.

Yes, it'd been *all* me.

I'd snapped his control. I'd whimpered into his mouth. Ordered him to touch my breast.

I'd done all of that while insisting we were friends and while dating Daniel.

Shit.

I once accused him of playing games with me, but it appears like it's me who's into them. What I can't do is toy with the man across from me. I've waited too long to be truthful with him. I tried to start this conversation with him at Cyrus's surprise engagement party. Now I have to finish it.

"I don't think I need to ask if you enjoyed the ghost tour." Daniel grins, picking up the menu off the table.

I laugh, and though it sounds a bit strained to my ears, he doesn't seem to catch it. "How could you tell? My very undignified scream or the way I almost climbed you like monkey bars?" I snort. "In my defense, though, I'd just like to point out that Cheesman Park is creepy as hell at night."

"Duly noted." He solemnly nods. "The capitol building too."

"Right?" I shake my menu at him. "I'm sure it was just the cold that had you shivering. Don't worry. I won't tell any of your boys."

He chuckles. "Deal." Dipping his chin, he asks, "See anything you like?"

I get down to the business of perusing the menu and am impressed. And again struck by how well he seems to know me.

"Everything on here sounds so good," I murmur. "And I've worked up a good appetite after all that walking." Several minutes and some internal debating later, I settle on a swiss mushroom burger, extra grilled onions and mushrooms, with a side of fries. After passing my menu and order on to our waiter, I cock my head and say, "I know at first you were really worried about this whole dating thing. But you shouldn't have been. You're incredibly good at it." I fold my arms on top of the table, even though I can hear my father in my head scolding me about bad manners. "I swear you have this knack of looking into my head and plucking out all my favorite things. I feel so . . . special. Like you pay attention to all the details about me or just somehow know me. I tell you what. You need to hold a webinar and teach all of your teammates your secrets. Maybe then they wouldn't need BURNED's services so much." I scrunch up my face. "Uh, wait. Never mind. Forget I said that last part. They're making me rich."

I laugh, and I expect him to join me. And he does, but it's small, tight. Frowning, I reach across the table and cover his hand.

"What's wrong? Did I say something—"

He shakes his head and slides out his hand from under mine, then holds it up, palm out. "No, no. It's all good. I'm . . . just glad you're enjoying yourself. It means a lot to me that you are. And thank you for giving me a second chance. Especially considering that first date was a complete disaster. It was really important that I show you the real me. The side that other people saw."

"I'm glad you called back."

And I am. Daniel is special. And any woman would be lucky to be able to call him hers.

I'm just not that woman.

But part of me wishes I was.

God, it would be so uncomplicated. So easy.

"Thank you for tonight," I say.

Suddenly, it's important for him to understand how much I appreciate him for his kindness. Yes, I have a bias against athletes. But between Jordan and Daniel—and even some of their teammates—it's changing. That preconception had been entrenched for years, so it's not entirely unearthed; remnants of the bitterness, the hurt, remain. But the sensitivity, compassion, and respect they've shown me have shone light into the darkest corners.

So though I'm saying *thank you* for tonight, I'm grateful for so much more.

"You're welcome."

"I . . ." I pause, wanting to give him some truth but unable to give him all of it. Jordan deserves that first. He's my friend, has been closest to me, there for me the longest. I can't give that to Daniel without offering it to Jordan. I lean forward on my crossed arms, meeting his hazel eyes. "I need to thank you for more than tonight, though. I don't know if Jordan told you, but I was initially . . . reluctant about going out with you. It wasn't personal. I just had a thing about seeing athletes. But I can honestly say I'm thankful I didn't allow that prejudice to keep me from going on the date with you. I would've missed out on meeting and spending time with an incredibly sweet, considerate, and just good man. Thank you for changing my mind and showing me I can't paint one group of men with one tainted brush."

Even as the words sit out there between us, I brace myself. I wouldn't blame him if he's offended.

But he's Daniel.

"I'm sorry, Miriam."

I sit back in my chair. Correction. Fall back. Blinking. And not just because the waiter arrives with our food. Once he sets our plates down and disappears, I murmur a thanks but don't touch my burger or fries. Instead, I stare at him.

"Sorry for what?"

"For whoever hurt you in the past."

Here's where I should make a flippant, dismissive comment to downplay his comment or the meaning behind my words. But the teasing dies on my tongue. That's beneath him . . . and me. I won't render my experience inconsequential. I was hurt, scarred.

"Thank you. Not that it was your fault and you need to apologize."

"No, but the person who should isn't here and, if he or she was, probably wouldn't. So here I am, doing it in their place. Because the point is you deserve one."

"Now you're trying to make me cry," I whisper. "And didn't Jordan tell you I have a reputation for being crazy? Crazy doesn't cry."

He snorts, picking up his beer bottle and leaning back in his chair. "Sometimes I would question if my wife had an ace missing from her deck, and she'd cry over any commercial about puppy-and-cat shelters."

"Sounds like your wife was not only fun but had a huge heart." Something tells me I would've really like hanging out with Jerricka Granger.

"She did," he murmurs, his eyes getting that distant glaze they adopted every now and then. It didn't take a genius to suss out his wife occupied his thoughts.

"Daniel." I reach for the hand not holding the beer, skirting our plates and skimming the back of his with my fingers. "I need to . . ." I shake my head, drawing my arm back across the table and settling my hands in my lap. "I'm not being fair to you."

He lowers the beer to the table, his hazel eyes sharpening. Yet his voice remains even, gentle, as he asks, "What do you mean?"

"I've enjoyed your company so much these last couple of weeks that I haven't been honest. You are such a good guy and a good . . . friend. And that's all we will be. I'm sorry I wasn't up front about that from the beginning. I wish I did feel more, want more. Maybe that's another reason I didn't say anything. Because I wanted it to be different. But I refuse to lie to you anymore. Especially if it means you can find a woman who can give you what I can't." God, I want to look away from those intense hazel eyes, duck my head in guilt. But I won't. That's a coward's way out. "I'm sorry, Daniel."

Quiet wraps around our table, and even the din from the other diners can't penetrate our semiprivate corner. Anxiety rises within me, and I part my lips to apologize again, to try and . . . explain? I don't know, do anything to alleviate the pain of rejection I've inflicted.

"Daniel—"

"It's okay, Miriam."

"It's not—"

"If you're going to say, 'It's not you; it's me,' please don't do that."

My chin jerks back into my neck. "Well, hell no, I wasn't going to say that," I say, offended. Then I glimpse the corners of his mouth twitch, and I narrow my eyes on him. "Very funny."

He chuckles, and though it's low and soft, it is a chuckle. Relief pours through me, and I exhale. Oh God. Am I going to cry? Because yeah, I'm that damn relieved.

"I was going to say it's not okay. What I did wasn't okay. I should've been up front from our second date. I strung you along, and that was cruel, even if my intentions were far from that."

"Miriam, I know that," he says, and his voice is kind. But I notice he doesn't reach for my hand. And that's fair. Though my chest squeezes. Hard. "There's nothing cruel about you. Look, you have nothing to feel guilty about. I don't know if I could've offered you a relationship; you are my first date since Jerricka. Even going out with a woman is a step for me, and I appreciate you for it. Yes, I'm attracted to you; you're a gorgeous woman. And yes, I was hoping to become your lover. But you don't need to be sorry for not feeling the same; you can't help that. And you definitely don't need to apologize for wanting to spend time with me. I've enjoyed it, Miriam. I've enjoyed you. And if you want to continue that, I'm here."

"Okay," I whisper.

"Good." He picks up his burger and nods at me. "Now, let's finish dinner. I promised you the best burgers in Denver, and these are it."

Smiling, I pick mine up and bite into it. He's right—this burger is damn good. But I can't enjoy it like I should. Guilt and a sadness sit in the pit of my stomach.

I'm not attracted to the man who looks at me with heat and smoke in his eyes.

And I can't have the only other man who knows me inside out and makes my heart sing like a gospel revival.

Daniel might've absolved me of my guilt and sorrow, but I can't pardon myself.

For the second time in a number of weeks, I arrive at Jordan's house unannounced. By now, I'm no stranger to his gated community, so after the security guard waves me through, I park, and my feet carry me up his driveway, sidewalk, and porch by pure muscle memory. Was this how he felt a couple of days earlier when he showed up at my house, desperate to get to me? After Daniel dropped me off, I didn't even go into my town house. I waited until his headlights disappeared, then got into my car and drove here. To the one person I could count on to . . . what?

Make the hurt go away?

Make me forget?

Yes and yes.

I knock on the front door and wait. Then silently curse under my breath. Shit. It's after ten o'clock. He might not even be home. Jordan is a hot-as-fuck man and, according to every online gossip site, enjoys a very active sex life. Not that we talk about that. Not that I want to even *think* about that.

God, I'm such a hypocrite.

Still, he could be out in someone else's bed or even have that person in his, and here I am, pounding on his front door, cockblocking. Yeah, I should go. Right now. Feet, *move*. Why are we not *moving*?

The front door opens.

"Are you fucking someone in there?"

The question blurts from my mouth without my permission, and any minute now, mortification will catch up with my anger. But at the moment, anger is driving the bus, because *honestly*. He just had his tongue in *my* mouth and his hand on *my* titty not two goddamn *days* ago.

He doesn't reply, just props an arm against the doorjamb and arches a dark-blond, pierced eyebrow. That's when I really take notice of him. All of him. The plain gray, thin hoodie stretched over his wide shoulders and chest. The faded black sweatpants hanging to his slim hips for dear life. The bare feet.

Not exactly an outfit intended for seduction.

Though to be fair, Jordan Ransom could wear a unicorn onesie with footsies, and women would drop at his feet, legs spread.

I sigh. "Let me try that again. Am I disturbing anything, or can I come in?"

Instead of answering, he steps aside and sweeps an arm in front of him, inviting me inside. Exhaling, I accept the invitation.

Unlike the other times I enter his palatial home, I don't take a moment to peruse the breathtaking, two-story foyer with its crystal chandelier and small fireplace and mantel. He claims every bit of my attention.

I wasn't expecting this.

Of course, I'd wondered if there would be any awkwardness in our first meeting after The Kiss. But I hadn't predicted this damn near raw awareness. As if the very thin shields I'd erected after our night together had been eradicated with one wild, passionate mating of mouths. His sexuality vibrates against my skin, and I rub my arms over my jacket, which is no protection against that vitality.

Or the sight of that ass in black sweatpants.

"I hope you don't mind me just dropping by. Again," I add, with no small amount of chagrin.

"I never do."

"Why?"

He glances over his shoulder, that eyebrow arched once more. And I don't blame him. I'm on a roll, it seems. As if the stress and self-directed anger and guilt from my evening with Daniel have stripped me of the filter on my mouth. And truth? That filter was flimsy to begin with.

"Why?" he repeats, leading me past the grand workmanship of a freestanding staircase, the formal living room, the great room, and the dining room to his study.

He moves through the room to an open pair of french doors and out to a deck with no less glorious views of soaring mountains, even though it's dark outside. Leaping, crackling flames in a firepit provide warmth and an orange glow while additional small lamps along the deck floor throw soft illumination around the perimeter. It's an intimate space, and the early-November night air doesn't reach us here.

"Miriam." He sinks into the padded deck chair, his gaze on me. "What do you mean *why?*"

Already regretting letting that one word loose, I follow suit and lower into the chair next to his, holding my hands out to the flames. "I mean, why do you never mind me dropping by? You are a reasonably hot thirty-year-old basketball player who's popular with the ladies."

He snorts. "Reasonably hot?"

"If you expect me to stroke your ego, Ransom, you got the wrong one." I'll forgo the obvious joke about stroking something else, because yeah—been there; done that. "So where was I? Right. Reasonably hot. Popular. Ladies. You're famous, got money, a pretty good job. So why are you always home and available when I drop by here? And a better question that has been plaguing me—"

"Plaguing you?" he interrupts again.

"Hating on my vocabulary is really beneath you." Once more, I avoid looking at him because I've been beneath him. Only two days ago. This conversation thing is tricky as fuck. "Why haven't you used BURNED's services? Your boys have. Repeatedly. But you? Not once. What's up with that?"

"Maybe because I can break up with my own women without any help," he drawls.

I finally look over at him, studying those elegant yet stark facial bones and the lush mouth. Strands of dark-blond hair escape the bun at the top of his head, and my fingers itch to push them out of his face. Trace the strong line of his jaw that's half-hidden by thick scruff. I lift my gaze and am immediately ensnared by electric-blue eyes. And I can't look away. Don't want to look away.

"So you do have women?"

Why am I talking?

"Is this why you came here?" he throws at me. "To question me about what women I'm fucking and not letting you break up with for me?"

"It's not *not* why I came over," I shoot back, then groan and scrub my hands over my face. "I'm sorry," I say into my hands, my voice muffled. "I don't know what's wrong with me. And if you haven't guessed, I don't know why I'm here." I spread my fingers and peek at him like he's a horror show I'm afraid to look at. Or maybe I'm the horror show. That's a bit more accurate. "That seems to be our MO lately."

"What's wrong, sweetheart?" he presses, and it's that gentle tone that unravels the knots inside me.

"I hurt a good man tonight," I whisper, lowering my hands and crossing my arms over my chest. "He told me I didn't, that he was okay, but I saw his eyes. What kind of person does it make me to lead someone on knowing I don't share the same feelings that he has? Selfish," I answer before Jordan can. "Because it made me feel special to be wanted, to be seen. To know that someone paid so much attention to me that they went out of their way to discover the things I enjoyed and cared about. But I did that at the expense of his feelings. A man who risked stepping out there after losing his wife, and his first attempt is me. How cruel is that?"

I don't allow him to answer that either. Giving a short, serrated laugh, I shake my head and rock back and forth, staring into the fire so I don't have to witness the disappointment in his gaze. The disappointment at how I treated his friend.

"This is why I'm not cut out for relationships. Relationships." I loose another caricature of laughter. "They're bullshit anyway. Utter and complete bullshit. No offense to Zora and Cyrus, and I really hope they make it. But this is why I don't buy into them. Either one person is always more invested than the other and pain and betrayal are inevitable. Or they're staying out of obligation or duty. Doesn't matter if they no longer love one another and are making everyone around them miserable. No thank you. I don't want any part of that shit."

"That's not always true," he says, and the softness of it has my chest tightening.

"How can you, of all people, say that?" I'm honestly curious. "You've told me about your childhood. Your parents are a perfect example of what I'm referring to. And what about the fucked-up relationships your mother had after your father? Plus, neither one of us has experienced real commitments. Not any that survive past the orgasms. And even they get tiresome after a while."

"I can say that because the examples you've named aren't all I've seen." He bends his legs and props his forearms on his thighs, his hands falling between his knees. The fire is reflected in his eyes, and I'm captivated by the dance of the flames there. That intense gaze seems alive, rendering it impossible to glance away. "Yeah, those are all true. But my old college basketball coach and his wife have been married for over forty years and are still in love and going strong. You didn't see Daniel and his wife, but those two were soul mates. I've played with men who were married in name only, and road trips were excuses to fuck anything that showed up at a hotel room. Not Daniel. He was devoted to Jerricka. No other woman existed for him. They weren't just lovers but friends. And Cyrus loves your sister. They may not have been together for years, but he adores her, and I believe, God willing, they will be like my coach and his wife one day."

"That's beautiful," I whisper. "Do you believe in it? Is that what you want for yourself?"

"Yes, I believe in it. And, Miriam, I don't just want it for myself. I'm *demanding* it for myself."

I swallow. How can words rip a hole out of me and leave me so hollow and brimming with yearning at the same time? Yearning for what he described. Too bad I know better. If only I didn't know there's no such thing as the beautiful fairy tale he depicted—I might . . .

Yeah. But I do know better.

"Have I ever told you how I got my name?" When he shakes his head, I force myself to continue meeting his gaze. "Zora and Levi are twins, so Mom and Dad each had a child to claim. Mom named Zora after Zora Neale Hurston, and Dad chose Levi's out of the Bible. Leviticus. No fighting. But with me, the story goes they fought Mom's entire pregnancy over who would have the right to name me. I was just one more battleground of the many they'd had and the many that would come after. When I was born, they still hadn't resolved the argument. But Mom waited until Dad left the hospital to go home and check on Zora and Levi, then filled out the birth certificate behind his back. She named me after Miriam Makeba, the South African singer and activist.

"To this day, Dad brings it up and throws it in her face. And to this day, Mom gloats over the fact that she got one over on him. That's the kind of marriage my parents have. One where they use an occasion as special, as sacred, as naming their child as the ultimate gotcha. I'm sure at one point they convinced themselves they loved each other. But they're proof that love, commitment . . ." I pause, a shiver running through me despite the heat from the firepit. "You can't trust them.

They're what we tell ourselves to justify being emotionally out of control. To explain why we're afraid to be alone. I'd rather trust in myself, be by myself, and stand in my own power than depend on someone who will abuse that faith I place in them."

The crackle and snap of the fire punctuates the silence, but my breathing echoes in my head, and it's deafening. I never intended to say all of that. Especially about my parents. I love them—God knows I do—but they robbed me. And it started with my name. And it continued with a stable, calm homelife. Hell, they ruined my first and only sleepover. For a kid who could count on one hand the number of friends she had—because when you were always the youngest kid in your class, hanging out with girls your age didn't happen often—a sleepover had been a rite of passage. And their bickering and fighting in front of my guests had spoiled it. I'd been afraid to invite anyone else over—that is, if I'd even had more friends to invite.

Still, I'm a grown woman now. I've moved on. Doesn't mean I've shared it with anyone.

Until now. With him.

Humiliation crawls through me, and inside I scramble backward away from him and that scalpel-sharp intensity in his gaze.

"I should—" In my head, I've already made it to my car. My body just hasn't caught up.

Jordan rises, and before I can move, he's standing in front of me, hand outstretched. I take it, and he pulls me to my feet.

In moments, I'm lifted in the air, in his arms, and settled on his lap in the deck chair he just vacated. He cradles me, tucking my head under his chin as he tenderly rocks me back and forth.

"I'm not letting you run away," he says into my hair, his embrace tight.

"I wasn't—"

"Don't bother lying." His arms tighten around me as if he can squeeze off my lie. Because yes, it's a lie. "Why were you about to leave?"

Then he brushes his lips across my forehead, leaving a trail of fire in his wake. "No, let me guess. Got too close for you. Too real. And what do two people like us, who come from fucked-up homes where we saw the worst people had to give to each other, know about intimacy, right? It scares the hell out of us. Or it should. And normally, it does. But not with you, Marilyn. And you can feel safe with me. I won't hurt you. Won't use whatever you share with me against you. So don't run. Stay."

Stay.

A shudder ripples through me, and I don't try to stifle it. *Stay.* I've been wanted for several reasons. My IQ. My talent. Sex.

But no one's ever asked me to just *be.* And not with them.

For how long?

The question sits on my tongue like a five-hundred-pound anvil, but I don't voice it, too afraid of the response. Besides, for once, I'm also content to just be.

Tilting my head back, I rest it on his shoulder. This up close and personal with him, I can catalog every detail on his face. The black pupil with the very thin ring of brown. The tiny scar on the edge of his right cheekbone. The deep dip above his top lip that lends it the bow shape. The almost-there-but-not-quite cleft in his chin.

I've drawn him countless times in the last few weeks. So many that his face is as familiar to me as my own. And yet, I could analyze him for hours and still find new elements that would fascinate me. Jordan Ransom could become a new field of study, and I would easily earn my doctorate in him.

"Tonight, I told Daniel I couldn't see him any longer."

His eyes narrow, but he doesn't speak. Yet my heart pounds in my chest, and the beat grows louder, the volume so deafening I can barely hear my own voice.

"It wouldn't have been fair," I whisper.

"Why not?" he asks, and that dark, low timbre is midnight and sin. Temptation wrapped in sex.

"You know why."

He bends his head the scant inches separating us and only stops when his mouth hovers a breath above mine. "Say it," he orders, his lips so close they nearly brush mine.

"Because he isn't you."

Jordan doesn't move, and I can taste his kiss, but he doesn't eliminate the remaining space between us. Doesn't take my mouth and give me what I can now admit I came here for. No, instead he stares at me, his expression inscrutable. Unease twists inside me, and for the first time since he placed me on his lap, I want to climb off, insert space between us.

"We're going to fuck," he states, and while the word sends a lightning bolt of heat straight between my legs, it tightens the screw on my unease, deepens it. Because his tone is flat, almost disconnected.

"Yes." We are. I need him tonight. And I won't be able to stop at a kiss. I'm too empty, too hungry. I haven't felt complete since the last time he filled me.

"And I'm going to be your mistake." His fingers thread through my hair, sifting before fisting the curls and bringing them to his nose. He inhales, his eyes closing and, for a moment, freeing me from their hold. It's in this instant that a flicker of emotion flashes across his face. Pleasure. Pain. Both. But when his lashes lift, his expression is back to being a mask of inscrutability. "Don't misunderstand me. I'm still going to fuck you. I find I'm so goddam desperate to be inside you I'm willing to have you any way I can. But I just want to make sure I know where we stand."

Oh God.

Regret pierces me in the chest, sliding between my ribs like the sharpest blade. I have a lot to answer for. The latest being from a couple of nights ago. I run the moments after our kiss through my head. I never called him a mistake, never said I regretted what happened on my couch. But viewing my actions, my silence, through his lens, I can see how he'd interpret them that way. And coupled with how I friend-zoned him after the first time we had sex, calling *that* a mistake . . . well, damn.

Briefly closing my eyes, I hate myself for causing this bold, beautiful man even a second of self-doubt. He's no one's mistake. No one's regret. And I can tell him that. I could write him a fucking sonnet about that.

Or I could show him.

Maneuvering out of his arms, I straighten, straddling him. But only for a moment. I slide down his big body, shifting until I'm kneeling between his powerful, toned thighs.

"What the . . . ? Miriam." His hands cup my shoulders, and a glance up his torso reveals he's lost that enigmatic expression. It's replaced by a mixture of shock and stark lust. His eyes, bright as a summer sky, are hooded, and his thin nostrils are flared. That full carnal mouth is pulled into a taut line, and he shakes his head. "What are you doing? This isn't . . ."

"Shh."

I stroke my hands up his legs, and when I reach the juncture where his thighs and torso meet, I angle inward, skating my palms over the rock-hard, thick length of his cock. My breath whistles out of my parted lips, and my belly spasms, echoing in my sex. Curling my fingers over the top of his sweatpants, I tug the waistband down, baring him. And *holy hell*, he's not wearing any underwear. God, he's every woman's fantasy.

No, screw that. I don't care about anyone else.

He's *my* fantasy.

With barely any coaxing, his dick pokes above the band, the head stretching to almost kiss his navel. My feminine flesh flutters, both in anticipation and a little anxiety. I've had him inside me—several times, as a matter of fact—and yet each time had required a little bit of time and patience. Because Jordan is a fucking *beast*.

And I loved every stretching, burning second of it.

A wide, aching pit yawns at the bottom of my stomach, and I'm insatiable.

Circling his flesh with both fists, I arrow him toward my mouth and swallow as much of him as I can take. His cock slides along my tongue, the tip bumping the back of my throat. His groan caresses my ears, and I ease him out, then pump him with my hands. As soon as he clears my lips, I brush a kiss along the engorged, plum-shaped head and lift my gaze to him again.

Passion has incinerated all vestiges of shock from his face, and his eyes gleam. Without breaking his visual hold, I trail my lips down his cock, releasing him only long enough to yank his sweatpants farther out of the way. Then I retrace my path with my tongue.

His lush mouth seems fuller against the lust stamped on his features. Shifting his hands from my shoulders, he drives them into my hair, gripping my hair in his big fists, knuckles pressing into my scalp.

On the tail end of a moan, I follow his silent but very clear instructions, and I lower my head again. His cock breaches my lips, and I allow him inside. His snarl rips through the air like an enraged animal, and the sound rumbles over my skin, breasts . . . clit. My sex clamps down around emptiness and quivers in complaint. Whimpering, I suck and lick him, my hands stroking faster, harder. Yes, my actions telegraph the rise in my need, the delirium crawling through my blood. What started as a demonstration of my feelings for him has swept me up, and the threads of my control are thinning, unraveling.

I raise higher on my knees, the better to take more of him. And his hands guide, lifting and lowering me over his cock, then holding me still while he feeds me how much he wants to give me. Shifting, I squeeze my thighs together, attempting to alleviate the ache high and deep inside me. A place experience has taught me with startling and vivid detail only he can reach and satisfy.

His tip nudges the back of my throat once more, and I inhale through my nose, relaxing and permitting him entrance into the narrow channel.

"Fuck, Miriam." The rasped praise or plea empowers me. Though I'm kneeling before him and his hands are buried in my hair, *I'm* leveling *him*. "Sweetheart . . ."

Again and again, I swallow as much of him as I'm able. And he's a big man, so it's impossible to take all of him, but from the way his huge body trembles and his muttered, guttural curses and encouragement, he loves it. And so do I. Every bit of it. His heaviness and taste in my mouth. His uninhibited surrender to me. His un-self-conscious show of his pleasure.

I crave it all. And more. I'm ravenous for everything Jordan has to give me.

"Sweetheart." His grasp on my head tightens, though he doesn't pull me free of him. "I'm about to come. Back off if you don't want me to finish here." He rubs a finger down the front of my throat.

I reply to this by tightening my fists on his cock and sucking him deeper. And with a gravel-roughened groan, he pumps into my mouth and, moments later, lets go. I take all of him, swallowing until he's spent and his harsh breaths pound against my hair. Only then do I permit him to slip free from between my lips.

"You coming into my life wasn't a mistake; it was fate. This between us"—I press a tender kiss to the base of his only slightly softened, damp flesh—"is hot, sometimes overwhelming, and a little scary but not a mistake. And you could never be one."

As I speak, the haze of pleasure dissipates from his gaze, and it's clear, sharp . . . on fire.

He cups me under my arms and lifts me. In seconds, I'm sitting in his chair; my boots, jeans, and panties are gone, and he's buried between my thighs.

Holy shit.

His tongue dives between my folds, licking a path that has a scream clawing its way free from my throat and echoing on the night air. I really hope his neighbors believe coyotes inhabit these mountains, or else they might call 911. And they wouldn't be far off. I could die from the pleasure threatening to splinter me apart.

He palms my thighs, widening them, making room for his shoulders. And oh God, does he need the room. Because he pulls me up close like I'm his favorite meal and he's about to enjoy every. Fucking. Bite. There's nothing hesitant or exploratory about his mouth. He dines on me, devours me. It's messy, wild, raw. It's hot as hell. And I'm at his mercy. I can't move, his big hands holding me still for this marauding.

I shake, one hand clutching the arm of the chair, and the other tangled in his long hair. He sucks, nips, laps at my flesh, his growls of pleasure vibrating through me. I glance down my body, and the sight of him, his mouth opened wide over me . . . squirming, I cry out, teetering on the edge of a cataclysmic release. The pleasure drives me close to insanity, and when his lips close around my clit, flicking, circling, I almost believe I've lost my claim on reality.

"Jordan, please," I beg. Because no, I'm not above it. Not when my belly cramps with the need to orgasm and sweat dampens my face and the pretty sweater I'm wearing. Not when a tremor ripples through my legs like an earthquake. "Jordan, I need it. Give it to me. *Please.*"

I don't need to define *it*. And he doesn't ask.

But he does provide it.

He lifts two fingers to my mouth, and I eagerly open for him, swirling my tongue over and around the digits, wetting them. So lost in my task, I hardly realize my eyes are closed. Not until he slowly, so slowly withdraws them do I lift my lashes, and my gaze clashes with the blue fire in his.

"Beautiful," he murmurs, painting my lips with his damp fingertips. "Good girl."

Then, without looking away, he lowers his arm and unerringly finds my entrance. And drives inside me. Strokes deep. Driving the breath from my lungs. I release a broken gasp and punch my hips up to take more. Demand more.

He breaks our visual connection and kisses a path back to my sex, his lips closing around my clit once more. He plays me, tonguing the engorged bundle of nerves and finger-fucking my core. And I'm his instrument, built, molded, and bent for his hands. And he draws the perfect melody from me. With a curl of his fingertips against a spot too high inside for me to reach without a toy, he shatters me.

I explode.

Right on that chair, I fragment and am left in pieces.

It's pleasure, pain, relief, and so much more.

And it's not enough.

My sex still spasms with the aftermath of my orgasm, and still, that burn isn't completely extinguished. The ache hasn't disappeared, hasn't been assuaged.

Jordan cups my face, grazing his lips across my forehead, down the slope of my nose, over my temple.

"Are you still with me?" he asks, and though there's an audible strain in his voice, it's gentle, patient. Letting me know the decision to go forward or stop here is completely mine.

There is no decision to make.

"Yes." I wind my arms around his neck, tunneling my fingers up into his hair, under his bun. "I don't have condoms on me," I whisper.

Something flickers in his eyes, there and gone before I can decipher it. But he brushes another caress over my cheekbone, his lashes lowering and hiding all emotion from me.

"I have some in the house." His muscles bunch as he prepares to stand, but I tighten my hold on him, stalling his movement.

"No." I shake my head for added emphasis. "I'm on the pill. And I'm clean. I wouldn't lie to you about that. I've also"—I pause, wetting my lips—"never been with anyone without a condom."

Including him.

That night months ago, we'd used them each time. But now, I don't want anything between us. I just want . . . him.

His answer is to notch his cock at my entrance and push inside.

A cry wells up in my throat, and I arch my back, neck straining, eyes closed. One of his hands tangles in my hair, pulling my head back up. He waits until my lashes lift, until our gazes meet and catch fire together.

"I'm clean, and I wouldn't put you in danger," he says on a low rumble.

He pulses his hips, burying more of himself inside me. Stretching me. Claiming me. It might as well be the first time we've had sex, and my flesh flutters around his cock, accommodating him. Welcoming him. He drives forward again, taking more of me, and his mouth closes over mine, capturing my gasp. I chase his tongue, his lips, and when he lifts his head, I'm panting. And he's completely seated inside me.

"Look at me, Miriam." He lifts his hand from my hip to grip my chin. "I haven't been with anyone since you."

Surprise wings through me, but he doesn't allow me time to dwell on that announcement, and damn, do I want to dwell.

But he drowns me in ecstasy, mastering my mouth and my body. Greedy, almost manic hands shove up my sweater and bra, cupping and molding my breasts, tweaking my nipples. Currents of electricity zigzag down my belly to my sex, and my core clenches around his flesh, grasping at him as he thrusts and strokes. Burying himself in me over and over. Fucking me into oblivion.

I twist beneath him, opening my mouth to his voracious kiss and my body to his driving dick. He dips his head, pressing a hard kiss to the top of my breast, then sucking the beaded tip into his mouth, pulling hard. I sob. Honest-to-God sob. Because I'm a living, breathing ache that needs to come for him. For me. For us.

The last release shattered me. This one will decimate me. Leaving nothing but ash.

I grasp at his head, gripping his hair, holding him close, pulling him away. I'm a mess. A crying, throbbing, right-on-the-edge-of-losing-it mess.

"I can feel you, sweetheart," he mutters against my wet skin. "I can feel your perfect little pussy squeezing me, ready to let go. Let go, Miriam."

He reaches between us, rubs his thumb around my clit, across it once, twice, and not another firm caress is needed before I'm coming so hard the scream can't leave my throat, though my lips part wide. The ecstasy traps everything within me, locks my muscles, my breath—hell, my mind—down, freezes me in a single perfect second.

Then I detonate.

His "Oh fuck" dimly reaches me, and I hang on to him, my sole port in the chaos that I've willingly thrown myself into. More tremors shake me, but they're not mine. They're Jordan's. And I tighten my embrace, welcoming the triggering of another orgasm as he pours into me.

And we fall.

Together.

Tomorrow I'll worry about who will be there to pick up our pieces.

CHAPTER ELEVEN

MIRIAM

"We fuck. And we fight. I think that makes us the best of friends."

—Sarafina Rose to North the Woodsman, Ravaged Lands

"Well? Aren't you going to offer me coffee? I'm cold, and my ass is numb from sitting on your porch for the last hour."

I draw to a halt as I approach my house, my breath forming a small cloud in front of my face in the chilly morning air. My heart pounds against my chest like a wild thing, and only the swift recognition of my sister's voice and the vague shape of her shadow prevent me from throwing my huge purse at her and running for my car. Exhaling a loud sigh, I move forward again at a halting pace.

"Uh, not to sound ungracious, but what the hell are you doing here?" Okay, so I sound ungracious. But it's cold and dark out—the sun hasn't risen yet since it's just six thirty in the morning—and my heart still thinks my sister is Michael Myers bent on my imminent death.

Zora stands on my top step, dusting the back of her jeans off, but her narrowed brown gaze is fixed on me.

"You haven't been answering your phone since last night. I had Cyrus call Jordan to see if he'd talked to you, and surprise, he's not answering his either. But I'm thinking to myself, that's not right. She can't be with him because she was just out with Daniel Granger last night. And your business is your business—"

"And yet you seem okay with airing my business for all my neighbors to hear," I mutter, marching up my steps and past her to my front door.

She follows me inside the house, closing the door behind us. I drop my purse off on the couch and make a beeline for the kitchen. Jesus be a fence, this is not how I imagined my morning after a night of the hottest sex ever. Would it be too much to ask for some privacy to think over what happened the night before . . . well, not too closely. I might not make it into the office if I go over *every* detail. But after leaving with Jordan—him to the arena, and me home—I looked forward to some quiet time to consider where we go from here. We can't go back to what—who—we were. I meant what I said to him. This wasn't a mistake. I could use the excuse of falling on his dick the first time. But last night? It was a deliberate, conscious decision.

So are we still friends? Lovers? Friends with benefits?

I swallow a snort. Right. Because every romantic comedy ever filmed depicts how well that arrangement pans out.

But that's not going to happen with my sister sitting at my breakfast bar, staring at me with her all-too-knowing eyes.

"What was so urgent you needed to show up at my place and wait on me in the dark?" I ask, glancing at her over my shoulder as I slide a pod in the coffee maker and a cup underneath. "The times when you waited up on me to make sure I came home safely are long gone. Oh wait." I tap my bottom lip. "That's right. You never did that."

Zora bends her fingers, making grabby hands toward the mug of coffee. "Hurry up with that. I'm going to need caffeine if we're going to have this conversation."

I finish brewing her a cup and then set it down in front of her. After retrieving the creamer from the refrigerator and grabbing the sugar off the opposite counter, I leave her to doctor her coffee and turn to fix another one.

"You sound a little bitter about that."

I shrug a shoulder, my back to her. "Do I?" I pause, examining the snarl of emotions tangled around my ribs like messy yarn. "I didn't think I was. But I don't know, maybe a little? Then again, is that fair? When most girls were dating in high school and having their older brother and sister checking in on them, I was thirteen or fourteen, too young to do any of that. And in college . . ." I shift my gaze to the steadily brewing coffee, the dirty string pulling tighter, snarling more. "Well, we weren't in the same house, so that was a moot point. Wasn't like you could run interference when you were living your own lives."

"And the one time you needed me to be there, I wasn't," she murmurs.

I turn around, scowling. "Don't make me regret telling you about Robert Sampson."

After picking up my mug, I carry it over to the breakfast bar and snatch her spoon away from her. With jerky movements, I sweeten my coffee to the perfect blend of can-I-get-some-coffee-with-that-cream-and-sugar and set the utensil back on the bar top. I'm still glaring at her as I lift the cup for my first hit of the day.

"News flash, Miriam. I'm not ever going to *not* feel guilty about you going through that shit alone."

"That's like me feeling guilty for not warning you that douche-canoe accountant you dated would stick his dick in anything that moved."

She rolls her eyes. "That's so not the same thing, and you know it."

I prop my forearms on the bar top, leaning forward and arching an eyebrow. It's my know-it-all expression that pisses her off, and I have time today.

"How isn't it the same? Did you know he was a serial cheater when you first met him? No. Did I know you were dating a serial cheater? Also no, not until long after the fact. And did I feel helpless that the motherfucker hurt my sister and I could do nothing about it? Yes." I cock my head. "Parallels, ma'am. Parallels."

"I hate it when you use logic to prove your points. It's irritating as hell," she grumbles.

I grin. "Right? It's a gift."

"Using logic or pissing people off?"

"Both." I shrug. "Why must I choose?"

She chuckles and lifts her cup, takes a sip. "To answer your question, I don't really know why I decided to wait it out on your porch this morning. I couldn't sleep. And Cyrus wouldn't let me drive up to Jordan's house. Told me to stop being a nut. So hanging out on your step it was." She eyes me over the rim of the mug. "I was worried. Call it sister intuition or whatever. But I needed to make sure you were okay."

"I'm . . . okay."

"That sounded very convincing."

Zora doesn't say anything, just sits there and continues drinking coffee, letting the silence stretch until it fairly screams. And so do my nerves.

"I had sex with Jordan," I blurt out. "Again."

More sipping. And eying.

"Say something. You came all the way over here at the butt crack of dawn and sat in the cold for an hour. So say *anything*."

"I thought you said the first time was a mistake and wouldn't happen again. I believe you said you'd never partake of community peen ever again, if my memory serves me. Which is why you friend-zoned him. That, and he's an athlete. And you—"

"Don't do athletes," I finish in unison with her. "I know, I know." I groan. "I might not, but my vagina is all-aboard the athlete train."

Sighing, I straighten. "I can fool myself into calling that first time a slip, a lapse in judgment, or scratching an itch. But the truth is I've been attracted to him from the start. And it's more than physical—although, I mean, c'mon. Look at him. But I've never had friendships with my one-night stands. Jordan . . . scares me, Zora."

My whispered admission echoes in the kitchen like a shout. Zora slowly lowers her cup to the breakfast bar, and her expression softens.

"You remind me of Cyrus."

I scoff. "What? No offense, but I think love has pickled your brain. Or maybe good dick has. I like the guy, but I'm nothing like your anal, rule-loving, corporate fiancé."

"Oh, no offense taken," she says dryly. "But yes, you are. You both have your ideas and your plans, and they're set in stone. And once they are, it'll take an act of God to change them. And I don't even know about that. You two might look at a burning bush and want to examine the quality of the pyrotechnics and thickness of the bush before calling it a miracle." Her mouth twists wryly.

I mean, she's not wrong.

About the burning bush.

But her opinion of me? Oh yeah, she's way off on that.

"That's so untrue. For example, I've backed off my view of athletes. I let my experience from college color my opinion on all of them. But after spending time with Jordan and then Daniel, I've realized I judged them against the behavior of a group of assholes. And I can't continue to live viewing people through the lens of my anger and hurt. It's not fair. And I might've missed out on getting to have two wonderful men in my life."

"Oh, Miriam, that's amazing." She reaches across the bar top but hesitates at the last second, her hand stopping several inches short of mine. I get it. Ours isn't a demonstrative family. But maybe that's another thing we should be changing. I grasp her hand. And squeeze.

She smiles, her brown eyes lighting up. "I'm happy for you. Fuck Robert Sampson. And he shouldn't influence your life—not one more damn day."

"You're right." Revelation dawns on me like the sun that's beginning to crest in the sky. By letting his actions affect how I interact with people, treat them, and corner a part of myself off from them, I have been allowing Robert to impact my life. And that sickens me.

And it stops today.

He no longer has any power over me.

Oh hell, that's freeing.

"You're still wrong about the other stuff, though," I breathe.

She laughs, flipping our hands and returning my squeeze. "Hear me out. Maybe the reason Jordan scares you when none of the other guys you've dated, including Daniel, have is because he threatens those ideas you have, those plans. And I'm not talking about the moratorium on athletes. I'm referring to the one on relationships. On commitment. You think I haven't noticed how you never let yourself get too close, get too invested in a person? To an extent, you're even like that with me and Levi. Almost as if there's a line drawn, and that's as close as people are allowed to come. And if they dare try to cross? You shut them down. Cut them off."

I shake my head. "That's not true—"

"It is. I grew up in the same house you did. Had the same example of relationships. Learned about what marriage, relationships, shouldn't be. Then sought out the very men who ended up leading me into what I witnessed growing up. You, Levi, me. We're all fucked up in some way. We just have to make the decision if we're going to stay that way." She releases my hand and cradles her cup of coffee, staring down into it. "I want so much more for you, Miriam. You deserve everything."

You should have everything you want. I'd give it to you if I could.

Jordan's voice echoes in my head.

"He believes in love, Zora. In the happily ever after." I chuckle, and it's almost . . . breathless. Definitely incredulous. "That's what's scary about him. He could make me believe too," I murmur.

"What's so bad about that?" Zora smiles, and it's small but full of so much joy it's almost luminescent. "What's so bad about letting someone else carry the burden of having faith until you catch up? Let me tell you; I've had a long, good look at Jordan Ransom's shoulders, and he looks like he can bear that weight pretty damn easily. And he wouldn't mind it either. As a matter of fact, I think it would be his pleasure to do it."

"And if he can't? If he . . . won't? What then?"

"But what if he will?" she counters softly.

She's asking me to take a chance. Like she did with Cyrus. She can encourage me to step out there, to take the risk because hers worked out. But I'm not that brave.

If I'd paid attention to what I saw growing up, then I never would've made the perfect naive victim for Robert Sampson. Adhering to the rules, standing behind the barriers Zora accused me of having in place, has kept me safe, protected. I haven't been anyone's fool since then.

And though Jordan offers me a place to be myself and makes my body sing, I can't leap for him. The past has shown me no one will be there to catch me.

"Since you're here, you can wait until I get dressed. I'll ride into work with you, and we can go to breakfast. Your treat."

Zora studies me, and I hold my breath because she looks like she's not going to let this subject go. But then she nods.

"Hurry up. I need to go home, shower, and get dressed first. I can't meet clients in sweats and bedhead."

Ravaged

I head out of the kitchen, and as my foot hits the bottom step, I pause and glance over my shoulder.

"Zora?"

"Hmm?"

"Thank you. For sitting on my step looking like who-did-it-and-why at six thirty in the morning."

She smiles around the rim of her coffee cup.

"You're welcome."

CHAPTER TWELVE

JORDAN

"I trust you."

—Sarafina Rose, Ravaged Lands

I turn my wrist over and glance at my watch, checking the time. Impatience skates through me. Miriam texted me five minutes ago letting me know she was *two* minutes away. Now I know she's a genius, but how does she mess up simple math like that?

Just as I'm about to grab my cell, her car pulls up to the curb. Shaking my head, I walk over and open the driver's door.

"We need to have a serious discussion about time management."

She grins at me, and I'm dangerously close to pressing my fist to the aching spot over my chest. The lust that throbs in my body runs a close second, and as she slides her hand into mine and lets me help her from her vehicle, the hum in my blood dials up.

It's been two weeks since we became lovers, and by now, with as much fucking as we've been doing, that greedy, gulping need should be at least a little toned down since it's been satisfied on the regular. But nope. If anything, every time she allows me inside her with nothing separating us, every time I come with her tight, sweet pussy milking and wringing me dry, the hunger only intensifies.

I'm an addict.

"I'm doing just fine with time management." She gives me a little sniff. "It's everyone else on the road who won't let me be great."

I snort and lead her up the ramp to a back entrance of Ball Arena.

"What're we doing here?" she asks, then gasps, drawing up short and jerking on my hand. So I stop. It's either that or drag her along. "The physical therapists approved you to play."

I grin. "Yes, just got the green light today." Her squeal of delight pierces the night air, and I laugh; my happiness bubbles up, spilling out alongside hers. Yeah, I'm fucking thrilled over that news too. It seems like I've been waiting forever to hear it, and I almost kissed our team therapist when he delivered the words "You're cleared." Three days from now, I'll be back on the court with my team. Where I belong. But . . . "That's not what tonight is about."

She frowns, holding up her free hand. "What the hell else could it possibly be about? And why didn't you call me as soon as you got the news?" She jabs me in the abdomen with her finger.

"Hold up." I block the third poke, chuckling. "I intended to tell you tomorrow. I wanted it to be a surprise. Tonight is about you."

"Tonight?" She leans around me and peers at the door. "What's so special about tonight?"

Instead of answering, I finish leading her to the door. As soon as we reach it, one of the staff members opens it, allowing us in. Nerves grind my gut as we follow him down a hall and through the bowels of the building until we emerge in another well-lit hallway. We pause before a door, and the nerves in my stomach surge upward to play man-to-man defense with my tonsils.

Shit.

This could go really well.

Or really, really bad.

God, I want this to go well.

"Okay, before we go in," I say, turning to her. "Just know that I . . ." *Might've fucked this up, although I had the best of intentions. I wanted to show you how brilliant and talented you are and how much I believe in you. I wanted to see you smile.* "Well, you'll see. Let's go in."

"Wait." She lays a hand on my forearm, halting me from opening the door. "Whatever is behind that door, Jordan. I love it."

The nerves dissolve, and I can breathe.

Because this is Miriam. How could I forget that?

Curling a hand around the nape of her neck, I bend over her and kiss her. Aware of our audience of one, I keep it light, tipping her head only slightly to stroke past her lips once. Enough to taste and savor.

"Let's do this." Clasping her hand in mine, I open the door and walk through.

Being a basketball player here affords me a couple of connections, and I pulled on them. And shelled out some money. But it was all worth it to reserve this large hall usually booked for weddings and receptions. Tonight, huge floor-to-ceiling boards occupy different sections of the room. We draw closer to the first one; a panel from the first omnibus of Ravaged Lands covers the board. It's an integral turning point in the series. Sarafina Rose defeats the creature who killed her parents, and she discovers her demon half.

I know this because I've devoured everything Ravaged Lands since she shared the truth about it with me. And goddamn, it's *phenomenal.* Especially the current issues. Reading about North and his relationship with Sarafina . . . how she sees him as this fierce, strong, and noble fighter and leader not in spite of his heritage but because of it . . . knowing that's how she views me? It's humbling.

But this . . . this is not the efforts of a superfan.

This is the work of a man who wants to see the joy in the eyes of the woman he loves.

Even thinking that terrifies me because I don't delude myself into believing she feels the same. She doesn't. And she's told me that. Hell, she doesn't even believe in love or long-term commitments. In the two weeks we've been sharing a bed, we haven't talked about what we are or where we're headed. And I, who am not afraid to get on a court and battle it out with fucking giants over a ball, am scared of one five-foot-two woman.

Because she can do what those men on the court can't.

She can break me.

A knot lodges itself behind my sternum, and I ignore it. At least for tonight.

For tonight, it's about her.

"Jordan," she rasps, slowly shuffling forward. Shock widens her eyes, and her fingers flutter at the base of her throat. That slender column works up and down, but for a few seconds, no words emerge. Then she whispers, "What is this?"

"This is for you." That's all I've got because the nerves have returned with a vengeance, bringing along buddies. "There's more." I nod toward the panel.

Just as she turns back, astonishment still glazing her eyes, people surge from behind the panel as if doors were thrown open.

But not just any people.

They're actors dressed as the characters from Ravaged Lands. The demon Baldar. Hannah and Manassah, Sarafina's parents. Dani and Hiram, her younger brother and sister.

And then Sarafina Rose.

Wow. I blink.

I'd chosen the actors myself from the portfolios, but in costumes . . . my pulse thuds so loudly the sonorous beat almost drowns out the dialogue. It's almost as if they climbed directly from the pages of the graphic novel and into this hall in Ball Arena. Especially the woman playing Sarafina.

I glance at Miriam, and she's mesmerized. Utterly transfixed, and my heart soars.

The scene closes, and every character freezes except for Sarafina Rose, who stalks through a freestanding door to the next panel. We walk over, and this panel depicts another pivotal moment in the series. When Sarafina breaks free from the cage several men imprisoned her in to harvest and sell her blood. Days of their taunting and insults tortured her nearly as much as their devices to steal her essence. She battles her way free, reclaiming her freedom and her power, the dialogue as well as the action breathtaking and heartbreaking.

After she slays the last man, Sarafina moves on to the next scene.

And the next one.

The last act I deliberately chose because it depicts when Sarafina meets North. As they circle each other, weapons raised, the chemistry between them is palpable. Each parry and thrust equals foreplay, and fuck if I'm not getting hot. This scene sets these two on the path to becoming lovers as well as partners in their battle against evil.

It's brilliant.

By the time the last performance concludes in front of the remaining panel, I want to cheer, whistle, clap. But I do none of that. Instead, I turn to Miriam. And my knees nearly buckle.

Tears stream down her face.

She doesn't make a sound. Neither her shoulders nor her chest shudders. But the moisture tracking down her face is unmistakable. And she doesn't try to hide it as she looks up at me.

"You make me believe," she whispers.

"Sorry?" I ask, confused.

Shaking her head, she dabs at her face with her fingertips. "Thank you, Jordan. No one has ever done anything so beautiful and thoughtful just for me before. I'm . . ." She spreads her arms, her hands palms up. "I don't . . ."

"Good God, you're speechless. I probably need to be recording this," I tease.

She smiles, but it melts away, and her eyes darken, the brown nearly black. "You really do have big shoulders."

I frown at her second enigmatic statement in as many minutes. "Excuse me?"

"I was afraid to share this side of me with you," she admits. "But no one has ever seen me the way you have. Truly *seen* me. And then accepted me. But you did. You *do*. In your eyes, I'm bold when I want nothing more than to hide. I'm brave when I'm scared shitless. I'm brighter than the sun when I feel invisible. I don't know why I was ever afraid to share this"—she turns and waves a hand toward the panel and actors—"with you. Before, you said Narnia showed you how to dream big. Showed you the greatness in yourself. You do that for me. You're my Narnia."

Holy fuck.

I blink. She's robbed me of speech, of thought, of breath. No one— and I mean *no one*—has ever made me feel so important, so vital to them. And goddamn, are my eyes stinging?

"Now." Moving into me, she reaches up and cups my face, tilting it down. "Do you have any more plans for tonight?"

"Dinner," I rasp. "I have sushi—"

"Is it something you can pack up and have moved to your house? I need you inside me ten minutes ago."

I go still, noticing the hot gleam in her eyes and the rise and fall of her chest.

Grasping her wrists, I lower her hands from my face and turn to the staff member standing behind us, ready to guide us over to the corner of the room where our dinner is set up.

"Hey, I hate to be an ass. But do you think you can box all that up to go?"

"Oh my God. Either I'm really freaking starving or this is the best dragon roll I've had in my life." Miriam pops another piece of sushi into her mouth and groans, eyes closing.

That sound and the sight of her in my T-shirt has my cock stirring beneath my basketball shorts. But after enjoying hot, mind-bending sex for the last hour, my dick is going to need to take a back seat to my stomach. I'm hungry as hell.

I select a rainbow roll for myself, and yeah, she's not wrong. This might be the best sushi I've had. But then again, glancing around at the blanket spread on the floor of my living room, with the lamps turned down low and the furniture pushed back to make room for this impromptu picnic, I suppose it might be the intimate atmosphere with this woman that influences the taste.

I have a feeling Miriam would make paste taste like ambrosia.

"Here." I reach for the edge of the blanket, where I'd discreetly set a gift bag, and pick it up. "For you."

She pauses in the middle of plucking up another dragon roll and stares at me. Her gaze shifts to the bag, then back to me.

"Another gift?" She lowers her arm, her hand resting on her bare thigh. "Jordan," she breathes. "You've given me so much tonight. Nothing could possibly top what you did in that conference room . . ."

"I'm not trying to top it. Just add to it. Here." I hold the bag out to her. "Take it, sweetheart."

She accepts the gift bag, though it is with reluctance. After setting it down in front of her, she reaches inside and pulls out a bottle of imported plum sake. The cobalt-blue bottle with pink cherry blossoms is engraved with her name in Japanese. I had it specially ordered weeks ago.

"It's beautiful." Her voice is barely a sound, and she handles the gift with a reverence that should be reserved for a relic. A warm glow radiates inside me, and my fingers curl into my palm. "It's absolutely beautiful." Her fingers trail over the cherry blossoms. Over the engraving of her name. "How do you do it?"

"Do what?"

"Make me want to forget?"

I cross my legs, set my elbows on my knees, and lean forward. "That's not the first time today you've made a mysterious statement like that. What are you talking about, Miriam?"

She turns her head, staring out the window, but I doubt she's seeing the mountains or the miles of preserve land.

"Do you know why I agreed to join Zora and Levi in opening BURNED?" she asks.

"Yeah, it offered you stability, and you wanted that. Especially with your brother and sister." Every conversation we've had is branded on my brain. There's nothing about her that I don't remember.

"That's true, but it's not all of it. I wasn't completely honest. I haven't . . ." She swallows, and her gaze swings back to me, and the bare pain in her eyes punches me square in the throat. "I haven't told anyone this except for Zora. And she found out by accident."

"Sweetheart, what?"

What the hell causes that kind of stark look? My limbs turn to leaden weights, but I push to my feet and circle the platters of food between us. My first instinct is to scoop her into my lap, hold her, cradle her against my chest, and shield her from whatever ghosts seem to be haunting her. But this isn't about me. Like all of tonight, it's about her.

"What do you need from me?" My voice is damn near a croak, the effort of holding back the fear and worry clawing at me almost a physical ache. My muscles fucking quake with the strain of it.

She tips her head back, brown eyes studying me. And maybe she sees I'm on the edge and takes pity on me. Or maybe she needs me beside her as much as I need to be there. Because she sweeps a hand over the spot next to her.

"Can you sit next to me? Let me lean on you?"

Anything.

I lower beside her and draw my knees up, then rest my arms on them. She scoots closer, pressing her shoulder against mine, and though I want more—like to haul her against me—I grant her exactly what she requested of me.

She doesn't immediately speak, and I don't rush her, although the protector in me roars to *fix it*. Whatever stole the joy of the evening from her—make that pain go away, and *fix this*.

"When I entered college, it was scary. Sixteen, still a child. And a sheltered one at that. Most sixteen-year-olds had experienced boyfriends, parties, football and basketball games—hell, friends. Some had experimented with alcohol and sex. Other than a couple of friends, I'd had none of that. While I can attribute some of that to my own shyness and being the youngest kid in all of my classes, my parents—especially my mom—had a good part to do with it. She might as well have wrapped me in a bubble. I understand she was afraid I would be taken advantage of because of my inexperience, but in turn, it was my inexperience that allowed me to be taken advantage of."

The fear digs its talons into me. I don't like the direction this is heading, and I draw in a deep, hopefully quiet breath. *This is about her.* I repeat the mantra, silently reminding the anger kindling in my gut.

"So yes, entering college was scary, but God, I was so excited too. Even though I still lived at home instead of at the dorms, I had a certain freedom missing until then. No teachers to report back to my parents. No bullying in the hallways. The campus was bigger, not so insular as high school. There were students from all over the country—hell, the world. And that's what it felt like. I had finally entered the world for the first time. I even had friends. A very small group, but they were more than I'd ever had before. College had started off really great for me, even though the more independence I seemed to gain, the more my mom tried to tighten her hold on me. She didn't allow me to go to mixers and would only approve university activities if Zora or Levi attended with me. She hated my friends and refused to let me date. If paranoia had a poster child, Monica Nelson would've had that endorsement." She huffs out a low puff of sound that I think is supposed to pass for laughter. "That's why when I fell for a football player, I didn't tell her. I didn't tell anyone in my family because they wouldn't approve, and I liked him. No." She pauses, and she goes still, as stiff as a statue next to me. "I loved him."

A sense of foreboding yawns wide in my chest. So big I could fit inside it. It doesn't take a prophet to divine that Miriam's aversion to athletes originated here, within the seeds of this story. I'd always wondered whose sins I was paying penance for—now I'm about to find out.

"His name was Robert Sampson. He wasn't a starter on the team or even one of the stars. But I didn't care. What started as me tutoring him in Advanced Algebra turned into more, and he liked me. He didn't care that I was a seventeen-year-old sophomore or what some people considered an oddity. For the first time, a boy—a young man—showed genuine interest in me other than to tease me or use me for grades. When we spent time together, he listened to me, showered me with attention and affection. And I fell. Hard. I gave him my virginity."

She goes quiet, and my breath stutters and stalls in my lungs. Since she can't see me, I close my eyes, bracing against the blazing tide of fury that batters me. Because I know what's coming. Maybe not the details, but the result? Oh, I know. The result is her pain. Her rejection.

"The couple of days after we had sex—or made love, because that's what I'd believed we'd done—I didn't hear from him. But I chalked it up to his busy schedule. Then, worried about him, I headed over to the football house to check on him. The door to his room had been cracked, and I almost knocked when I realized he wasn't alone. Several of his teammates were with him, and I heard my name. He was telling them about 'smashing the freaky geek' and that it was time for them to pay up. Apparently, I had been a bet for him to get in with the more popular players. While I'd been giving him my heart and body, I'd only been a prank to impress his asshole buddies."

"Sweetheart," I rasp.

Pain and rage. That's what I've become, and even though it's ten years later, I want to hunt down this motherfucker who would take advantage of a child. *A fucking child.* Because that's what she'd been, if not by law—and just barely by law, as seventeen is the age of consent in Colorado—then definitely in experience, in mentality.

The name Robert Sampson is stamped on my brain with a mental cow brand. I'll never forget it. Never forget the name of the person who stole her innocence. And I'm not referring to her virginity. I'm talking about her trust in people. Her belief in love. Her faith in the goodness of people.

The guilt of that lies on his shoulders.

"I hated him. Hated his friends. They made me feel so . . . small. But as I left that football house, I promised myself no one would ever do that to me again. Have that kind of power over me again." She shook her head. "But my virginity and my heart hadn't been enough for him. He wanted my pride too. Looking back, I think something in him needed to break me, to drag me to the ground. Because he called me later that night and left a message inviting me to a party the football players planned on throwing after the game that Friday. That probably wasn't the only thing on their agenda. Humiliating me was too."

She straightens, and when she looks at me, the shadows of pain linger in her brown eyes, but a smirk rides her face. My fingers itch to trace it even as a cautious pleasure trips through me at the sight of it.

"But unfortunately a stink bomb going off right in the football house ruined their party plans. Also had the house—and its tenants—smelling like shit for weeks. Or so I'm told."

I stare at her. Then snicker.

"That's fucking savage."

"I don't know what you're talking about." Her smirk deepens but then fades. "I guess I should thank Robert and those other football players. After that, I stopped giving a damn what people thought. Stopped letting people walk over me, make decisions for me. I stopped hiding in plain sight. That's when people started calling me a little crazy, loose. Didn't bother me. All that meant I was finally living my life out loud and by my own rules."

"You don't owe those assholes a thing, and for damn sure you shouldn't be thanking them for anything." I plant a hand near her hip and lean over her, lowering my face to hers. This close, I can taste the oyster sauce and wine on her breath, and I want to lick it off. "No, I take it back. You want to be grateful to them? Be grateful that they revealed the strength that always existed beneath. Be thankful that their pettiness, immaturity, and just shittiness of character only highlighted the integrity and beauty of yours because you would never think of treating another person that way. Be grateful that they showed you that you could be bent but not broken."

It makes sense now. The theme of empowerment, consent, and choice that runs through Ravaged Lands. How Sarafina defends other people, but she's also her own champion. It all makes such heartbreaking and awe-inspiring sense.

I lift a hand to her face, letting it hover there, and only when she captures my wrist and presses my palm to her cheek do I cradle it. And my whole body sighs.

"You don't have to tell me why you joined BURNED," I murmur, stroking my thumb underneath the full curve of her bottom lip. "I get it. You believe in the mission of the company. And while you're there, you want to give someone what you didn't receive. The gentleness, the carefulness, the honesty."

"Why am I not surprised you understand?" she asks, the faint smile on her lips also in her tone. She briefly closes her eyes. "Thank you for being my friend. Because of you, I've started to let go of the past. As it was pointed out to me recently, I'm refusing to allow what happened with Robert to dictate my choices, my perceptions of people, even how I enjoy life. I've been going through the years mistrustful and suspicious. It almost prevented me from getting to know you. It almost kept me from being here, in this moment." She turns her head into my palm, kisses it.

I'm reeling from the *my friend*. Those two words stab me in the chest like the sharpest knife, and it's hard to believe I'm not bleeding out on the carpet in front of her. It's one thing to be friend-zoned when we've known each other for a couple of weeks.

It's another to be relegated to that hellscape when I'm in love with her.

Because I love this woman.

She's the fairy tale I've been waiting for, that I refused to settle for. And I'm her . . . friend.

A despair surges within me, swelling so quick, so furious, that my already flimsy defenses crumble under it. Fast on its heels is an urgency to grab at this moment, at the present, with greedy, grasping hands. To hold on so I can preserve it as long as it's able to last.

I lift my other hand to her face, tip her head back, and brush my mouth over hers. Her hands circle my wrists, and she hangs on to me, parting her lips and taking me inside.

God, she's so sweet. Sweet sin.

Our tongues tangle, indulging in a dance that my dick is weeping to bust in on. But it has to wait. Because I'm not ready to release this wicked treat of a mouth. I dive deeper, licking, sucking, worshipping. I need to seek out every part of her and pay its due. And she returns the sentiment. She releases my wrists and buries her hands in my hair, thrusting into my mouth, lapping at the piercing at the corner of my lip, tugging at it, entering in an erotic duel on my turf.

I rise to my feet, bringing her with me. In one seamless motion and with no effort at all, I hike her into my arms. A fierce satisfaction barrels through me at the differences in our frames, our physical makeup. It probably labels me an asshole caveman, but it doesn't stop the primal glee at being able to lift her petite body, cup her gorgeous ass, and hold her against me. Our mouths still fucking each other, I carry her over to the couch and, turning, sink down, arranging her over my lap so she's straddling my thighs.

We groan into each other. On reflex, my hips grind upward, stroking my cock against her bare pussy. My shorts provide no protection against her wet heat. Tunneling one hand into her hair to keep her mouth fused to mine, I grasp her hip with the other, guiding her movements. Back and forth. Tight little mind fuck of a circle. Back and forth. That circle. She's messing up my shorts with all that soaking wet, and they're officially my favorite pair. My cock pounds as she rides me, and I can't help myself. Jerking my head back, I fist the bottom of my shirt that she's wearing and twist it up and out of the way, granting myself an unrestricted view of that perfect glistening sex stroking up and down my cloth-covered dick.

It's almost as good as feeling it.

Yeah, that's a lie.

Nothing is better than that hot, slick flesh directly on mine.

And I need it. Now.

Squeezing her hip, I halt her movements and reach into my shorts, pulling my erection free. I fist the base, holding myself for her. Clenching my jaw at the damp kiss of her sex across the very tip. "Take me in, Miriam," I demand. Beg. *Take me home.*

Eyes meeting mine, she curls her fingers into my shoulders and slowly sinks down. I yank the T-shirt over her head, and the blonde curls spring about her head. Lust glazes her hooded eyes, has her teeth sinking into her bottom lip. As her pussy slowly inches its way down my cock, claiming more and more of me, I pull that full curve loose and push my thumb between her lips, sliding it over her tongue.

Withdrawing it, I circle her nipple, watching it pebble, feeling her pussy flutter and spasm around me. On a groan, I cup both breasts, squeezing, molding, plumping.

"Jordan." She presses her forehead to mine and, with a shudder, swallows the rest of me. "God, I can feel . . ." Another shiver, a full-body quake, rolls over her, and it echoes in her sex. My eyes nearly cross as it ripples over my cock.

"Nothing feels as good as you, Miriam. Nothing . . ." Nothing ever will. "Fuck me, sweetheart."

And she does.

She rises and falls, dragging that perfect tight sex up and down my cock, fisting me, sucking at me. I cup the back of her neck, yanking her forward, crushing my mouth to hers. Her rhythm stutters but picks back up, and she's taking us there, racing for that line that's the ultimate goal. Pleasure.

Reaching between us, I sweep my fingers over her clit, circling, rubbing. And when she stiffens and her sex clamps down on my cock, I growl, ecstasy nailing me in the back of the head. Gripping her hips, I thrust up into her, fucking her through the orgasm, shoving me head-first into my own.

As she sags against me, I plunge again and again, pistoning through her grasping core until it comes for me. Rapture.

Oblivion.

Home.

CHAPTER THIRTEEN

JORDAN

"I've faced men, demons, wizards, and revenants. None have terrified me. Just you."

—North the Woodsman to Sarafina Rose, Ravaged Lands

"Like Linc needed another reason to throw a party," Miriam mutters as a valet opens her door and she twists in the passenger seat and sets her hand in his.

She allows him to help her from the car, and I step out and hand his partner my keys. When the guy pulls off and I send up a small prayer that my vehicle is returned in the same condition I passed her off in, I extend my hand to Miriam.

"Well, the one he's giving tonight is for my return to the team, so I'm going with it." I give her a little tug to get her moving toward the massive front door.

Being back is . . . amazing.

It was only practice, but it's been so long since I've been able to get on a court, play with my team, get physical, and not feel like fucking china—being suspicious of my own body—that I'm damn near giddy.

So when Linc had announced the impromptu "get-together" in my honor in the locker room at the end of practice earlier this evening, I'd been cool with it. Since the day after tomorrow begins a three-game on-the-road series, most of the guys were fully on board too. Honestly, though, if it were up to me, I'd spend this evening and tomorrow with Miriam at home since I'll be away from her the next few days.

And though I've been anxious to play again, the last few weeks off have spoiled me in terms of spending time with her. Now, my days and evenings are about to revolve around basketball, press, and traveling. With the other women I've dated, basketball was always the wife, and they, the mistresses. For the first time, it's the other way around. At least in my mind and heart. The game might consume the majority of my time, but in my heart, she's the priority. Even though I can't tell her that or show it. Not if I don't want her to run screaming for the hills.

But soon, that's a risk I'm going to have to take. Not just because this relationship limbo we're stuck in confuses the hell out of me. But also because living this half life with her—having her body but being uncertain and fearful about her heart—is doing what I told myself I would never do.

I'm settling.

If there's a chance I can have all of Miriam, that she will have all of me, then I'm going after it. After us.

"You're looking a little too thoughtful over there for someone who's about to enter a den of debauchery."

I glance down at her, grinning. "Den of debauchery? Don't tell Linc that. He might have a banner made and strung across the front of his house."

She snorts. "It's sad that I agree with you."

I draw to a halt at the top of his stairs and guide her to the side of the door just in case anyone walks up behind us.

"Answer me honestly, yeah?" She frowns but nods, and I slide my hand under her curls and cup the nape of her neck, squeezing. "Are you uncomfortable around . . . ?" I wave a hand toward the house behind me. "Are you okay being around them?"

Since she shared her past with me, I understand her disdain of and aversion to athletes. That she accompanied me to different parties and events awes me. With another woman, cynicism would argue she did it for her own personal and business reasons. But I'd asked her to go with me to all those places; she wouldn't have gone on her own. She'd agreed because of me. And that kind of sacrifice, especially now that I have all the knowledge about what occurred in college, humbles me.

And gives me hope for us.

"Yes, I'm fine." She smiles and slides her arms around my waist, tipping her head back and smiling up at me. A warmth softens her brown eyes, and breathing becomes an option. "It didn't take long for Linc and the others to grow on me."

"Good." I tug her toward me, pressing a kiss to her forehead. "They love you too. You're like a cross between their little sister who they're protective of and their mother who has no problem giving them shit because you're not at all impressed by them."

"Aww." She bats her eyelashes and splays her fingers wide over her chest. "That's the sweetest compliment ever."

Laughing, I wrap my arm around her neck and pull her closer—

"Hey, Jordan. Miriam. It's good to see you again."

I look up to see Daniel standing on the top of the stairs, staring at us. As I meet his shuttered but sharp gaze, one thought flashes through my head.

He knows.

Fuck.

Music, laughter, and loud chatter crowd Linc's house, along with his guests. It's more of a toned-down version than the last party I attended.

But that just means there are about one hundred people here instead of three hundred. Still, it's loud, and everyone's having a great time.

Except me.

Guilt will do that to a person. Suck all the good time right out of him.

Goddamn.

Not for the first time in the last hour, I curse myself out. If I could reach behind me and kick my own ass, I would. I've had weeks to tell Daniel about me and Miriam. That first week, I can blame it on being caught up in her, in the change of our relationship. But after that, I have no excuse. Especially when I found out about returning to the team. All of us coming face to face was inevitable. And because I kept putting off calling Daniel and telling him the truth, he found out in the worst way possible.

Now, in his eyes, I'm *that* guy. The one who would sneak behind a friend's back and pursue the woman he wanted.

Because right now, to the man who mentored me, one of the men I respect most in this world, I'm that man.

A shaft of pain slashes through me, and I stare down into the bottle of water I've been nursing for a half hour. I wrap mental arms around that slashing ache, absorbing it into my muscles, my bones. It's no less than I deserve. Doesn't matter that I knew her the longest . . . loved her first. I wronged him, hurt our friendship, and need to make it right.

"Jordan, got a minute?"

As if I summoned him with my thoughts, I turn around to face Daniel. That pain blazes brighter, hotter, and as I stare into his unreadable, closed expression, the words of regret, of explanation, crowd into my throat, climbing on top of each other.

But nothing emerges except "Yeah, I do."

Daniel nods and turns. Before following, I scan the room for Miriam, locating her in the far corner with Linc and a few other people.

Satisfied she'll be safe with Linc, I pull my phone out and shoot her a quick text about leaving to talk with Daniel.

Tucking my cell back in my pocket, I join him. We wind through the throng of guests, not stopping until we come to Linc's library. Daniel opens the door, and we step into an almost suffocating silence compared to the cacophony happening outside the room.

This library is my favorite room in Linc's house. Some people use libraries as showpieces and have no clue what books occupy the spaces on their bookshelves. Not so with Linc. The man is a complete book-worm and has probably read every title on the nearly floor-to-ceiling shelves that cover three of the four walls. There's a sense of calm and peace in here along with the familiar scent of the cherry-and-choco-late-flavored cigars he enjoys every once in a while.

Somehow it seems appropriate that I'm about to be handed my ass in a room that was a safe haven.

Turning to face him, I thrust my fingers through my hair. "Daniel, look. I—"

"You're in love with her."

The bald, abrupt statement echoes in the room, almost startling in its bluntness. Only the press of the shelves at my spine prevents me from stumbling back a couple of steps. I've admitted those words, that truth, to myself before. But hearing them aloud and voiced by someone else . . . fear locks around my throat with meaty, thick fingers. So tight I can barely breathe past its brutal grip.

"Yes," I rasp. Then, because saying it once aloud seems to unlock something inside of me, easing the grasp on my throat, I say, "Yes. I am."

Daniel remains quiet so long I can pick out snippets of conversation from the voices filtering through the walls. He glances away from me, but a muscle tics along the hard line of his clenched jaw. Tension tautens his shoulders, and his body bristles.

"For how long?" he asks, swinging his attention back to me, the cool tone belying the stiffness of his frame.

I consider lying. No man wants to admit to a pitiful case of unrequited love for their friend. But I've kept enough from Daniel, and he deserves the truth from me, no matter how pathetic it makes me look.

"Almost from the beginning."

"You've been in love with Miriam almost from the moment you met her, and you didn't say a word to me? Not when I asked you to set me up with her? Why the hell did you even go through with it?" Now the anger seeps into his voice.

I push off the shelf, take a step toward him. "Because Miriam didn't—doesn't—feel the same for me. She doesn't even know that I'm in love with her." I flex my fingers, straighten them. Seeking something to do with my hands, I then tuck them into my front pockets. "As for why I set you up . . . for the first time since Jerricka died, you showed an interest in dating a woman. And Miriam is special. If anyone knows that, I do. And just because she didn't see me as more than a friend didn't mean she couldn't with you."

He frowns. "Yeah, and that doesn't answer my question. Why didn't you tell me you had feelings for her?"

Frustration and embarrassment mingle, temporarily ensnarling my voice. After a moment, I say, "Because you wouldn't have reached out to her if I had. And dammit, how I felt for her had nothing to do with it. It wasn't about me."

"The fuck it wasn't," he snaps, and the uncharacteristic curse telegraphs the enormity of his anger. "You lied to me."

"I did," I admit. "But not to hurt you. You're my friend. I loved Jerricka. I just wanted to help—"

"No, you were playing God. At the very least playing a damn martyr." One corner of his mouth curls, and he shakes his head. "Yes, you might've done this for me, I believe that. But you damn well did it for yourself too. Don't even try to fool yourself into thinking you didn't."

I frown, slashing a hand in front of me. "That's not true. I—" Fuck, I can't even continue the sentence. I stare at him, at the truth as it sinks inside me. "I did. But not for the reason you think."

Not to be some messed-up puppeteer with a God complex. Not to watch them dance to strings I pulled. That he could think I'm capable of that . . . bile churns in my stomach, climbing for my throat.

"Then why?" he demands, cocking his head, eyes narrowed. "You owe me an explanation other than 'You're my friend.'"

Now it's my turn to look away from him. But then I look back. Because I can't be a coward in this moment. He deserves better than that. And I owe myself more than that.

"If I saw with my own eyes that you two were happy together, then I could move on. I could finally let her go and move on."

He lets out a harsh bark of laughter. "You hear how fucked up that sounds, right? I don't even know what the hell to do with that." He raises his hands, palms up. "You used me. Do you get that? You didn't just use me to get over her, Jordan. You used me to have her the only way you could. True, I asked for the advice, the tips. But she didn't really have a chance to know the real me because I've been showing her you all this time. You've been dating her through me."

I don't have shit to say.

I'm stunned. Because he's right. That *is* what I was doing.

Shame slides through me in a slick, oily glide.

"That's not what I intended," I tell him.

He laughs, and the serrated edges of it punctuate the air. "Intentions. We all know about intentions, right?" He lifts his arms, dropping his folded hands on top of his head. "You know what's the most fucked-up thing about this, Jordan? I know you're a good man and friend. And I'm not even angry about you being in love with Miriam." He drops his arms, pinning me with a stare that has lost most of its heat but is weighed with more shadows. More disappointment. And that punches me, leaving me sore and desperate to rub the place on my sternum. "I'm

upset you lied to me. We're better than that. *You're* better than that."
He shakes his head. "I don't care what justifications you gave yourself,
Jordan; you lied. To me, to Miriam. And if you love her like you say, you
can't begin a relationship with her with that deception between you."

"You lied to me about what?"

We both jerk toward the new but very familiar voice in the room.
Miriam stands just inside the doorway, her lovely face carefully blank.

Except for her eyes.

Her dark-brown eyes are watchful. Cautious.

Hopeful.

As if she's longing for us to tell her she misheard. That I hadn't lied
to her.

God, I wish I could. I'd give anything if I could.

But I can't. Because I've betrayed the cardinal rule of our friendship.
Of my love for her.

I've lied with no ill intent, with no malice, and with only her happiness in mind. But it was still a lie.

Staring into Daniel's anger and disappointment has punched a hole
in my chest.

But confronting the heartbreaking blend of emotions suffusing
Miriam's face drives home the knowledge that I didn't understand the
concept of pain until this moment. Not until terror and grief mixed
with it to saturate every tissue and tendon in my body.

Not until I breathe it.

"Jordan," she says.

"I'm going to leave and let you two talk," Daniel murmurs.

He nods at me and strides toward the library door, pausing next
to Miriam.

"I'm sorry, Miriam." He glances at me over his shoulder. "I had the
opportunity to be honest with you, but I placed my wants above that.
And I'm not proud of it. Especially knowing you're going to be hurt by
our decisions." He lifts his hand as if to place it on her shoulder, but it

hovers there. And at the last second, he lowers his arm back to his side. "I hope you can forgive us both."

With one last look at me, he exits, closing the door behind him.

"What the hell is he talking about?" she asks, and it's impossible to miss the note of panic creeping into her voice. "What decisions am I going to be hurt by?"

"Miriam," I breathe, taking a step toward her, my hand outstretched to do . . . what?

I don't know. Like what I suspect happened with Daniel, I can't touch her. Not with this bomb sitting here between us, waiting to detonate. Not when I'm not sure if she will want my hands on her again.

Maybe she's thinking the same thing because she moves farther into the room but sidesteps me and my hand, claiming Daniel's former position. Her arms fold around her chest, but then, with a frown, she drops them to her side.

"Tell me."

"I asked you to give Daniel a chance and date him. After the first date went so horrible, he came to me for advice and . . . tips on how to win you over. To show you he could be the perfect man for you." I think back on that day. How I should've stopped to be honest with her. If I had, maybe I wouldn't be here looking into her eyes as understanding slowly dawns. Understanding, hurt . . . and betrayal. "So I did. I helped by telling him your hobbies, likes, dislikes. He wanted to—"

No. I shut down the rest of that sentence. No excuses. None for myself or Daniel. And she doesn't want to hear them anyway. Not from the way she frowns, crossing her arms. And this time she doesn't lower them. And I interpret the gesture correctly. She's protecting herself.

From me.

I try to inhale past the blow of agony that kicks me in the gut. Try and fail.

"So the anime-website subscriptions, the ghost tour, monster museum . . . that was all you," she says, her voice low, vibrating with . . .

anger, disbelief, pain. A nauseous mix of all three? "That was all you feeding him information about me." She barks out a harsh, ragged laugh that's ugly and breaks my heart. "That's a lot of fucking trouble. Were you that desperate for your friend to get laid? Was he?"

"What?" My chin jerks back, the verbal fist of her words slamming into it. "What the fuck? *No*, Miriam. That's not how it was at all."

"Right," she drawls; her mouth twists into a terrible caricature of a smile. "I'm sure it wasn't. And there I was going on and on about how well Daniel seemed to know me. How it made me feel special that he paid attention to all the details about me. How he *cared*. Shit." She thrusts her hands into her hair, fisting the curls and stalking several steps to the window offering a view of the lit pool. "You two must've gotten a laugh out of that one."

"Miriam, please look at me. Please," I beg. Because I'm not above it. She slowly—reluctantly, it seems—turns to me. As if the sight of me pains her. Disgusts her. "We never wanted to hurt you. Sweetheart, that never even crossed our minds. You *are* special. That's why I—"

"Save it," she says, voice flat. Then she gives another of those awful, jagged laughs. "*God*. It's like goddamn déjà vu. Except instead of Daniel fucking me, you did."

I almost drop to my knees; I reach behind me and clutch the edge of the bookshelf just in case. How is it possible to still be standing when the pure agony has me flayed wide open like some gruesome science experiment? I run a hand over my chest and abdomen, inanely making sure I'm still in one piece. Flinching because even my own touch is too much.

"I did it because I love you," I rasp.

Yeah, my voice sounds hoarse from the silent roar I locked down. She stiffens, her shoulders damn near rising to her ears as if she's severely offended by my announcement. And her eyes narrow, her head already shaking, denying the veracity of my words.

But I'm hollow, and I have nothing to lose.

No one to lose. Not anymore.

"You love me?" she repeats, disbelief dripping from her tone.

"Yes." I meet the anger, the dark hurt, in her gaze. I don't flinch from it. "I have almost from the moment we met in the Bacon Social House parking lot. From the instant you asked me to carry you away to my mansion for a carefree life of domestic bliss, Jimmy Choos, and orgasms." In spite of the emptiness yawning wide in my chest, a faint flash of humor flickers, and I barely smile before it disappears. "I was in love with you the first time we made love—or I did—and the first time you told me we could only be friends. I've never stopped. Even when I wanted to. Even when I tried to. And Daniel? He was my attempt at trying to. But I failed."

I flip my hands over, peer down at my palms as if they contain the answers to how everything has become so incredibly screwed up.

"I failed because it would be easier to quit breathing than it would be to stop loving you. One is possible; the other isn't. You are under my skin, entrenched in my heart, my soul. If I'd been honest with you about my feelings from the beginning, maybe none of this would've happened. But if I'd been honest with you, we both know we wouldn't be standing here because you would've cut me out of your life."

"Is this the transference-of-emotion portion of the program?" She waves a hand between us. "This is the part where this bullshit is somehow my fault?"

"No. All of this—lying to you, hiding the truth from Daniel, betraying your trust—is on me. I own that. But you need to own yours too. Give me that. Especially since I have the feeling when we walk out of this room, I won't have another opportunity to talk to you."

Because she would do what I accused her of—excise me out of her life.

"Be honest with me, Miriam. Be honest with yourself. How many men have you had sex with, then, before the damn sweat dried, demanded either friendship only from or nothing? You were already running scared. Something about me, about us, terrified you. A part of you, on some level, whether you want to admit it or not, knew I loved you. And that same part knew I wasn't a man you could easily control. Because that's what your flings are about, aren't they? Control. Leave them before they leave you? But love is the one thing you can't plan, can't dictate or manipulate. You weren't expecting me, and that scares the hell out of you. And that's okay, because you terrify me too. But the difference between me and you? I'm not running away from you. I'm running toward you."

She doesn't speak, and in a way, that says everything.

Nodding, I turn but draw to a halt and pivot back to face her.

"I'm sorry I betrayed your trust. I could give you reasons and excuses, but I won't. That cheapens the apology. And, Miriam, I am so sorry. I never meant to traumatize you again, and it's ripping a hole in my chest that I'm the cause of your pain. If you don't believe I love you, if you don't accept anything else I've said here in this room, please believe that."

Then I stride out, a wild, red-tinged desperation propelling me toward the front door and out into the dark. After pausing only to arrange a way home for Miriam with Linc, I practically bolt out of his house.

I don't know where I'm going.

And it doesn't matter. I just need away from here.

Away from her. Away from the source of my pain.

But unfortunately no one's invented a way for me to escape myself yet.

CHAPTER FOURTEEN

MIRIAM

"They won't allow me in heaven and revile me in hell. But you? You've always taken me just as I am."

—Sarafina Rose to North the Woodsman, Ravaged Lands

"The Men's Ministry is volunteering at the soup kitchen the day before Thanksgiving," Dad announces, cutting into his prime rib. He slides a look in Levi's direction, who doesn't even glance up from his dinner plate. "It would be nice if you'd join us, Leviticus."

"Why?" Levi forks mashed potatoes in his mouth, not even commenting on Dad's use of his full name. The name he despises. Something I suspect Dad knows and gets secret pleasure out of using anyway to needle my brother. Their relationship lands somewhere between complicated and toxic as fuck. "I don't believe in organized religion, so why would I join an activity hosted by one?"

Oh shit.

Silently sighing, I pick up my wineglass and down a healthy swallow. Something I've been doing often for the past five days, but Sunday dinner with my parents just offers a different excuse.

Yeah, best not think about why my alcohol consumption has risen lately, or I might steal the bottle of merlot off the table and go cuddle up with it on the living room couch. That'll definitely give Dad a reason to take my name to altar call.

"Are you telling me you refuse to serve your community and those less fortunate than you?" Dad demands, his eyebrows dropping down in that ominous scowl that heralds a storm of biblical proportions. Literally. Bible verses are imminent.

"No, that's not what I said. I questioned why I needed to join under the umbrella of man-constructed religions and denominations when I don't believe in them. The word for that is hypocrisy. The Bible speaks on that." Levi swallows more potatoes, his gaze still focused on his plate. "Negatively."

Dad's face darkens, fury gathering in his brown eyes. His lips screw up, deep brackets appearing on either side of his mouth. *Oh boy.* When will he learn that Levi gives as good as he gets? And often better?

And why won't my brother just admit that he *does* give back to his community? He's not flashy with it, but he tutors at one of the local community centers and, through BURNED, sponsors a program that mentors young Black men entering business-related professions. But instead of saying any of this, he eats mashed potatoes like they're manna and about to disappear in a few hours.

And wow. Look at me with the biblical metaphors.

I return my wineglass to the table, peering at it suspiciously. Jesus juice, indeed.

"Oh, for God's sake, Reggie, leave him alone," Mom says from the other end of the table. "I swear you do this at every dinner. Can't you give the Holy Roller routine a rest for one Sunday?"

"Don't take the Lord's name in vain at this table, Monica," Dad snaps. "And maybe if you were more of an example of a virtuous woman, our children wouldn't balk at doing something as selfless as giving back to others."

Slope $= y_2 - y_1 \,/\, x_2 - x_1$. *Slope formula. It determines the angle of a line that connects two points on a plane.*

I begin to sink into my head, slip away into my comfort place that even wine can't provide as Mom and Dad start to snipe back and forth with each other.

$x = -b \pm \sqrt{b^2 - 4ac}/2a \ldots$

You weren't expecting me, and that scares the hell out of you. And that's okay, because you terrify me too. But the difference between me and you? I'm not running away from you. I'm running toward you.

Jordan's voice snatches me back to the present, and like every time I've tried to find forgetfulness in the past five days, I can't. He pursues me, not leaving me alone. Not letting me . . . run.

God, I could hate him for planting that in my head.

I could if I didn't hate myself for finding an element of truth in it.

Pain thrusts itself into my chest, making its presence known even though I've tried to suffocate it with wine, work, food, anime—damn near anything that will occupy my mind. But nothing has helped. Nothing has erased my memory of Jordan's voice telling me he loves me. Has loved me since we met in that parking lot and I propositioned him with being his sugar baby. And a bargain basement sugar baby, at that.

Nothing has wiped clean the image of his face just before he turned around and walked away from me. The sorrow. The regret. Pain.

The resignation.

No matter what I drink or do, it's the resignation that sets off the clawing panic inside me. I've tried and, so far, succeeded in not analyzing the reasons behind that panic too closely. But like the judgment day Dad keeps sermonizing about, I know the time is approaching when I won't be able to run away from my reckoning.

Run away.

Two words I'll be happy to never hear or say again in life.

"Zora, I still can't believe we weren't invited to your engagement party. I have a very big bone to pick with your new fiancé. Where is Cyrus, by the way?" Mom arches an eyebrow. "I invited him to dinner."

"He had a business trip and is out of town for the next couple of days." She slides me a glance, and I have no idea what that's about. Okay, fine, I can guess. "The engagement was a surprise, as was the party."

"That young man should've come over here and asked for your hand in marriage from me first. What happened to that? Respect in your generation has been abandoned. That's the reason we weren't invited to that party, Monica," Dad says, stabbing his fork at Zora even though he directs his comment to Mom. "He knew he was wrong and I would have something to say about it."

Zora sits there, her usual placid, Sunday-dinner smile on her face, taking this verbal lashing because that's what Zora does. Her MO since we were kids. Keeping the calm. The peacemaker. Although Cyrus has stepped into the breach lately, and Zora has retired most of the unwanted duties thrust upon her. But old habits die hard. If anyone knows that, it's me.

It's not fair.

My parents aren't satisfied with the venom in their own relationship; they have to plant seeds in Zora's. Suck her joy from her. And they don't care. They don't see. They never *see*.

Levi sets down his fork, anger gleaming in his eyes. "It's not enough that—"

"Maybe the reason Cyrus didn't ask for her hand in marriage is because this isn't the 1950s and she's a grown woman perfectly capable of making the decision on her own of whether or not she wants to marry the man she loves. And maybe the reason he didn't invite you to the party is because he wanted to give the woman he adores a happy evening with joy-filled memories and not one filled with resentment, bickering, and toxicity. Those are just my immediate thoughts."

Silence permeates the room, and I swear, even the world beyond the house has gone quiet. Inside, that small voice in my head squeaks an "Oh shit!" and shuts the hell up.

Across the table, Levi stares at me, and for the first time, my older brother looks at me with something other than strained patience and confused affection, as if he has no idea what to do or make of me. Admiration brightens his gaze. And understanding. For the very first time in my twenty-seven years, I think my brother and I understand one another.

Zora, seated next to him, smiles at me and mouths, "Thank you."

For not sinking away and disappearing.

For speaking up.

For defending her.

"Excuse me?" Shock and a looming anger deepen Mom's voice. "Excuse me?"

"Did you really just speak to us like that, young lady?" Dad snaps, his fork clattering to his plate. "And at our own table?"

"You should've waited until we were in the living room, Miriam," Levi, back to his usual sardonic self, adds.

"That's enough out of you," Dad thunders. Then, to me, he demands, "What has gotten into you to even dare talk to us like that?"

"I know what it is," Mom mutters, throwing her napkin down beside her plate. "That business they're all involved in. None of this . . . behavior began until they started it. Especially you, Miriam." She shoots me a look, and I'm not immune to the anger and hurt there. But I can't allow it to dictate my life anymore either. "This isn't *you*."

"Meaning it's us," Levi says to Zora.

"Levi," my sister murmurs, though the corner of her mouth twitches.

"Actually, Mom, this *is* me. I'm mouthy, no filter, a little offensive even when I don't mean to be, and often a little unapologetic about it." My voice shakes because, *oh my God*, I can't stop talking. But it's like a dam has broken inside me, and everything I've held back out of fear of their rejection or hurting their feelings, out of insecurity, comes rushing out. "I'm also sensitive with a big heart, even if it's bruised. I'm a good friend, sister, and daughter, though far from perfect. I'm more than my IQ. I like math, but I love art. I'm an artist."

Just saying those three words aloud has a weight lifting off my chest, and I suck in a deep, cleansing, healing breath. And I smile. Big. I meet the gazes of every member of my family.

And I say it again just because it feels so wonderful and liberating.

"I'm an artist and author. And a damn good one. Just ask my publisher and my many readers since Ravaged Lands, my graphic novel series, are among the most-downloaded issues on their app—"

"I fucking love Ravaged Lands," Levi says. "Especially Zadok. He's a badass."

Shock damn near knocks me back in the chair, and I stare at him, mouth hanging open.

"Levi! Language," Mom yells. Oh yes, she's just about reached her limit. And she proves it by pushing her chair back and shooting to her feet. "This is ridiculous. Art? Graphic novels? Since when, Miriam? And what next? God, I'm afraid to ask." She pinches the bridge of her nose.

"I don't know what's next," I say. She drops her arm and glares at me, but I don't avoid the heat there, don't duck my head. "But I'm not a child, and whatever choices I make are for me. If you approve, that's nice. But if you don't, that's okay too. This is my life, Mom. And I can no longer allow my past to influence my future . . ."

That includes my childhood.

And their marriage.

Their relationship issues are just that—theirs. And it doesn't mean it's like some generational curse where I'm doomed to repeat their history.

For so long, I've possessed this attitude of "If I don't give a fuck, then people can't fuck me over." But that's a lonely existence. Even though I've dated and had short-term boyfriends, I've never let them close. Yes, I've allowed them inside my body, but never my heart. I was too scared that once they glimpsed the sometimes-goofy-nerd, at-times-insecure woman behind the ballsy exterior, they wouldn't stay. They'd see the only thing special about me was my Mensa membership.

But Jordan saw behind the curtain, and not only did he stay, but he was my friend in spite of—no, because of them.

He *loved* me because of them.

My breath stalls in my lungs, my heart pounding against my rib cage as if auditioning for the drummer position in a rock band.

Jordan loved me.

That night in Linc's library, I couldn't hear that, couldn't accept it. And now, in a moment of clarity so clear it stings, I get the reason, the why. For so many years, art has been my cathartic joy, and my stories a place where that joy was protected. Where I was safe to be me without criticism, rejection, or fear. Because I was in control. As the storyteller, I dictated what happened to the characters, how they extricated themselves from trouble, how they triumphed. As the creator, I could be a part of the fantasy, immerse myself in it, yet still maintain enough distance to ensure everything happened the way I wanted.

But Jordan, by involving me in his own plan with Daniel, in a way made me a character in a tale I had no control over. I couldn't influence. That night in the library, I felt . . . violated. My sanctuary had been tainted, exposed as not quite as secure as I'd always believed. And that fucking hurt.

Because now I have to face the reality, the truth. That I used my stories as crutches. I lived vicariously through them so I wouldn't have to *live*.

I wouldn't have to hurt. I wouldn't have to fail.

I wouldn't have to love.

So in that library, instead of admitting that about myself—that I'm a big ol' coward—I focused on the lie and how I'd been flung back to that shitty football house on campus, overhearing how I'd been tricked by another person I'd trusted and given myself to.

But Jordan is nothing like Robert Sampson.

He's nothing like any man I've ever met.

He's my friend. He's my lover.

He's my love.

I love Jordan Ransom.

"I think she just had a breakthrough," Levi says to Zora, though his gaze is pinned on me. "And I didn't even have to threaten Jordan." He shrugs. "Damn."

Zora snorts, although her soft smile lights up her eyes. "Don't kid yourself, Leviticus. Jordan Ransom would bench-press you." Pushing back her chair, she stands. "Let's go get some Froyo. My treat. And you can tell us how you plan on winning Jordan back. I have some ideas, and Cyrus is on board, FYI."

Levi stands, tossing his napkin to the table. "I'll get the frozen yogurt but pass on the planning."

"What the hell is going on here?" Mom throws up her hands, then glares at Dad. "Say something, Reggie! Don't just sit there like a bump on a log, dammit."

"Don't you curse at me, Monica," he snarls. "And this is what I call chickens coming home to roost. If you hadn't—"

I don't stick around for the replay. And neither do Zora or Levi. We walk out of the dining room, leaving my parents to do what they do best. We really don't need to be here for this.

Besides, there's always the next Sunday dinner.

We grab our coats and within moments are standing outside in the cool November-evening air. I feel a hundred pounds lighter leaving this house than I did walking in. And I have a mission.

To get back the man I love.

And if there's anyone who I trust to have a plan, it's Zora . . .

"One more thing." I abruptly stop at the bottom of the stairs. "I'm quitting BURNED."

Zora and Levi stare at me. Blink. And stare some more.

"What're you talking about?" Zora asks.

I squint. "So *quitting* is probably the wrong word. I plan to stay as a partner and have a hand in the big-picture decisions for the company. But the day-to-day operations as far as being over marketing and promotion? I'm resigning, and Dani can be promoted to my position." When both of them *continue* to stare at me, I smile. "Trust me. Let's talk over Froyo."

CHAPTER FIFTEEN

JORDAN

*"Don't ever make the mistake of forgetting what I am.
Changeling. Not human. Thank the goddess."*

—North the Woodsman, Ravaged Lands

Cyrus stares out the driver's side window at the entrance of the chain hotel. Even though I can't see his face, I have zero doubt a frown creases his brow. He's emanating Big Frown Energy.

And yeah. I'm never saying that again. Not even in my head.

"Are you sure about this?" he asks.

No. "Yes. Besides, it's a little too late now."

His head swings toward me, and I witness that scowl firsthand. "No, it's not. We can drive away right now, and no one would know the difference."

I blow out a short breath of laughter. "You make it sound like we're *Thelma & Louise*-ing it. We're not criminals. You're too shitty behind a wheel to be anyone's getaway driver, and I'm too pretty to go to jail."

"And you're stalling," he points out. Damn him. "Which only emphasizes my argument that maybe you should put this off for another time. At least until you're sure you—"

"Cyrus, I'm sure." I study the hotel, looking up to the third floor and the row of windows there. "I appreciate you worrying about me, but I need to do this. Now. It's been overdue." I pull on the door handle and push open the car door. "Thanks, bruh. I'll be back shortly."

In moments, I walk into the hotel lobby, tugging down on the brim of my baseball cap to try and conceal my face. Not breaking stride, I head straight for the bank of elevators and, once inside, press number three. Nerves tangle inside me, and I stare at the numbers above the doors as the floors slide by. Too soon, the three lights up, and the doors slide open with a small hiss.

I step out and follow the arrows directing me to room 323. It's all the way at the end of the hall. Giving me just enough time to talk myself out of this decision, back into it, out, and back in. I thrust my fingers through my hair, fisting the strands as I stare at the closed door with the fake-gold numerals on it.

Cyrus is probably right; maybe I should've put this off until I wasn't so raw about Miriam. When my emotional skin still didn't feel like a third-degree burn afflicted it. But it's been only days. Getting over Miriam Nelson? How long does it take to measure forever?

Clenching my jaw, I briefly close my eyes. Anxiety spikes inside me like a crazy-ass pogo stick, and I'm back to asking if I'm really ready to do this shit when I whisper, "Fuck it," and knock.

A minute later, the door opens.

And I come face to face with Michael Jones for the first time in ten years.

It's like staring into a mirror. Same blond hair, dark-blond brows, facial features, towering height, and big build. Although the last decade hasn't been kind to him. Deep lines fan out from the corners of his eyes, and they're not from smiling or laughing. More grooves cut under his cheekbones and dent either side of his mouth. Gray liberally sprinkles his beard and hair, and weight sits in his gut, straining the front of his white long-sleeve shirt.

Life has not been kind.

I wait for the dark glee or satisfaction at the signs of wear and tear to fill me. But I feel . . . nothing. Not happiness at his rough-around-the-edges state. Not the need to punch him in the face. Not sorrow over his abandonment.

Just nothing.

"Son." Michael breaks out in a grin, his arms outstretched. "I'm so glad you—"

I step back. "That's not what this is. I'm sorry if you got the wrong impression."

The smile bleeds from his face, and his arms slowly fall to his sides. "At least come inside so we can talk about this."

"Actually, we can do this right here, thanks." I hold up a hand, forestalling anything else he might have to say. "I didn't come here for a kumbaya moment, and if that's what you thought, then let me get that out of your head. I didn't even come here for a conversation. This is going to be a monologue, not a dialogue." I inhale a breath, release it. "I needed a father when I was three, six, and even thirteen. I needed you to teach me how to pee straight, not hit girls, control my anger, be a damn man. I needed you to be there for Mom so she didn't have to work two or three jobs to make rent and pay bills and make sure I ate and had clothes on my back. I needed you to be there so she wasn't exhausted all the time and I didn't blame myself for it. But since you weren't, since you walked, never looked back or sent a dime, Mom picked up the slack in every area of my life. And where she couldn't, my coaches did.

"So what I'm trying to say, Michael, is this . . . I needed a father then, not ten years ago after I was drafted. And not now. It's not about forgiveness. I forgive you, if that's what you need, although a part of me doubts it is or that's why you came back here. But if it is, you have it.

But it's all you'll have from me for now. And don't come through Mom again. Leave her out of this. You've done enough damage there, and she doesn't need to be reminded of it. If I need to talk to you, I know how to get in touch with you now. But understand this and respect it, Michael. *I'll* contact *you* if and when I decide to. That's my decision, not yours. You forfeited that right when you walked out and didn't look back." I take another step away. "Goodbye, Michael."

This time, it's me who walks away and doesn't look back.

Minutes later, I exit the hotel and find Cyrus parked exactly where I left him, the motor running. I smirk. He took the getaway-driver thing a little too seriously. After climbing into his car, I shut the door and exhale a deep breath.

"Everything good?" Cyrus asks.

"Yeah." I smile. "Everything's good."

And for the first time, when it comes to anything pertaining to my father, I mean it.

CHAPTER SIXTEEN

JORDAN

"Fine. If you've got to get technical. I love you. Happy?"

—Sarafina Rose, *Ravaged Lands*

"Good game, Jordan!" Linc slaps me on the shoulder. "It's so fucking good to have you back!" he yells, even though I'm standing right here in front of him.

I grin, the adrenaline still pumping through my veins, even though our game against the Pistons ended thirty minutes ago. Giving him a one-arm hug, I pound him on the chest, then release him. Around us, the rest of the team shouts back and forth, all in various states of undress, some having hit the shower. There's a frenetic energy in the locker room that's particular to winning. Especially when you're home. Tonight there will be parties, drinking, and fucking. Lots of fucking.

"Twenty-four points and ten rebounds. You're such an under-achiever," Daniel says, clapping me on the shoulder.

I grin at him, relief a cool balm spreading through my chest. It's been a little over a week since our confrontation about Miriam. When he left that library, I didn't know if we would be on speaking terms again, much less be cool. I don't know if we're as tight as we used to be, but in the last few days, since we've been playing again, he hasn't been as cold. And I have been hopeful.

Tonight, I have even more hope.

I shrug. "I need to have goals." After stripping off my jersey, I tip my chin up. "Thanks, man."

"You're welcome. Now bring that same energy tomorrow night."

Laughing, I bump his fist. "Yeah, bruh."

He walks off, and a peace soothes one of the raw places in my heart. One of them. The other one? Well, it's going to take more than a fist bump and team bonding. I head to the showers, the high from the win fading, replaced by the weight I've carried around for days.

I have the press conference and then home. Finally. I'm tired. And lonely.

A part of me had hoped, maybe even prayed a little, that Miriam would reach out to me. Call. Text. Fucking skywrite. But nothing. And with each day that's passed, I've lost more of my hope that she'll forgive me.

That she'll love me.

I can't make her fall in love with me.

And fuck. I've become a country song.

Standing under the shower's stream, I bow my head and wash away the sweat and dirt of the game. Only a little while longer.

An hour later, seated behind the table and microphones on the podium, I feel like that "little while" is eternal.

A reporter gives his name and identifies his station. "Jordan, how's your groin pull? Are you back to full health?"

It's only the fifty-first time it's been thrown at me since my return. Sometimes, I wish they'd come up with more original questions. Or listen to the answer I gave the last guy. But this is the job.

Forcing a smile that I hope appears real, I give my patented reply, "Thanks to the team's great physical therapists, I'm at one hundred percent."

The next question is for Daniel, and I relax but only slightly. And just for the moment. While my name and face end up on ESPN, blogs, and gossip sites often, this part of the job is my least favorite. One slipup, one mistake, and suddenly you've insulted another player's game or wound up married to the Loch Ness Monster's niece. Shit can get unpredictable quick if you go off script.

Another question comes at me after a reporter introduces herself and her paper. "Jordan, that drive in the last twenty seconds of the fourth quarter, you got the rebound and scored the layup, cinching the five-point lead to win the game. What were you thinking?"

I mentally sigh, hating these "What were you thinking?" questions. Because "That I wanted to win the fucking game" is never the right answer. I checked with Coach. He said it wasn't.

"Mainly that if I miss this layup, Coach is going to run me in practice, and I'm never going to hear the end of it," I joke. The room fills with laughter. I wait until it dies down a little before adding, "You can't give the Pistons a chance to come back. Twenty seconds or two. If you can take the shot, you take the shot and put points on the board. We don't stop playing until the game is over."

Hands shoot into the air, but a woman in a white blouse and dark-blue pants beats everyone else to the punch. "Jordan, Kyle Rappaport with the *Denver Oracle*. Can you comment on your position regarding the graphic novel series Ravaged Lands?"

I blink, certain I didn't hear that question right.

"Uh, excuse me?"

"Your position regarding the Ravaged Lands graphic novels?"

I frown, more than a little confused. Like a fuckton confused. Maybe someone on the Ball Arena staff had let it slip about me arranging the mini Comic-Con exhibition here?

"I love the series."

Before another reporter can ask a question, this Kyle is back at it. Or, rather, back at me. "And what about graphic novelists? What is your position on graphic novelists?"

My heart starts to pound in my chest, my mouth going dry. My gaze sweeps the press room, but for a moment, all I see is a blur of faces. Focusing back on the reporter, I study her face, but her expectant expression gives nothing away. And I don't recognize her.

"Jordan? Graphic novelists?"

A murmur ripples through the room, as if they, too, realize this shit is unusual. Because it *is*.

"I can't speak for all graphic novelists, since I only know one," I slowly say, leaning into the microphone. "But my position on that one? She's pretty damn amazing."

I scan the room one more time, and how can these people not catch my pulse magnified times a thousand in all these damn microphones? Hell, I can barely hear my own voice. Shit. Leaning back in my chair, I drop my hands onto my thighs. My suddenly sweaty hands.

"And said graphic novelist? If she'd made a mistake, jumped to a wrong conclusion, and wanted your forgiveness, what would you have to say on that?"

The room bursts into loud chatter, and cameras click as a wild, crazy joy sings through me. I clear my throat of the hope crowding into it. Straightening and flexing my fingers on my thighs, I desperately peruse the room again. Nothing. Nothing. She's not here. She's not . . . a slight movement and—*there*.

There she is.

Miriam steps out of the exit's shadow, and it's like a beacon shines down on her. Logically, I acknowledge it's just the track lighting, but no, she's fucking glowing. Another small movement, and Cyrus moves into my line of sight, wearing a small smile.

Shifting my attention back to her, I meet her gaze and don't look away.

"I would have to say that she doesn't have to ask for my forgiveness. That it's hers. Anything I have is hers. Me included."

"Can I quote you on that?" Kyle asks—grinning.

The room erupts in reporters yelling my name and shouting questions about graphic novelists and whether I care to expound on my answer and who "she" is. But I'm not paying attention to any of them. Only Miriam has all my attention.

It's always been only Miriam.

Standing, I push my chair back, then skirt the table and my teammates. In seconds, I'm off the podium, not even caring that I'll be paying a hefty fine for disrupting this press conference. All that matters is the woman at the back of the room and getting my arms around her.

The reporters part like the Red Sea, still yelling their questions. Flashes go off, and as I reach Miriam and swing her up in my arms, holding her tight, the world . . . stills. Quiets. I close my eyes, inhale her spicy-cinnamon-and-vanilla scent, savor the press of her body to mine, feel the beat of her heart against my chest . . .

God. I bury my face in her neck. I didn't know if I would be here again. Didn't know if I would touch her again.

"Sweetheart." It's all I can get out as I set her on her feet, cup her face, and tip her head back. Sweeping my thumbs over her cheekbones, the corners of her mouth, I shake my head and loose an admittedly shaky laugh. "What're you doing here? Well, besides giving me the best rom-com grand-gesture moment created?"

She grins, circling her hands around my wrists. "Just like Cyrus's friend asked, I'm here to ask your forgiveness."

"Miriam, you don't need—"

She releases one of my wrists to press a finger to my lips, shushing me. "Yes, I do. Jordan, I have prided myself on living for myself and not caring what other people thought. But the truth is I've been so tangled up in my past I've allowed it to color my present and almost wreck my future. From my parents to Robert, I've never let go. And by holding so tight to what happened then, I made no room for you or a possibility of you. Of us. Worse, I punished you for another person's sins when I knew you weren't him. You, Jordan, are nothing like him. You're . . . everything. My Narnia. All this time you've seen me. When my own family didn't, you did. And I'm so sorry for wearing blinders when it came to you. For not seeing your heart. I'm sorry for assigning you blame that wasn't yours. I'm sorry for not trusting you with my heart when there's no place, hands, it's safer in. Mostly, I'm sorry it took me so damn long to say I love you."

She slides her hands up my chest, then wraps her arms around my neck and rises on her toes. I meet her halfway.

"I love you so much, Jordan Ransom," she whispers against my lips. "And thanks to you, I believe in the fairy tale. You *are* the fairy tale. You're mine."

Goddammit, she's going to break me. I crush my mouth to hers, not caring who's watching, listening, or taking pictures. Not one more second can pass without her taste in my mouth. Without me confirming this is my forever.

She is my forever.

Her fingers tangle into the hair at the nape of my neck, holding me to her, and our lips part, tongues greeting, welcoming each other, and I sigh into her mouth. This. This is home.

She is home.

When she draws back to brush a kiss over my chin and jaw, the noise around us penetrates, and I lift my head, blinking against the glare of the cameras thrust into our faces.

Laughing, I wrap my arms around her, lifting her off her feet again and smacking a hard, quick kiss to her lips.

"I think we might've made a spectacle of ourselves," I murmur.

She tips her head back, grinning up at me. "Just a little." Then the grin fades a bit, and her teeth sink into her bottom lip.

"What, sweetheart?" I ask.

Her lashes sweep down for a moment before they lift, and a hint of uncertainty glints in her brown eyes. "Before, in the library, you said you were running toward me. Have you stopped?"

I shake my head, then chuckle softly and brush a kiss over her forehead, cheek, and finally her mouth. "Sweetheart," I breathe against her lips. "I'm a cross-country runner, not a sprinter."

She stares at me, and the moment the meaning of my answer dawns, a beautiful, blinding smile spreads across her face, and damn if I don't fall just a little bit more in love with her.

"I love you, Miriam Nelson. I've never stopped. And I never will."

"I love you more, Jordan Ransom. Thank you for not settling."

And with the press clamoring around us, our happily ever after begins now.

EPILOGUE

MIRIAM

"I'm yours forever. And for an immortal, that's a long time."

—North the Woodsman, Ravaged Lands

Six months later

"Damn, I'm good."

I grin down at the finished panel of the latest issue of Ravaged Lands. Also, coincidentally, the last one of what will be the fourth omnibus. Satisfaction and joy flood me, and it's like a hit of adrenaline, energizing me even though I've spent the last six hours working nonstop.

Since leaving the everyday operations of BURNED six months ago, I've been able to devote more time to my full-time career as Rayland Penn. Which has meant releasing biweekly issues of my series instead of monthly. The more-frequent releases have meant an uptick in downloads and readers. And they are absolutely loving Sarafina Rose and North. The buzz has generated even more interest from publishers, and my new agent is negotiating a distribution contract right now that will see Ravaged Lands on not just indie bookstore shelves but in chain stores as well.

It's been a dream.

One I didn't know could be mine. I wasted so much time being afraid—of being open with my brother and sister, of standing in my truth, of letting others see the real me . . . of living. So I've vowed to myself to never live in the past again. To never pass another day in bitterness or fear. To spend every moment forgiving and loving myself.

And with the man who has brought such joy and completion to my life.

Sighing, I set down the stylus and hop off the high-back drafting chair and step away from the standing desk. Stretching my arms above my head, I glance around the airy, sunny room with the balcony french doors thrown open to allow the early-afternoon sunshine in. An array of windows claims one wall, while framed art from Ravaged Lands mounts the others. Besides my desk and chair, a couch, chairs, a table, a bookshelf, and other office equipment claim space in the huge room.

It's my office.

In Jordan's house.

He created this place for me. Not as a bribe to get me to move in with him . . . although I cannot lie—it worked. Still, he wanted me to have my own space in his home. Little does he know, I already did. Him.

He's my place that I call my own.

I give the screen one last glance; then I cross the room and leave the office. In moments, I'm down the stairs, moving through the wardrobe, and yelling into his man cave.

"Hey, Jordan!"

"What's up?" He appears at the bottom of the stairs, hands clasping the ends of the railings. Arching an eyebrow, he cocks his head. "Listen, I have not even dared to breathe on the closed door of your office. You're finishing your book, and I've left you alone."

"And I appreciate you for that, Ragnar." I grin. "But I've officially finished, and I have something to show you." I wave at him. "Come here."

He bounds up the stairs, and I step aside, but he doesn't stop. Instead, he aims straight for me, slinging me over his shoulder in a fireman's carry. With a scream, I slap my hands on his firm, delectable ass.

"Put me down, crazy! Do you know how much coffee I've been drinking?"

He laughs and pays me no mind, carefully but swiftly climbing the stairs until we're in the doorway of my office. Gently, he sets me on my feet, steadying me until the blood rushes back to other parts of my body.

"I've missed you," he murmurs, wrapping me up in his arms and burying his face in the crook of my neck. I embrace him, holding him tight and breathing in that mountain-fresh-and-earthy scent that is a comfort and stimulant. He's my personal intoxicant. And he's been on the road for the last three days. God, I've missed him too. "And congratulations on finishing."

He brushes his lips over the base of my throat, right over my racing pulse.

Groaning, I push his head up and move back. But not before grazing his jaw with my teeth. It's a promise for later. As a groan rumbles in his chest, I'm assuming he understands it.

"Thank you. I can't believe I'm done." Enfolding his much bigger hand in mine, I lead him farther into the room.

He follows me to my desk, and I wait, anticipation and excitement coursing through me. I'm damn near dancing with it, shifting from foot to foot. And I know the moment he sees it.

He stills.

I grin.

"Miriam . . . ," he breathes.

Miriam, not Marilyn. Because it's that huge. It's that . . . us.

Sarafina and North have fought through many battles and wars. They've been hurt and separated and nearly died yet always found their way back to each other. And in this last issue of what will be the end of the omnibus, they stand facing one another under an arch of scarred tree branches. For once, she's out of her leather and is dressed in a simple green shift, and a white linen shirt covers his torso instead of his jacket. With no one but the sky and earth as witnesses, they bind a cord around their wrists and arms, pledging themselves to one another forever.

It's a reflection of us.

Except for once, fantasy is following reality instead of the other way around.

"It's beautiful." He clears his throat, then turns to me, blue eyes bright. "Now I'm yours there and here. No going back."

"I wouldn't have it any other way."

The corner of his mouth twitches, but the love in his gaze fills my chest so I almost don't have room to breathe. As if he's unable *not* to look at it, he returns his gaze to my tablet.

"You know, it's funny," he murmurs.

I wrap my arms around his waist and lay my head on his shoulder. He lifts his arm and winds it around me, holding me close. "What is?"

"I was once a little boy who escaped through a book to Narnia, and now, thanks to you, there's a piece of the man in your novels who's found happiness with the woman he loves. But"—he shakes his head and looks down at me, cupping my face, his thumb nudging my chin up—"nothing compares to the joy that man has found in this life—real life—with you."

I close my eyes, and when his kiss comes, I sink into it. Sink into the love that I know will always be there to lift me up.

"I love you," I whisper, opening my eyes and meeting his. "I love you, Jordan Ransom. More than I ever believed possible."

"I love you more, Miriam." He presses another kiss to my mouth, then smiles. "Now let's go have holy-shit-you-finished-another-book sex."

Grinning, I push off him and run for the door. Glancing over my shoulder, I yell, "First one to the bed does that thing with the tongue."

I hoot with laughter as he rushes past me and darts down the hall.

Little does he know I let him win.

After all, I *love* how he does that thing with his tongue.

Win. Win.

ACKNOWLEDGMENTS

Thank You to my Heavenly Father, who gave me strength, perseverance, creativity, drive, and sanity when I thought I'd lost all of that. The year 2021 was the most difficult of my life, and I leaned on You more because there wasn't even a rock bottom for me. And in my weakness, You always showed Yourself to be strong. Thank You for never leaving nor forsaking me. You're faithful, and I've never known the true extent of that until this past year. Thank You, Father, for loving me beyond my wildest imagination.

To Gary. Thank you for being my rock and so incredibly steadfast. When I said I couldn't, you didn't even bother saying I could. You just pushed food in front of me, left me alone with the laptop, and gave me space to be. Thank you for loving me through, well, everything and for not calling me crazy—even though you probably thought it a few times, LOL!—and for taking the dog out. I love you!

To Dahlia Rose, my writing partner in crime! Thank you for dinging me every morning and ordering me to get my ass in the chair and write. You've become more than a friend over the years. You're family now, and I'm seriously considering trading in that chick who shares my face for you! I mean, she's never helped me write books *and* sent me cookies!

To Monique Fisher. Thank you to a fellow author and an amazing graphic novelist for taking the time and answering all my questions about graphic novels, illustration, and publishing. You helped me add an authenticity to Miriam and Ravaged Lands that I'm so proud of, and I just can't thank you enough. Any and all errors are purely my own and due to my bad note-taking and ignorance in not asking the right questions! Because you, woman, are awesome!

Thank you to such amazing writers and, more importantly, friends Kenya Goree-Bell, Jessica Lee, and LaQuette for checking in on me to make sure I'm alive. LOL! I know it's not easy being friends with an introvert, but y'all have hung in there, and it means the world!

Thank you to Keisha Mennefee of Honey Magnolia Co. for pushing me outside my box. Well, actually, for blowing up that box and kicking the ashes. You've believed in me and supported me and have been more than just an amazing PR and media rep. You're a friend. Love you!

To Lauren Plude. Thank you for never failing to make me feel like a sparkly, bedazzled Nalini Singh. It's the best compliment I could give. LOL! With every email, note, edit, and comment, you're always so enthusiastic, encouraging, and invested. And each book is that much stronger for it. You're amazing, and I'm honored to work with you.

To Rachel Brooks. Frankly, I'm running out of ways to tell you how wonderful you are. The writer in me just said, "Hold my beer!" Thank you, Rachel, for being not just a truly great agent but also an unwavering and honest guide in this business. Thank you for your compassion as well as your strength and for giving me your knowledge with patience and kindness. I brag on you for good reason, because you really are Rachel Super Agent!

ABOUT THE AUTHOR

Photo © 2019 Poetic Images Photography / Avery Carter

Published since 2009, *USA Today* bestselling author Naima Simone loves writing sizzling romances with heart, a touch of humor, and snark. Her books have been featured in the *Washington Post* and *Entertainment Weekly* and have been described as balancing "crackling, electric love scenes with exquisitely rendered characters caught in emotional turmoil."

She is wife to Superman—or his non-Kryptonian, less bulletproof equivalent—and mother to the most awesome kids ever. They all live in perfect, sometimes domestically challenged bliss in the southern United States.